THE
CRIMSON
BUTTERFLY

The DANCING TUATARA PRESS
Books from RAMBLE HOUSE

CLASSICS OF HORROR

1 Beast or Man! — Sean M'Guire
2 The Whistling Ancestors — Richard E. Goddard
3 The Shadow on the House — Mark Hansom
4 Sorcerer's Chessmen — Mark Hansom
5 The Wizard of Berner's Abbey — Mark Hansom
6 The Border Line — Walter S. Masterman
7 The Trail of the Cloven Hoof — Arlton Eadie
8 The Curse of Cantire — Walter S. Masterman
9 Reunion in Hell and Other Stories — The Selected Stories of John H. Knox Vol. I
10 The Ghost of Gaston Revere — Mark Hansom
11 The Tongueless Horror And Other Stories — The Selected Weird Tales of Wyatt Blassingame Vol. I
12 Master of Souls — Mark Hansom
13 Man Out of Hell and Other Stories — The Selected Stories of John H. Knox Vol. II
14 Lady of the Yellow Death and Other Stories — Selected Weird Tales of Wyatt Blassingame Vol. II
15 Satan's Sin House and Other Stories — The Weird Tales of Wayne Rogers Vol. I
16 Hostesses in Hell and Other Stories — The Weird Tales of Russell Gray Vol. I
17 Hands Out of Hell and Other Stories — The Selected Stories of John H. Knox Vol. III
18 Summer Camp for Corpses and Other Stories — Weird Tales of Arthur L. Zagat Vol. I
19 One Dreadful Night — by Ronald S.L. Harding
20 The Library of Death — by Ronald S.L. Harding
21 The Beautiful Dead and Other Stories — The Weird Tales of Donald Dale
22 Death Rocks the Cradle and Other Stories — Weird Tales of Wayne Rogers Vol. II
23 The Devil's Night Club and Other Stories — Nat Schachner
24 Mark of the Laughing Death and Other Stories — Francis James
25 The Strange Thirteen and Other Stories — Richard B. Gamon
26 The Unholy Goddess and Other Stories — The Selected Weird Tales of Wyatt Blassingame Vol. III
27 House of the Restless Dead and Other Stories — Hugh B. Cave
28 Tales of Terror & Torment Vol. 1 — Edited by John Pelan
29 The Corpse Factory and Other Stories — Arthur Leo Zagat
30 The Great Orme Terror and Other Stories — Garnett Radcliffe
31 Freak Museum — R. R. Ryan
32 The Subjugated Beast — R. R. Ryan
33 Towers & Tortures — Dexter Dayle
34 The Strange Case of The Antlered Man — Edwy Searles Brooks
35 When the Batman Thirsts — Frederick C. Davis
36 The Sorcery Club — Elliot O'Donnell
37 Tales of Terror and Torment Vol. 2 — Edited by John Pelan
38 Mistress of Terror and Other Stories — The Selected Weird Tales of Wyatt Blassingame Vol. IV
39 The Place of Hairy Death and Other Stories — An Anthony Rud Reader
40 My Touch Brings Death — The Weird Tales of Russell Gray Vol. II
41 Echo of a Curse — R.R. Ryan
42 The Finger of Destiny — Edmund Snell
43 The Devil of Pei-Ling — Herbert Asbury
44 The Madman — Mark Hansom
45 Laughing Death — Walter C. Brown
46 The Silent Terror of Chu-Seng — Eugene Thomas
47 Death of a Sadist — R.R. Ryan
48 The Crimson Butterfly — Edmund Snell
49 Vampire of the Skies — James Corbett
50 The Back of Beyond — Edmund Snell

CLASSICS OF SCIENCE FICTION AND FANTASY

1 Chariots of San Fernando and Other Stories — Malcolm Jameson
2 The Story Writer and Other Stories — Richard Wilson
3 The House That Time Forgot and Other Stories — Robert F. Young
4 A Niche in Time and Other Stories — William F. Temple
5 Two Suns of Morcali and Other Stories — Evelyn E. Smith
6 Old Faithful and Other Stories — Raymond Z. Gallun
7 The Alien Envoy and Other Stories — Malcolm Jameson
8 The Man without a Planet and Other Stories — Richard Wilson
9 The Man Who was Secrett and Other Stories — John Brunner
10 The Cloudbuilders — Colin Kapp
11 Somewhere In Space — C.C. MacApp

DAY KEENE IN THE DETECTIVE PULPS

1 League of the Grateful Dead and Other Stories — Day Keene in the Detective Pulps Vol. I
2 We Are the Dead and Other Stories — Day Keene in the Detective Pulps Vol. II
3 Death March of the Dancing Dolls and Other Stories — Day Keene in the Detective Pulps Vol. III
4 The Case of the Bearded Bride and Other Stories — Day Keene in the Detective Pulps Vol. IV
5 A Corpse Walks in Brooklyn and Other Stories — Day Keene in the Detective Pulps Vol. V
6 Homicide House and Other Stories — Day Keene in the Detective Pulps Vol. VI

THE CRIMSON BUTTERFLY

by

Edmund Snell

Introduced by

John Pelan

RAMBLE HOUSE

2014

ISBN 13: 978-1-60543-749-1

Preparation: Gavin L. O'Keefe and Fender Tucker

Cover Art © 2014 Gavin L. O'Keefe

Dancing Tuatara Press #48

EDMUND SNELL: FATHER OF THE FANTASTIC THRILLER?

If you're reading this introduction then it's likely you are not a stranger to either Ramble House or my work. I've spent the better part of my adult life researching and reviving interest in authors who are mostly forgotten today. A while back I was asked who I would cite as the author that I would point to as being the best example of what we're trying to do here at Dancing Tuatara Press. Would it be the supreme author of weird menace fiction, Wyatt Blassingame? Well, Blassingame would certainly be near the top of the list. Would it be the master of the supernatural thriller, Mark Hansom? No, a half dozen books doesn't really make for a flagship author. Pulpmaster Hugh B. Cave? His contemporary John H. Knox? Cave is well published elsewhere and Knox, like many of his contemporaries has only a small output, enough for a set of five volumes.

The answer I came up with was Edmund Snell. I really can't think of any author who produced more of the type of fiction that we specialize in that is so little-remembered today. We tend to think of Walter S. Masterman as being a prolific master of the fantastic thriller and rationalized supernatural yarn, but Snell has him beat by well over a million words. It's hard to say today just how influential Edmund Snell was, but one thing is certain, starting with the present book in 1924, no one produced more work in the realm of the fantastic thriller between 1924-1944 than did Edmund Snell.

Best known today for his novels such as *The White Owl*, *The Yu-chi Stone*, *The Sound Machine*, and *The Back of Beyond*; many readers would be surprised to learn that Snell's output as an author of short stories and novellas far exceeded the wordage of his published novels. During the 1920s it was next to impossible to pick up a British fiction magazine and not find an Edmund Snell story therein. When the story papers came along with the format of *The Thriller* calling for a full-length novella every issue, Snell was really at home, producing an astonishing amount of work of mystery/adventure fiction ranging from the supernatural to tales of American gangsters to weird tales set in exotic locales such as Borneo and Singapore. *The Crimson Butterfly*, originally published in 1924 marks his first foray into blending the fantastic with the detective story. Records are unclear as to whether this or *Corrigan's Way* was his first published book; but he established his mastery of both the classic adventure story and the fantastic thriller in the same year.

In Snell's time there were no market categories such as sf/fantasy/detective, such fare was labeled "thriller" and could be anything from a straightforward crime novel (something Snell also excelled at), to a full-blown science fiction tale to a Gothic horror story or a rationalized supernatural tale wherein seemingly otherworldly actions are finally proven to have a human cause. Certainly the blend goes back as far as Poe, but Snell, perhaps more than any other author made the genre his own. While Sax Rohmer had his Devil-Doctor stalking the streets of Limehouse, Edmund Snell gave us the fiendish Chanda Lung, the fiendish Indian-Chinese super criminal whose adventures span two decades and a trilogy that began with *The Yellow Seven*. With Edmund Snell you never knew exactly what you were going to get . . . You might find supernatural horror such as *The White Owl*, straight-forward gangster action, bizarre science fiction such as *Kontrol* or *The Sound Machine* or murder and mayhem in exotic locales (something that the well-traveled author was superbly equipped to write about).

However, it was in the area of the "Asian Menace" and master criminals that Snell really excelled, whether dealing with warring tongs or aboriginal magic, Snell's tales of the Far East and master criminals stalking modern London are of a level far surpassing the quality of most of his contemporaries. As to why Edmund Snell seems to have been so universally ignored when it comes to reprints, it seems that the lack of heirs interested in preserving his work was the main culprit, certainly lack of quality was not a factor as the list of superior novels is a long one and I have already prepared four collections of previously unreprinted novelettes with more to come.

That said, I have to thank our Grand Poobah, Fender Tucker for leading the charge in the Edmund Snell revival well before I came on board with the publication of *Dope & Swastikas* and *The Sign of the Scorpion*. Going forward we'll be handling Edmund Snell much the same way that we're dealing with Walter S. Masterman: we plan on reissuing a number of his books and issuing several new collections. The material that ventures into the weird, sfnal, or Asian Menace arenas will be issued from DTP with new introductions. The material that is more straightforward crime/mystery will come out under the Ramble House imprint. As it stands, there are at least seven novels and a half-dozen collections that seem perfect for DTP and about the same number of volumes that would be more appropriate issued by Ramble House. In any event, prepare for a major revival of Edmund Snell.

Sadly, until Mike Ashley completes his index of the British magazines, there's really no definitive bibliography to speak of. *The Thriller* has been pretty well indexed as has *Detective Fiction Weekly,* but there are literally dozens of fiction magazines (mostly British) that we know (or suspect) that Snell contributed to that haven't been indexed at all and are fairly rare today. Considering how prolific the author was, it's very likely that there exists as much quality material that I don't *know* about, as there is of material that we do know of . . . Sadly, one volume that is very high on my list is the collection *Yellowjacket: The Return of Chanda-Lung.* The Chanda-Lung stories feature the title character, one of the most memorable super-villains of the pulp era. Rather than merely another clone of Fu-Manchu, lurking in the background while assorted henchmen carry out his plans,

Chanda-Lung is more closely akin to A.E. Apple's terrifying Mr. Chang (who also stalked through the pages of *Detective Fiction Weekly*. We anticipate being able to gather all the material necessary to release the Pennington trilogy some-time next year. Of course, this is just one of several projects with three or four collections already in hand and going through the editorial process. If you're an Edmund Snell fan already, than rest assured, there's a lot more to come; if you're just discovering this fantastic author for the first time, do check out the other titles available here at Ramble House and stay tuned for many, many more volumes.

John Pelan
Winter Solstice 2013
Gallup, NM

CHAPTER I

THE COMING OF ABU-SAMAR

JAMES BATTISCOMBE—district officer at Rembakut—emerged from the little courthouse that formed the ground floor of his bungalow, directed his monocle upon a group of natives that still lingered in the clearing, and, turning abruptly on his heel, negotiated the flight of steps that led to the verandah.

He sat down somewhat heavily and touched the bell.

"Bring me a drink—a long drink," he said to the *boy* who appeared in response to his summons.

At the sound of his voice Vera Battiscombe raised her head from the cushion upon which it had reposed.

"That you, Jim?"

The magistrate stretched himself and crossed the floor. He selected a portion of the wooden rail in the immediate vicinity of his wife's chair and leaned his broad back against it.

"Well?" he inquired.

She raised her finely marked brows.

"Well?" she echoed. "Had a busy morning?"

Battiscombe groaned.

"A confounded, interminable land dispute. The worst of native witnesses is that they go such a devil of a long way round, and if you attempt to interrupt 'em they never come to the point at all. Lord! isn't it hot?"

He mopped a large red face with a coloured handkerchief.

Vera had never been fearfully in love with James Battiscombe, but she simulated an intense interest in his affairs to suit her own ends. Her husband, on the contrary, still basked in the sunshine of fatuous contentment at having by some miraculous means persuaded so beautiful a creature to con-

sent to share his existence. A devoted, uncomplaining moun-
tain of flesh, normally content with the smallest of favours,
he vaguely wondered why she stopped with him out there at
all. These Borneo wilds, he was wont to reason, were good
enough in their way where mere man was concerned, but for
a woman—cultured and used to a lot of amusement, well,
hang it all—! He was oblivious of his wife's shortcomings to
such an extent that his friends were constantly divided between an anxious desire to kick him and an equally anxious
desire not to hurt his feelings—and consequently did nothing.

Whenever a particularly persistent rumour floated to Battiscombe's ears he would shrug his shoulders and explain
with wide-open eyes that anyway she was damn' good to
him, and, if he wasn't complaining, what the devil had it got
to do with anybody else?

"And his excellency the *Tuan-Hukim* gave his learned decision, I suppose, and everybody went off very pleased with
themselves?"

The magistrate laughed.

"Not the least bit like it. His excellency postponed the
hearing of the case until to-morrow, thereby neglecting his
duty in the interests of thirst."

He took the glass from the *boy* and winked broadly across
it at his wife.

"Well, here's all the best! Are not the waters of Abana and
what's-his-name greater than all the rivers of Israel, what?—
Jove, I wanted that!—Then, old thing, to cap it all, I was
forced into an unseemly dispute with a most extraordinary
creature." He drew a crumpled visiting card from his pocket
and read: " 'Dr. Abu-Samar'—and a whole string of letters
that I suppose stand for something or other."

Mrs. Battiscombe squirmed herself into a sitting position
and rested her chin on her hand.

"Dr. Abu-Samar!"

Her husband nodded.

"He pushed in just after I'd instructed Corporal Kuraman
to clear the court, and insisted on seeing me."

"What was he like?"

"Oh, a tall thin chap with a blue serge suit and a red *fez*, a brown face and an enormous pair of tortoise-shell spectacles. Apart from all this, he had an extremely unpleasant way of looking at one. Just a moment. I'll ring the bell."

Vera raised a hand.

"Not another one, dear! You know you don't want it."

Battiscombe grinned.

"I know I do!"

She shook her head.

"Not before lunch."

He shrugged his shoulders and deposited the empty tumbler on a small bamboo table.

"Right-oh, little woman; suppose you know best. Anyhow, about this Abu-Samar feller; he told me that he was an expert in tropical diseases and intended offering his services to the neighbouring planters as such. I suggested that the planting syndicates were already fully equipped with medicoes and that the Chartered Company had a few others of its own knocking around looking after the general health of the community—when they weren't playing golf."

"And—?"

"And, oh, he didn't seem to think any of 'em counted for very much. However, that's his affair. He pitched the usual yarn of being the son of a chief somewhere way-back, gave me to understand that he had pots of money and had returned to his own country to reform the notions of his fellow blacks as to the treatment of sickness. He indulged in a long rigmarole about removing the film from their eyes and uplifting the coloured inhabitants of Borneo until they were fit to rub shoulders with the more cultured European, and somewhere about that point I began to smell a rat. I was confoundedly hot and thirsty and I just itched to boot the fellow into the clearing, when he capped everything with a cool request that I should put him up for membership of the club!"

A ripple of laughter escaped Mrs. Battiscombe.

"And then you *booted* him!"

The magistrate set his jaw grimly.

"I booted him! I called upon the corporal first, but he didn't seem especially anxious—so I carried out the operation myself. He sat down on the grass outside and became abusive and threatening. Began a long preamble commencing with the statement that knowledge was power and concluding with a veiled threat to employ his marvellous knowledge in wiping out the entire white population of the island. I fancy he was annoyed really because I tore his trousers."

Vera slipped from her chair and joined him at the rail.

She leaned over, peering in all directions, but could discover nothing more unusual than a belt of mature cocopalms and a sky of infinite azure.

"What happened to him?" she demanded.

"He cleared out in the end, with a little boy in white holding an elaborate yellow umbrella over him and one hand wandering all round his neck to see if his collar was still there. I threatened to arrest him, and he ultimately realised that I meant it and was not at all impressed with either his letters or his wardrobe."

"Quite an exciting morning!"

"Oh, quite! My blood was up—and I let him have it hot."

Mrs. Battiscombe smiled.

"My cave-man!" she murmured, and patted his sleeve with a well-simulated affection that prompted the magistrate to squeeze her arm to indicate that in him also the fires of romance were not entirely burnt out.

He produced a cigarette and tapped it thoughtfully on his thumb-nail.

"I'm running into Jesselton this afternoon," he remarked suddenly. "Coming?"

"No."

He lit up and tossed the match into the clearing.

"Oh! why not?"

Mrs. Battiscombe coloured slightly.

"Because, my dear man, it happens to be Thursday, and you know I promised to ride over to Dick Moberly's to inspect the new clubhouse he's erected for his assistants. You've a terrible memory, Jim."

"I must have, for to tell you the honest truth I can't recall having ever heard that Moberly had built a clubhouse for his men or that he wanted you to inspect it." A shadow crossed his face. "I say, Vera, aren't you seeing rather a lot of Dick Moberly?"

"Jim!"

It was the first sign the proverbial worm had ever shown of turning, and—feeble as the effort was—it startled her.

"Well," pursued the magistrate with dogged persistence, passing a nervous finger round the inside of his collar, "you are, aren't you?"

She came right up to him and, resting her hands lightly on his tunic, gazed unflinchingly into his face.

"You're not suggesting that there's anything—*wrong* between Dick and me?"

A light flashed suddenly in his eyes and died down as quickly as it had come.

"Good heavens, no! Only—well, people will keep talking. I suppose it's because they've nothing else to do. If I'd listened to a tithe of the yarns that are going around about you, I'd have booked your passage home long ago. Perhaps it's a good thing I don't jump at conclusions."

Vera Battiscombe suppressed a smile. She could not imagine her husband jumping at anything.

She stared hard at a cluster of scraggy fowls picking for sustenance in a scattered heap of straw.

"And what are they saying about us?" she demanded.

The magistrate cleared his throat.

"Oh, the usual things. Look here, Vera, don't think I'm complaining, because I'm not; but try and vary things a bit; you know what I mean. People notice you; they can't help it, because you're so confoundedly good-looking. I didn't tell you at the time—I didn't think it was worth repeating—but over a week ago I overheard a scrap of conversation in Sandakan—and knocked a man down for his share in it."

Vera's head came sharply round, and if he had looked he would have seen that she was paler than usual.

"Well? What was it?"

"That you deliberately pushed in between Mrs. Moberly and Dick—and that that was why she went home so suddenly."

Her eyes flashed.

"How wicked!"

"Damnable! Another planter feller picked my man up. He was drunk, but he knew what he was saying: 'I'm mighty sorry for you, old man, and if I were in your place I'd do the same; but if that's your line of action you've got your work cut out. You'll have to fight the whole island!' "

"He didn't say that!"

The D.O. nodded his head slowly.

"He did, old thing. To the best of my belief, those were his exact words. Well, there you are, dear. I've given you the whole grim story for what it is worth. I suppose the average man would have rowed you about it; but I hate rows. It's too hot, for one thing, and for another, I'm confident in my own mind that you wouldn't let me down."

The cook-boy appeared at a doorway.

"*Makan* is served, *Tuan*," he announced.

Battiscombe nodded in his direction to indicate that he had heard. He turned to find his wife the picture of injured innocence.

"I thought it was only women who talked scandal," she declared with a fine air of contempt.

The magistrate did not trouble to defend his sex.

"Well, it isn't, you see, and under the present circumstances it's up to us to face facts. Cut down your visits to *Bukit-Serang* to, say, once a month, and blow in occasionally upon some of those faded women who have possibly had a hand in setting these rumours in motion."

She smiled feebly and spread out her hands.

"Must I?"

The magistrate patted her shoulder affectionately.

"It seems a rational sort of thing to do. Lord, Vera, if we could afford it, I'd clear right out of here."

Mrs. Battiscombe started.

"And that wouldn't be rational at all. Everyone would think we'd made things too hot for us and were afraid to stick to our guns."

He held his head on one side.

"I'm not so certain about that. It'd show 'em, at least, that you didn't care a rap for Moberly and would leave Borneo with me as readily as you came."

"Would I?" she ventured.

Battiscombe slipped his arm round her and piloted her gently towards the living-room, laughing to himself all the while at what he imagined to be the finest joke he had heard for many a long day.

CHAPTER II

THE CRIMSON BUTTERFLY

HE LOOKED UP AT HER from the foot of the steps.

"Good-bye, little woman. Give my regards to Moberly. Perhaps it's just as well you couldn't come. The Commissioner sent word this morning that he wanted to see me, and I expect we shall indulge in a long pow-wow."

"Don't be late," said Mrs. Battiscombe, perhaps just a little anxious to know how late her husband would be.

When considering a question of time, however distant, the magistrate instinctively sought enlightenment in the dial of his watch. He did so now.

"I'm counting on Matthews to fix me up with a trolly. Unless I'm delayed, it should bring me back by about ten. Cheerio!"

She watched his great form amble across the clearing and disappear presently where the path wound between the trees. She returned to her chair and sat for some moments, her hands clasped in front of her, gazing into space. Presently she arose and went with quick determined steps to her room.

As she regarded herself in the long mirror of the wardrobe Jim Battiscombe had taken so much trouble to import for her, she found time to reflect that, after all, there were consolations even for having married a fool. She had once calculated on there being other consolations, but these had been speedily modified by the suddenly revealed meanness of James Battiscombe senior and his only too evident intention of living to a ripe old age.

She bit her lip. In spite of the easy way in which he laughed things off, an inborn instinct told her that doubts were beginning to form in her husband's slow-working brain, and these germs, once firmly seated, had an unpleasant habit of increasing with an alarming rapidity. The thought made her angry. She had contemplated a pleasant afternoon in Moberly's bungalow at Bukit-Serang—and now all those cherished moments would have to be devoted to a tiresome review of their respective positions.

A second survey of her own image in the glass gave her food for further reflection.

Drop Dick Moberly! It wasn't quite such a stupid suggestion after all. It would have to come to an end sooner or later, and there were times when his incessant protestations bored her intensely. Vary things a bit, Jim had suggested. Well, why not? There were still a score of loopholes for escape from the monotony at Rembakut. Her husband was agitated solely on account of her visits to the planter, and her insatiate desire for admiration and conquest swiftly turned her thoughts in other directions. After all, there were more attractive men in Borneo than Dick Moberly!

The picture that her blue eyes were surveying so critically was that of a slight, slim woman in the early thirties, with all the freshness of a girl of nineteen, an aureole of light fluffy curls, and pouting lips that required only the slightest artificial attention to keep them amazingly red.

Her riding-breeches of white drill added a certain piquancy to her appearance of which she was not entirely oblivious, and the broad white solar topee she affected became her wonderfully.

Deliriously attractive, daring to the point of recklessness, such was she whom the adoring Jim Battiscombe persisted in regarding as his devoted better-half, whom Cranley·—who had a gift for apt expressions—had christened the *vest-pocket adventuress* and whom the Commissioner of Police labelled as a *damned dangerous woman*.

She rode off presently through the cocopalms and took a path which led through fields of rectagonal pools where vivid green paddy-shoots thrust their heads timidly above the surface. Great water- buffaloes, browsing in the open, raised their broad snouts at her approach; ugly, formidable creatures with lashing tails and a legendary objection to the white man because of his fondness for soap! But Mrs. Battiscombe had passed these particular beasts a score of times and grown to regard them merely as familiar landmarks on the road to Bukit-Serang.

On the white wooden bridge that spanned the Ayer River she met Dr. Abu-Samar.

He was standing at the far end of the bridge, a cigarette between his lips and his tortoiseshell glasses reflecting the rays of the tropical sun. As she drew closer, she saw that he was taller and more powerful in build than her husband had made it appear; his fingers were long and tapering and his complexion was sallow rather than brown. There was something strangely compelling about the look with which he greeted her. It was as if his eyes were gifted with extraordinary magnetic powers.

"Good afternoon, Mrs. Battiscombe," he said, "I have been waiting for you."

The girl reined up her mount and sat looking down at him, an amused smile at her lips.

"Waiting for me," she echoed pleasantly. "What exactly do you mean by that?"

A memory dashed upon her of her husband's treatment of the doctor that morning and she wondered if the man's presence there were due to a desire for revenge.

"You are on your way to see Mr. Moberly of Bukit-Serang," continued Samar in the same measured tones. "I am a doctor here, you know, and Mr. Moberly has an appointment at my house at three. He instructed me to endeavour to intercept you and escort you there to meet him." In some peculiar way he seemed to read the doubts which lay in her mind, for he added, "If you would rather go on to Mr. Moberly's bungalow, I am to tell you that his servant will give you tea and Mr. Moberly will join you there later."

Mrs. Battiscombe was gazing down at the muddy waters of the river. She looked up suddenly.

"Very well," she returned slowly. "I will come."

Upon hearing her consent, Dr. Abu-Samar turned abruptly on his heel.

"If you will permit me, I will go on ahead and show you the way."

She touched her pony's flank with her heel.

"Is it far?" she asked.

"About half a mile," he said over his shoulder.

The path by which her guide took her was ill-marked, and after the first two hundred yards or so she was forced to dismount to avoid the overhanging branches.

They came presently to a small open space, waist high for the most part with *lalang*, in which stood a broad, squat house with a freshly-repaired roof of sago thatch and walls of dried reeds. A verandah had been added to the original structure and neat wooden steps, painted white, led up to this.

At the foot of the steps a native girl with sarong of bottle-green, and long cigarette between her fingers, lounged idly against a post, favouring the white woman with a look of insolent curiosity mingled with something Vera Battiscombe did not altogether understand.

Abu-Samar waved an eloquent hand.

"Here is my humble dwelling, Mrs. Battiscombe. Shall I take your horse? Or would you prefer to tether it yourself?"

He shouted something in a dialect unknown to her and the brown girl, with a flash of her white teeth, flounced off towards the back of the house.

Vera tapped her riding-boots with her stock.

"Do I go up here?" she inquired.

"If you please."

She found a cane chair and took possession of it without invitation.

The doctor offered to relieve her of her hat and whip, but she shook her head.

"No, thank you. It's already after three and I don't suppose Mr. Moberly will want to stop very long."

She accepted a cigarette, however, and lit it from the match he held towards her.

He flicked the match airily into space and strode off to the far end of the verandah, from which he continued to stare at her until she began to feel profoundly uncomfortable.

"Have you been here long?" she demanded at length.

"Not long," returned Samar briefly.

At three-fifteen she grew uneasy.

"You are quite certain Mr. Moberly is coming here this afternoon?"

He did not answer at once, but came slowly towards her, his head pushed slightly forward, his eyes never leaving her face.

"You are a very beautiful woman, Mrs. Battiscombe," he said suddenly.

She came quickly to her feet, her face flushed.

"Answer me," she commanded, stamping her foot. "Is Mr. Moberly coming here or not?"

"*Not*," confessed Samar with astonishing frankness. "I am afraid that the whole of my story was nothing less than pure invention, designed to induce you to do something which you would not otherwise have consented to do."

She stood for some moments aghast, trying vainly to collect her thoughts. Her eyes followed the encircling line of foliage, endeavouring to discover some gap wide enough for her to ride through and outstrip Dr. Samar, should he attempt to follow.

"Oh!" she ejaculated at length—and made for the stairhead. The doctor barred her path, a thin hand resting on either post. His disarming smile exposed a perfect row of white teeth.

"It would be impossible for you to get away from here unless I desired you to," he said; "but it may ease your mind to learn that I have not the least intention of harming you or of detaining you longer than is absolutely necessary for my purpose."

He smiled again.

"Very naturally you assumed that I wanted to make you suffer for the insult your husband put upon me this morning. I can assure you such is not the case. I am a cultured man,

Mrs. Battiscombe, not a savage. Confess, you don't in the least mind being here."

Mrs. Battiscombe laughed nervously.

"Not if you play square. I'm in rather a hurry though, really."

Samar raised his brows mockingly.

"To find Mr. Moberly—or return to your husband, who happens to be in Jesselton?"

"If you are going to insult me, Dr. Samar—!"

"I do not wish to. I merely desire to show you that I know everything. I am a strange man, Mrs. Battiscombe, with an extraordinary history—and extraordinary powers. The people here regard me as a magician, a miracle worker. They come to me when they are ill, but they are afraid of me, all the same. Frankly, I like to inspire fear. My ancestor was Sidi Samar, an Illanun and a pirate in the days when the English Rajah first came to Sarawak. Driven back into the interior by superior forces, he became, by reason of the vast wealth he had accumulated and the terror he inspired, chief of a tribe of warriors who existed by murder and rapine. A well-kept secret, handed down from father to son, made me eventually sole possessor of his fortune. My desire for knowledge was insatiable. I went to England—the home of the traditional enemy of my tribe—and added to the mysteries of the East the scientific knowledge of the West—"

"Why England?" interrupted Mrs. Battiscombe. "Why go to our country at all if you dislike our people?"

Dr. Samar screwed up his eyes.

"One goes to the bazaar for beautiful fabrics, for jewels, for wondrous ornaments—not because one has anything in common with those who sell. From England I went to Germany, Italy, Austria, and even to America. I have travelled far, you see, always accumulating knowledge—"

"And yet you are content to return to Borneo and live in a native hut with a roof of *ataps!*"

"I have come back to my home and my people," said Samar quietly, "to the island the white races have taken from us, and, if they could but realise it, so great are my powers that it would pay them to treat me with respect."

She glanced at her watch and held out her hand to him.

"Well, good-bye, Dr. Samar. I mustn't really stop a moment longer. Your story has been so interesting that I feel almost inclined to forgive you for having lured me here under false pretences."

Again that queer light had crept into his eyes.

"You are going to do more than that, Mrs. Battiscombe," he assured her in a voice that had dropped to a whisper. "You are coming here again and again. At first because I shall call you, and you will be compelled to come—and later because you will have learnt to prefer my house to the bungalow of the little planter at Bukit-Serang." He caught both her hands and drew her, feebly resisting, to the open doorway of an inner room. "Come. One look at the magician's palace and you will be free to depart."

They passed through heavy curtains of orange-coloured silk ornamented with silver beads and, as these swung to behind them, he released her. She found herself in a comparatively small apartment furnished with a strange conglomeration of Moorish, Chinese, and Indian furniture, and hung with bizarre Oriental draperies. A table inlaid with mother-of-pearl occupied the centre of the floor, and close to the far wall reposed an elaborate divan. The atmosphere was permeated with a sticky, resinous odour which she traced to a heavy bronze jar in a corner, from which issued a faint wreath of blue smoke.

Suddenly, as she gazed around her in bewilderment, Doctor Samar threw open the lid of an enormous cedar-wood box and tossed a jumbled heap of glittering ornaments on to the table.

"A little souvenir of your first visit, Mrs. Battiscombe," he suggested. "Choose what you will." Victim of a confused host of fears and suspicions, she backed towards the curtains, her eyes fixed on the glittering pile.

He lifted the table bodily and held it up to her eyes, but she pushed it away from her.

"No, no," she cried hoarsely. "It is quite impossible. You don't understand . . ."

"Very well; then I must choose for you."

He selected a pendant in the form of a butterfly, magnificently carved from a red, transparent substance the colour of ruby, with emerald eyes and swung from a chain of gold filigree. It was as thin as a wafer, and, almost before she was aware of it, he had clasped it round her neck.

She stared at him with frightened eyes.

"You mean me to keep this?"

He folded his arms.

"The Crimson Butterfly," he said softly. "A talisman to which native superstition has attributed strange powers. It is said that the wearer has but to express a wish—and it will most surely be accomplished." He laughed easily. "I warned you that I was a magician, Mrs. Battiscombe. Even our friend Mr. Moberly would scarcely be able to provide you with so wonderful a gift—in return for the many favours you so graciously bestow on him!"

The events of the afternoon had played the deuce with Vera Battiscombe's nerves, and she was on the verge of hysteria. Her face dropped suddenly into her hands and, with a wild outburst of sobbing, she staggered through the curtain into the clearer air of the verandah.

"How dare you!—How dare you insult me like this!—That man is nothing to me—nothing, I tell you!—I wish he were dead!"

Something made her look up.

Abu-Samar was standing at a little distance from her, and the stairway to her pony was within easy reach.

"One has to be careful what one wishes," the doctor reminded her, "when one happens to be the wearer of the Crimson Butterfly!"

She tore herself from his gaze with an effort, and, running madly down the steps, untethered her mount with trembling fingers.

Half an hour later she stumbled upon the white wooden bridge and rode headlong back to her husband's bungalow, haunted with the memory of Abu-Samar's mocking eyes.

Her servant's startled gaze directed at her chest drew her attention to the butterfly pendant that still hung there, glaringly magnificent against a white background.

She shuddered involuntarily and tucked it out of sight.

CHAPTER III

ARMOURER ENTERTAINS

A STRETCH OF POWDERY SAND, bleached white by a relentless Eastern sun, bordered on three sides by trees through which—to the eastward—ran a gleaming single track of railway line; a sea of deepest blue, shimmering in a vast crucible whose rim was the far horizon, like some strange metallic substance, which bubbled over on to the sand and on the surface of which a group of tiny islands clustered together like lumps of jade.

A sun hanging low in the western heavens, a breathless, sweltering stillness, broken at intervals by the shrill quarrelling of apes in the branches and the gentle plashing and sucking-back of a timid tide.

There were only two living creatures visible in the whole of this vivid tropical landscape; an Englishman in white drill who sat, pipe in mouth, on a grassy mound—and a small furry sloth whose brown eyes surveyed the biped from above with mischievous interest.

The man on the mound stirred suddenly and stretched himself and the sloth took instant flight, scurrying for the ample cover lent by the foliage.

Michael Armourer cocked his head on one side and listened.

A distant rumbling sound, accompanied by a discordant shriek, announced the approach of the afternoon train.

Battiscombe's colleague at Jelandang glanced at his watch.

"She's late this afternoon," he said to himself, and tapped out his pipe on his heel.

He had almost filled it again from a voluminous oilskin pouch when the catastrophe occurred.

The train—a jolting line of white coaches drawn by an ob-
solete engine that puffed and snorted asthmatically—
emerged from the trees on the one side at the same time as a
trolly—propelled by a group of perspiring natives—appeared
at the other. The trolly carried two passengers—an elderly
gentleman with a short grey beard, who had a camera fixed
on a tripod before him and was turning a handle vigorously,
and a young girl in white.

Either the engine-driver was short-sighted or his brakes re-
fused to respond, for before Armourer could reach the spot
the natives had scattered, the man and the girl had fallen off,
and the engine was pushing the trolly before it in the direction of Jesselton.

Armourer tripped up over the tripod, recovered himself,
and bent down over the girl. She sat up suddenly and rubbed
a bruised arm.

"I hope you're not hurt?" he inquired with genuine anxiety.

It dawned upon him at that moment that she was unusually
good-looking and that she was laughing.

"Oh, no. I'm not in the least bit hurt, thanks. Hadn't you
better have a look at father?"

Armourer rose to his full height and peered down into the
hollow into which the only other occupant of the trolly had
fallen.

The old gentleman was scrambling to his feet, muttering a
string of harmless expletives in a particularly definite manner, most of which appeared to be addressed to the train.

"Preposterous, I call it! An expensive instrument and a perfect panorama ruined all through the confounded idiocy of a
native driver! A man like that ought never to be permitted to
control an engine again!"

Armourer suppressed a sudden desire to laugh.

"As a matter of fact," he reminded the stranger, "trollies
are theoretically illegal."

The other surveyed him sourly.

"Who the dickens are you, anyway?" he demanded.

Armourer smiled.

"I happen to be the magistrate of this district. My name's Armourer—Michael Armourer. I hope you haven't damaged yourself."

The older man placed both hands on his hips, stared at the tail end of the train—a couple of hundred yards away, where a little group of natives and Europeans had gathered—at his daughter, and at the half-frightened coolies who were wandering back into sight again—then threw out his chest and laughed heartily.

"Well, Joyce, here's an adventure for you! You always declared you wanted one—and now you've got it!—Are you hurt?"

"Oh, dear me, no! I've grazed my arm; that's all."

"Splendid! And now, Mr. Armourer, do you mind sending that train of yours on? I think we've had all the publicity we require this afternoon."

"And the trolly?"

"Of course, I was forgetting that. You might ask those grinning lunatics to get it off the line until the train has gone, then put it on again and push it back to Jesselton. I'll pay 'em when they're ready to start."

"You're not going on?"

The older man shook his head resolutely.

"I'm not going on one of those ghastly things again—in the interests of science or anything else. You can make your mind quite easy about that."

"But, father," protested the girl, "how are we going to get back?"

He stroked his beard.

"We shall place ourselves unreservedly in the hands of the local magistrate. I'm not so certain he oughtn't to arrest us both in any case. We appear to have been breaking the law!"

He crossed the line and picked up his camera.

"I suppose I ought to tell you, Mr. Armourer, that I'm Professor Herbert Standen and this is my daughter Joyce. I'm interested in a good many things, but my pet subject is Poisons. And," he added, "if I knew of a suitable one at the moment, I'd cheerfully administer it to the Director of Railways—or whatever he styles himself—who beat me at golf yesterday and suggested this infernal trolly-ride!"

He examined the camera and, setting it down tenderly at his side, straightened a leg of the collapsible tripod over his knee. Apparently satisfied that the total damage to his property was small, he cast an appreciative eye over the landscape.

"This is certainly a very beautiful spot—very beautiful. What do you think of it, Joyce?"

The girl was standing a few paces from them, shading her eyes with her hand.

"It's simply glorious," she said at length. "I love it."

Armourer excused himself and hurried off to stimulate the coolies into action. He returned in half an hour to find the professor and his daughter down by the water's edge.

"It's all clear now," he explained, "and I've taken the liberty of squaring your men for you. I'm afraid I didn't give them all they had expected; but it was a good deal more than they deserved. You'd better come up to my place and see if you think you will be comfortable enough there."

The professor stuck his hands in his pockets and favoured the younger man with an amused smile.

"You don't for one moment suppose I'm going to plant myself and family on you at a moment's notice?"

"I'm afraid it's Hobson's choice. You see, there's only one train up and one down a day—and that's the last of any sort until to-morrow morning."

He indicated a faint line of grey smoke that still hung above the trees.

Standen looked startled.

"But, bless my soul, we ought to have taken that, then?"

"Certainly, if you wanted to get back to-night. But you told me to send off the trolly and the train and indicated at the same time that you didn't desire publicity, so I thought the best thing you could do was to stop the night at my bungalow."

The professor called to Joyce.

"Do you hear that, my dear? Mr. Armourer says we've to put up with him, as there's nothing to take us to Jesselton until to-morrow."

Joyce gasped and spread out her hands.

"But I haven't brought a thing—not even a tooth-brush!"

Armourer laughed.

"We can fix you up with that all right," he assured her. "There's an estate shop within a mile of my house. If there's anything else you really require, you had better write a little note to Mrs. Battiscombe at Rembakut—and one of my men will run over before dinner."

He picked up the professor's camera and tripod and crossed the line.

"Does tea appeal to you at the moment, Miss Standen?"

The girl nodded enthusiastically.

"Then follow me. I can promise you a cup in ten minutes."

The professor took up the rear, shaking his head at intervals.

"I'm extremely grateful to you, I'm sure," he panted, as they reached the summit of a steep incline, "but I hate putting anybody to an inconvenience."

"You're not," the magistrate laughed back at him. "You're doing me a great honour. It's three weeks since I had a visitor of any sort."

He extended an arm and pointed to a spot where the shingled roof of a new bungalow showed amid a veritable forest of growing rubber.

"That's Moberly's place. He's the manager of the estate I told you about when we were discussing tooth-brushes. It's one of the best bungalows out here."

"It looks simply topping," commented Joyce, who was by this time thoroughly reconciled to the prospect of a night spent without her luggage and secretly exultant that the accident had put an end to what had promised to be a dull and uninteresting afternoon.

"His rubber looks well," said Standen. "There's been a lot of good work put in there."

"Oh, he's thorough," agreed the magistrate. "That dreary-looking atrocity right ahead of us is my shack."

Joyce looked.

"It seems quite a big place."

"Oh, it's not the size I complain of. As a matter of fact it suits me pretty well, but when visitors come along its many defects have a habit of becoming apparent. However, you'll see what it's like for yourselves."

As they crossed the wide stretch of grassland in which the building lay, a couple of terriers bounded down the steps and came scurrying to meet them.

It was somewhere between tea and dinner that Armourer, returning from an excursion to Moberly's estate shop, found Joyce alone on the verandah.

He dropped quite a fair-sized parcel into her lap.

"Well, there's your tooth-brush," he said.

She wrinkled her forehead.

"But this isn't all tooth-brush!"

"No," admitted the magistrate, "it's not; but it all comes under the category of toilet requisites—except the chocolates—and they're supposed to be bad for teeth! Where's the professor?"

She shook her head.

"I haven't the least idea. He's wandered out somewhere."

Armourer scanned the landscape.

"Does he often do this?" he inquired.

"Oh yes; more often than not, in fact."

"What a singularly convenient sort of parent!"

Her dark eyes met his and they were full of merriment.

"It's not always convenient, you know, to be left like this. Father's quite capable of dumping me anywhere—and forgetting where he's put me, just like he does with his umbrella."

"But he *will* come back, of course?" inquired Armourer with mock anxiety.

"Of course. Don't you want him to?"

He sat down opposite her and, clasping his hands over one knee, he appeared to be thinking deeply.

"My proper answer would be—yes, most certainly; but what I really want to say is that, if I am to be employed as a left-luggage office by absent-minded professors of poisons—er—well, it occurs to me that you're rather the sort of baggage I should like to be left behind and never claimed! Now, that was really clever; wasn't it? Do look at that sunset! It's the only decent thing about here I've got to show you."

She sprang to her feet and ran to the rail. Armourer stood close behind her, and for a matter of seconds an exceedingly beautiful brunette and a particularly good-looking young man remained in close proximity, the last eerie rays of a departing sun bathing them in an unearthly pallor.

The glory of the heavens—now that the sun had gone—left her breathless and trembling.

She looked up at him.

"I have never seen anything like it," she murmured. "Isn't it just wonderful?"

"By Jove, it is," averred Armourer; but he was looking at her, and for him the glories of the Eastern sunset were forgotten.

CHAPTER IV

A Dance at Rembakut

It was towards nine o'clock when Vera Battiscombe, immersed in the contents of a paper-covered volume, heard a horseman come flying across the night-shrouded clearing and slither to a standstill immediately under the verandah.

She glanced up sharply, wondering if it could be Dick Moberly, anxious to discover what had prevented her paying her intended visit.

A cheery voice from the blackness swiftly disillusioned her.

"Hello, there! Anybody alive?"

She went to the rail.

"Is that you, Mr. Armourer? Yes, I'm very much alive, thanks; but Jim's in Jesselton. Won't you come up?"

He handed his pony over to one of Battiscombe's men and came up the steps three at a time.

Michael Armourer was one of the few men with whom she had never been able to make headway, and probably for that reason more than any other she unconsciously sharpened every weapon in her armoury at his approach. He was handsome, broad-shouldered and essentially virile, but invariably left her with the impression that he liked her very much and found her excellent company, but that, according to his notions on life, the fact that she was Jim Battiscombe's lawful wife presented an impenetrable barrier to anything that savoured of intimacy.

He came into the radius of the lamplight and extended a large hand.

"How are you, Mrs. Battiscombe. Sorry Jim's away. I should like to have seen him. As a matter of fact I've come over on rather a delicate mission. I was going to dispatch an orderly on the job, but got it into my head he might muck it up. I should never have forgiven myself if he'd rolled up with a pair of Jim's pyjamas instead of a nightie!"

Vera wagged an admonishing finger.

"I know what it is, Mr. Armourer; you've been drinking."

The magistrate shook his head.

"Not unduly. I did open a bottle of bubbly for the professor, but he mopped up most of it himself."

"Then what on earth are you talking about?"

"This," said Armourer, and thrust a sealed envelope into her hand. "I've visitors at my place. They got tied up in a trolly accident and hadn't brought any *barang*. I managed to fix up the old man; but the lady presented difficulties. I haven't the remotest idea what's in that note, and I am given to understand that the parcel is to be duly secured and sealed before it's handed over to me."

Mrs. Battiscombe perused the contents of the letter with an amused smile.

"Shall I read it out to you?"

He retreated across the floor, waving his hands in front of him.

"Heaven forbid! Have pity on my youth and innocence, please!"

Vera laughed.

"But, my dear man, what on earth could a woman require for a single night that an average man shouldn't hear about?"

"I don't know," returned Armourer, "I haven't even bothered to think. In any case, I don't suppose it amounts to anything much, but the fact that I am conveying the confounded paraphernalia from one woman acquaintance to another makes me prefer to remain in a state of blissful ignorance."

She dashed a sidelong glance at him.

"Is she pretty?"

Armourer pretended to reflect on a subject upon which he had long made up his mind.

"As a matter of fact, I suppose she is."

"Fair or dark?"

"Dark, I suppose you'd say."

"Well, she must be one or the other, mustn't she?"

"Certainly—unless she happens to be something in between." He bent forward earnestly. "Does your husband allow people to drink on his verandah when he's away? I mean when people happen to have ridden rather a long way and swallowed a fair amount of dust?"

"My poor man. I'm so sorry!"

She touched the bell.

"Hoon-Kit," she said to the servant who shuffled in, "the *Tuan-Hakim* of Jelandang is thirsty. Bring in the decanter and a glass."

"Why not in the plural?" demanded Armourer.

Vera smiled.

"Because I don't care for whisky—and my husband doesn't like me to drink with strange men—even if they have ridden a long way and swallowed a lot of dust!"

She accompanied the latter half of the remark with a grimace.

Armourer looked at the ceiling.

"It really is refreshing," he retorted, "to discover a woman who is actuated solely by her husband's desires. Er—does Jim know about this?"

"I don't think I altogether like you," declared Mrs. Battiscombe.

The *boy* brought in the decanter and Armourer helped himself.

"Did Jim go down by the train?" he asked suddenly.

Vera nodded.

"Then the Lord only knows what time he arrived in town. She was an hour and a half behind time when she passed my place."

"You don't mean that?"

"I'm afraid I do. That seems to indicate he'll be late back."

She shuddered.

"I loathe sitting up here all alone," she said. "Isn't it just too annoying! I haven't spoken to a soul except Hoon-Kit since tea. Be a Christian and sit down and talk for a bit."

He shook his head.

"Sorry, Mrs. Battiscombe, but I've got to get back to my guests. Besides, you're forgetting the parcel!"

She came right up to him, putting every ounce of pleading she knew how into her eyes.

"Half an hour!"

He picked up his hat.

"Can't be done. You see, Miss Standen's probably tired and waiting for her kit, and—"

"You're just itching to get back to her!" she concluded for him.

He held his glass to the light.

He was in a queer mood that night, a state of mind that had obsessed him ever since that look he had exchanged in the brief twilight with a girl he had known but a handful of minutes. The thought flashed across him that the professor and his daughter were only awaiting his return to go to bed and that, even if they stopped up with him for a while, it was highly improbable that Joyce and he would be permitted to remain alone for a second time. And here was a superlatively attractive woman begging him to perform a common act of charity.

"All right," he said; "I'll stop. One of Jim's men can take the stuff."

"It's awfully good of you. Just a minute and I'll get the things. Do you want to send any message?"

Armourer rubbed his chin.

"Better tell the professor I'm delayed here on business, but hope to be across in an hour or so. He needn't trouble to wait up unless he wants to. Shall I write it down?"

"Oh, no. I'll see that Corporal Kuraman sends somebody with intelligence."

As she passed the long mirror she looked into it and smiled.

She found Armourer presently, leaning over the rail, smoking.

"Give me a cigarette, please."

He held out his case.

"What are we going to do?" he inquired.

"What do you want to do?"

She insisted on lighting her cigarette from the glowing end of his cigar, a process that brought them into such close proximity that he found it embarrassing.

He had always pretended to himself that he despised Mrs. Battiscombe for the flagrancy with which she conducted her amours, but, under present conditions, he caught himself in the act of reconsidering this opinion. It was only a step from this to tacitly admit that Jimmie Battiscombe was rather a stodgy companion for an endless succession of breakfasts, dinners and teas, and it was scarcely to be wondered at if a girl with some *go* in her should seek to relieve the tedium of tropical loneliness with an occasional flirtation.

Vera had somehow succeeded in infusing into his veins a pleasurable feeling of comfort and self-satisfaction, combined with a dash of recklessness.

"I don't know," he laughed. "What is there to do?"

She possessed herself of an arm and led him towards the gramophone.

"Let's dance. Let's pretend we're in a really smart restaurant in a really big town and that we've had a really nice dinner!"

Armourer grinned.

"Anything else?"

"And that you're dancing with a really nice girl—that you really like!"

He fell into the trap.

"I shan't need to pretend that," he said.

She pounced on this first rash admission and used it for all she was worth.

"Won't you?"

He hedged.

"Won't I what?"

"You know what you said."

"What did I say?"

"*I* haven't forgotten," said Mrs. Battiscombe, contriving to blush.

She delved into a pile of discs.

"Let's have a fox-trot. *Eastern Stars* is good."

She poised the needle carefully on the record, gave it a little sideways tap with her finger and closed the lid.

For the first time he noticed her frock. It was a greeny-blue clinging affair, and it dawned on him that she had slipped it on while making up the parcel for Joyce.

As she stood there, waiting for him to take her, the devilry of all the witches of mythology danced in her eyes.

"Are you ready?" she whispered.

He passed a moist hand over his forehead.

"I suppose so," he stammered, and awoke to discover that they were dancing.

From that moment his enthusiasm grew until they raced back to the machine at the conclusion of each tune and the records overflowed on to the table and the floor as they were played and discarded.

A sudden thought made him glance at his watch. They were in the middle of a one-step, and she held his wrist, trying to stop him looking. He succeeded at length and his face fell.

"What is it?" she asked.

"Quarter past eleven."

"It can't be."

"It is, by Jove!"

He held it so that she could see for herself.

"Just one more," she pleaded.

He hesitated.

"Right-ho! The very last, mind."

They ran to the gramophone and his fingers sought the handle a second only after hers. In the excitement of the moment he allowed them to remain longer than he had intended.

"Michael!"

He was aware of the sensation of something cold trickling down his spine. He turned to find her upturned face so close to him that he felt her warm breath on his cheeks. Those lips of hers were the very devil!

He hadn't the remotest idea why he did it. Never in his wildest imaginings had he ever intended to supplant Dick Moberly. He could have sworn that, without any effort on his part, those lips came closer—until they touched his . . .

A voice came from the stairway:

"Hello, you two! What on earth are you up to?"

Armourer brought his head up with a jerk and turned awkwardly to greet James Battiscombe.

Vera was coolness itself.

"Hullo, Jim! Back at last? I didn't go over to Bukit-Serang after all. I just stopped here on my own, until Mr. Armourer rode over for some clothes for a girl who'd got stranded with her father. He told me the train was late and I made him stop. We've been dancing."

Her husband stood in the centre of the floor, his topee at the back of his head, swinging his monocle on its string.

"So I see," he remarked, in a tone that was entirely new to her. He nodded to Armourer.

"Well, Michael! Playing the good Samaritan?"

The younger man felt uncomfortable.

"I had to decide," he managed to say, "between my unexpected guests and Mrs. Battiscombe."

"You had no difficulty, I take it, in coming to a decision?"

Vera frowned.

"I persuaded him to stay."

He thrust his hands in his pockets and looked at her.

"I'll wager you did! Well, good-night, Michael. I'll try and drop over and see you one of these days. I hope you're not too tired, Vera, because I've quite a lot I want to say to you."

CHAPTER V

BATTISCOMBE ASSERTS HIMSELF

"JIM!"

"Well?"

She came closer.

"Why were you so rude to Mr. Armourer?"

A suggestion of the old weakness of character crept into his face. He remained for some moments blinking into her eyes as a man trying to accustom his gaze to the light. Presently his features hardened, and he regarded her squarely.

"Look here, Vera, how much longer is this sort of thing to go on? Do you expect me to be polite to these—harmless acquaintances of yours for an eternity?"

She flushed angrily.

"I don't understand you. What in the name of goodness are you driving at?"

He brought his fist heavily down on to the table and the glass Armourer had used rolled off and broke on the floor.

"You know very well what I'm talking about. Don't beat about the bush. Answer me!"

Completely bewildered, she racked her brain for some clue to the solution of her husband's changed attitude. Jumping at the most obvious conclusion, she repeated the suggestion she had made earlier in the evening to Michael.

"You've been drinking."

He nodded bitterly.

"Oh, yes," he retorted, "I've been drinking all right. I dropped in at Vance's place and had a couple on the way up. I've been treated to a considerable amount of undiluted hell on your account this evening—and I felt I was in need of something to steady myself. I can put up with a lot more than most men, I fancy—but there are some things I can't stand."

"Such as—?"

"Such as discovering my own wife kissing one of my colleagues on the verandah of my own house!"

She was trembling with fury now, her fingers clenching and unclenching themselves at her sides.

"That's not true; you know it's not true!"

"I wish to heaven it weren't; but, for the first time in all this miserable business, I have the evidence of my own eyes. Good Lord, Vera, haven't you some sense of decency? Leaving me out of the question altogether, aren't there sufficient scoundrels on the island without you wanting to seduce a decent boy like Armourer?"

She made a sudden movement towards her room.

"If you've nothing but these vile accusations to level at me, I'm going to bed."

He stepped between her and the door.

"Listen to me," he said sternly, "you're not going to leave this verandah until you've heard everything I've got to say."

She tried to push past him, but he caught her by both arms and forced her into a chair.

She sprang out of it again, her cheeks very white, her eyes blazing.

"How dare you treat me like that! How dare you bully me!" Her lower lip quivered and she buried her face in her hands. She collapsed in the chair again, seeking refuge in tears. "You—hurt—me."

He stood irresolutely over her, his features twitching. He was feeling uncommonly miserable, and, had she sought to retreat at that moment, he could not have mustered courage to detain her. A weak impulse prompted him to take her in his arms and comfort her, but that final scene between Armourer and his wife still rankled, and he choked it down.

Remembering something, he dived a hand into a side-pocket and threw a bulky packet into her lap.

She glanced at it through her fingers, but did not move.

"You will find some of your own letters there," he told her hoarsely, "letters from Moberly to his wife suggesting a divorce and letters from Mrs. Moberly to the Governor. I am counting on you to explain why Moberly should have imagined his wife had grounds for obtaining a divorce."

She gulped down something, withdrew her fingers slowly and turned a tear-stained face up to him.

"Where did you get these?" she asked dully.

He sat on the edge of the table and folded his arms.

"Mrs. Moberly has been in correspondence with the Governor for some time. She has known Sir Henry for a good many years. I am given to understand that he doesn't desire to pose in any way as a censor of morals, but that, wishing to put an end to what he regarded as a highly undesirable state of affairs, he forwarded these letters to the Commissioner."

Her fingers fidgeted with the tape that bound the bundle.

"That was why he wanted to see you?"

"Yes."

She dabbed her eyes with her handkerchief.

"And you believe all these horrible fabrications?"

He clasped his hands between his knees and swayed uncomfortably to and fro.

"What else am I to believe? You say you didn't go to Bukit-Serang this afternoon?"

"No."

"Why not? If you are going to tell me it was out of any sense of decent feeling for me, I'm afraid I can't believe it."

She was dangerously near tears again.

"Jim, why are you such a beast to me?"

"Why are you such a beast to *me*?"

"I'm not," she sobbed. "I've just tried to amuse myself; that's all. I did kiss Michael Armourer. I made him kiss me. You don't suppose I did that because I cared about him? Men are such fools!"

"I'm just beginning to realise it," said Battiscombe. "I'm not in the least bit blind to the fact that you've fooled *me*."

She shook her head sadly.

"You'll never understand me, Jim. You've brought me out to the East and you expect me to behave with all the absurd decorum of the suburbs. Spices, tropical sunshine—and colour! If you want to blame anything, you must blame the surroundings, the climate and the unutterable loneliness. You've had your work; I've had nothing to do but to bask in the sunshine and absorb! It's got into my veins—this Borneo of yours. I've caught the spirit of the place and, to all intents and purposes, I'm a head-hunter. I delight in these little conquests. Armourer was a real conquest, Jim, because in his heart of hearts he despised me—and he despises me still. Oh, I know I've sinned. In that respect I've sinned terribly. I've ridden back, flushed with excitement at my wrong-doing, like a naughty child expecting to be smacked; but you've never smacked me, Jim. You've just sat there, fat, contented, blind . . . until I could have shrieked at you—'Dick Moberly's kissed me; do you hear? What are you going to do about it?' You're lucky that that's all that has happened; but it is all!"

He glanced down at his hands.

"Do you swear that?" he demanded presently in a low voice.

She rose with a sudden movement and leaned against him, smoothing the lapels of his jacket between finger and thumb. She looked up at him, her blue eyes that seemed so honest brimming over with mute appeal—and Jim Battiscombe succumbed.

He crushed her to him—this beautiful penitent, swathed in the vampire frock she had selected to overwhelm Michael, and she was far too clever to complain of his roughness then.

"I've been a little rotter to you, Jim," she whispered. "You must be firm with me in future—ever so firm; do you understand?"

Her husband nodded. He was so utterly overcome, so profoundly optimistic that their married life had found its second wind, that he forgot she had evaded his question.

"Poor little woman!" he murmured presently. "I'm afraid I've been very much to blame." He caught sight of the pile of letters in their binding of official tape that had fallen to the floor as she rose. "We'll burn those damned letters—every blessed one of 'em. Anyhow," he added fiercely, "this affair's shown up Moberly in his true colours. You won't want to see him again."

"Never," she agreed with almost unnecessary emphasis. Moberly's indiscretion had led her into uncommonly deep waters—and she was not likely to forget it in a hurry. This would be a lesson to her for all time, and she would take care Michael Armourer did not commit a similar error. Besides, she remembered, Armourer was unmarried.

"I suppose he's given you presents?—brooches and things?"

She started.

"You want me to send them back?"

"Rather!—every one!"

"Very well, I will. I'll make them up into a parcel the first thing in the morning."

Battiscombe rubbed his hands together.

"We'll do it now and wash our hands of the whole affair."

He observed her tenderly.

"You're a wonderful little woman, Vera. I don't wonder fellows fall head over ears in love with you the minute they see you."

She was still nestling in his arms and there was a gap between her frock and her neck.

"Hullo!" he exclaimed, "what's this?"

His glance had fallen on the chain of gold filigree, and before she could prevent him he had drawn the Crimson Butterfly from its hiding-place into the lamp-light. "I've never seen this before."

He groped for the fastening with his great fingers.

A moment later he held the pendant in his palm and Vera stood a little away from him cudgelling her fertile brain for some excuse to account for its presence there.

As he pawed it wonderingly, struck momentarily dumb by the sheer beauty of the thing, a queer feeling stole over him.

He could have sworn that he was handling something unutterably unclean.

He looked up sharply.

"Did he give you this, too?"

Mrs. Battiscombe hesitated. She was on the point of explaining how Abu-Samar had stopped her, induced her to go to his house and forced her to accept the gift, when she realised the difficulties besetting any such confession. She had already told him that she had refrained from embarking upon her proposed expedition to inspect Moberly's newly-erected clubhouse. She would have to correct that statement, which would be a remarkably bad beginning to a rather improbable story. Jim had doubted her once that night, and, having put these doubts to flight, it would be a pity to risk arousing them again.

"Er—yes. It's pretty, isn't it?"

He dropped it on the table.

"Extraordinarily so. Wonder where he got it?"

She gave the faintest shrug to her shoulders.

"In some bazaar in Colombo or Singapore, I fancy. He did tell me."

Battiscombe slid from his perch, and, foraging for some moments in a cupboard, unearthed a sheet of brown paper. He spread it out and placed the pendant on it.

"That'll make a good start, anyway. Trot out all the other little tokens of affection, dear, and we'll get this job off our chests."

She sighed deeply.

"Must we do it to-night? I'm so tired."

For once he was firm.

"Absolutely. It won't take you a moment."

She went to her room.

Five minutes later he carried off a little oblong parcel to the back of the house. He came back smiling.

"And that's the end of Mr. Richard Moberly! I've given it to Kuraman, and our worthy planter will find it when he comes on to the verandah for an early breakfast. It'll help him to start the day well!"

She surveyed him doubtfully.

"Oughtn't I to have written?"

He shook his head.

"In future, whenever the necessity arises for anyone to write to Dick Moberly, it's going to be your lawful husband!"

She was arranging her hair in front of the glass when Jim's head and shoulders came round the door.

"I say, Vera!"

"Yes?" she responded through a mouthful of pins.

"I didn't tell you, did I? The Commissioners instructed me to watch that black feller closely."

She looked round.

"Black fellow?"

"Why, yes; the chap who styles himself Dr. Abu-Samar. I happened to mention our little encounter this morning and he got quite excited. As far as I can make out, Samar's not a doctor at all. He's a revolutionary of a most dangerous type and has already given trouble in Sarawak. He's believed to get a hold over the natives by sheer hypnotism. He can make 'em believe anything. Well, good night, little woman. Sleep well."

The door closed softly.

CHAPTER VI

THE MAGIC OF ABU-SAMAR

THAT NIGHT VERA BATTISCOMBE dreamed a peculiar dream; peculiar because she rarely dreamed at all, and doubly peculiar because she had no memory of ever falling off to sleep or, in fact, waking after it.

She had been lying, her hands clasped behind her head, staring up at the oblong patch of white cotton from which the mosquito-curtains were suspended, thinking over the events of the past twenty-four hours. It had been an eventful day, in all conscience, she reflected, and allowed the principal characters in a drama for which she herself had been primarily responsible to pass before her eyes in quick succession. Abu-Samar, Armourer, Jim—posing so ridiculously as the injured husband and coming conveniently into line in the end—and the sacrificed Dick Moberly, deservedly sacrificed at the altar of his own indiscretions.

She wondered idly what the planter would say when he discovered the Crimson Butterfly in the parcel—whether he would return it immediately or keep it until he had found an opportunity of seeing her and demanding an explanation. The thought of the Butterfly brought her back to Dr. Samar. If what the Commissioner had told her husband were true, the fact that he had merely induced her to accompany him to his house and frightened her was all the more to be wondered at. It flashed across her mind that his rather unusual conduct was not without its motive, but what that motive was she could not for the life of her discover.

A sense of uneasiness crept over her.

It was quiet outside, and the house was unusually still. The perpetual droning of insects, the shrill whine of a mosquito seeking some flaw in the netting, the deep, rhythmic snoring of her husband in the adjoining room—all these familiar sounds seemed to be receding into the distance. Suddenly a fierce gust of hot wind blew in through an open window, and the little lamp by her bed flickered and went out. She knew the wind was hot, for it fanned her cheek, and yet, by every known law, the breeze at that early hour of the morning should have been cool. The dog on the verandah gave a peculiar yelp and moved restlessly on the cane chair upon which it invariably reposed.

She shut her eyes resolutely and turned over on to her side and a queer noise broke upon her ears like the rushing of waters. There was a dry sensation in her mouth and the heat was becoming unbearable. She sat up, intending to reach for the quinine, firmly convinced by this time that she was in for a dose of fever. Her eyes hurt her, and, even before she raised the lids, she was conscious of a bright red light.

Groping for the bottle, she discovered that the mosquito-curtains had disappeared. She opened her eyes wide and, at the sight that met her gaze, endeavoured to scream; but no sound came.

It was as if, by some extraordinary miracle, everything with which she was familiar had been spirited away. The four walls within which she had lain secure—the roof even—had vanished.

She found herself reclining upon a divan, of orange-coloured silk, with the great stars blinking down at her from a violet dome, and in the red light from a tall brazier at the foot of her couch a myriad of winged creatures fluttered. By the base of the brazier a native girl lay asleep.

Gradually, as her frightened eyes accustomed themselves to the outer gloom, she discerned the vague outlines of rocky crags and the more distant tips of tall trees.

She dropped back on to her elbows and her voice returned to her.

She called to the girl in Malay, and the brown form stirred. Her face came round and Mrs. Battiscombe recognised the girl she had seen at Samar's bungalow.

"Goddess of the Crimson Butterfly, I hear!"

She uttered a little cry and clutched at her breast. Her fingers closed over the pendant that Battiscombe had insisted on sending to Moberly.

It was then that she saw that she herself wore a *sarong*—a sheath of shiny black powdered with gold that swathed her from her breasts to just below her knees—and that her arms, her neck and her ankles were hung with treasures that resembled those which Abu-Samar had produced from his cedar-wood coffer.

"Where am I?" she asked faintly.

"In your temple, O goddess!" returned the brown girl, and threw something into the brazier which sent its flames flaring to the heavens.

Mrs. Battiscombe sat bolt upright and beckoned.

"Come here," she said. "I want you to tell me why I am here and who brought me."

Brown eyes surveyed her strangely, incredulously.

"The goddess remembers nothing?"

Vera shook her head.

"Nothing; nothing at all. I was in bed at my husband's house—and the wind came . . . "

The girl drew closer and stood presently, with her arms folded, looking down at the white woman.

"Great goddess," she said, "I am Dara—and I obey. Once, before the white man came in his ships across the black waters, there was a white goddess in the temple of the Crimson Butterfly—so wonderful in her loveliness that all men who beheld her desired to possess her. She wore the emblem of the Sacred Butterfly at her throat and no man dared draw near to her because of it. After a little while, a strange man came who had not heard that the kiss of the goddess was death—and so died. There came another and yet another, each sharing the same fate, until the goddess, wearying of chiefs' sons, sought to entrap the Sun. Upon a certain night, the Sun dropped not into the western sea, but fell into the temple of the Crimson Butterfly—and for many moons there was nothing but darkness. The Butterfly—whose life was the

Sun—feared to destroy it, and when at last the Sun rose again it was seen that the goddess, too, had departed. Nevertheless, it was written that in a thousand moons she would return again to her people. To-night the prophecy is fulfilled; the fires of the temple burn once more and there is again a goddess at the shrine of the Crimson Butterfly."

Vera Battiscombe moistened her lips.

"And how do you know I am the real goddess?—I might be an impostor."

The girl shook her head.

"Those who sought you found the symbol at your throat."

She pointed to the butterfly pendant.

Vera moved impatiently.

"But that's perfectly ridiculous," she insisted, "I had never set eyes upon the Crimson Butterfly until this afternoon. Dr. Abu-Samar made me take it."

And still the brown girl shook her head obstinately.

"The prophecy is fulfilled!"

Mrs. Battiscombe sprang from the divan and shook her violently.

"Listen," she screamed. "This is all a trick, an act of vengeance because my husband unfortunately insulted Dr. Samar when he came to him yesterday. I am an Englishwoman. I was born in England. I should never have come to this wretched island if I hadn't married. Get me my proper clothes and take me back."

She threw the girl from her and looked up into the evil eyes of Dr. Abu-Samar.

Instinctively aware of the scantiness of her attire, she shrank back from him.

"Goddess of the Crimson Butterfly," he taunted her, "I have summoned you—and you have come. The dog is still sleeping, the little soldiers in the round hats have not stirred. To Abu-Samar those things are as nothing. You have sent my gift away, but it will come back to you; it will always come back—and the kiss of the goddess is death!"

She clapped her hands over her ears to shut out the sound of his voice and, turning on her heel, ran heedlessly into the darkness. The night air was cold and moist, and suddenly she realised that she was standing on the soft earth at the foot of the long flight of steps that led up to the bungalow.

It was almost light now and the feathery tops of the palm trees showed like phantom creations above a sea of billowy mist.

She was about to seize the wooden rail and commence the ascent when she discovered that her hands were full. She was staring with startled eyes upon a brown paper packet that had somehow become broken open and from which protruded the Crimson Butterfly.

The sound of quick footsteps above made her thrust the packet into the pocket of the pyjama jacket she wore.

James Battiscombe, his face very white, his hair on end, peered down at her.

"Vera! Where on earth have you been? You gave me the shock of my life."

He hurried down the steps and carried her up.

A minute later she was in a long chair, with a blanket wrapped round her, making faces at the brandy he insisted on forcing between her lips.

"I thought I heard you moving and went into your room," he explained, tapping the cork back into the bottle. "You weren't there. I didn't know what to think. It occurred to me that, after the row we had last night, you'd got snorky and bolted." He rested his hands on his hips and beamed down at her. "You don't usually walk in your sleep, do you?"

"No," she assented weakly, "I don't think I've ever done it before.

And then, an irresistible drowsiness stealing over her, she fell asleep.

CHAPTER VII

A Strange Insect

Vera Battiscombe blinked and looked up.

She was still lying in the long chair on the verandah and the blue sun-blinds had been drawn. There filtered up to her through the morning air the chattering of natives, the contented clucking of hens, the ring of an axe in the forest.

Still in a state of semi-coma, she dimly realised that Jim, with his accustomed thoughtfulness, had drawn the table to her side, so that the bell which would summon Hoon-Kit was within easy reach.

She yawned and was about to turn over and continue her slumbers when her arm touched the pocket of her pyjama-coat. A guilty feeling stole over her and she forced herself into a sitting position. With trembling fingers she fumbled for the contents, hoping to discover that the bulging contour of the pocket was due to an accumulation of handkerchiefs, to a bottle of quinine tabloids placed there by accident, to anything rather than the packet she imagined she had removed from the custody of Battiscombe's men in her sleep.

Her worst suspicions were justified. The parcel which should have gone to Moberly at dawn was still there.

She held it at arm's length, and, as she did so, the ghastly details of her nightmare built themselves up in her imagination with a vividness that set her trembling. It had not all been a dream, could not have been, for here was a portion of it—glaringly concrete—within her fingers. She was weary, too, thoroughly exhausted, as if she had undergone some stupendous fatigue. Her head throbbed, her eyes felt sore and watered in the light, and she was conscious of a dull aching from head to foot. How much, her reeling brain demanded, had been real—and how much illusion?

Her watch had stopped. Still holding the blanket round her, she crept to the living-room door and saw, by the clock that hung on the wall, that it was ten minutes past eleven.

Jim would be coming from the court-house at noon.

She unearthed a fresh sheet of paper and made the parcel up again. A strong impulse assailed her to withdraw the butterfly pendant and dispose of it in some manner when her husband was away, but she fought it down. The thing frightened her. She must get it out of the house or she would go mad.

In the seclusion of her own room she scrambled into some clothes and penned a hasty note to Dick.

"MY DEAR,

"Jim has come to his senses at last and, for a time at least, we must put an end to everything. Keep everything you find here. Some day I hope to be able to see you and explain.—VERA."

She was about to fold it when force of habit made her add her inevitable postscript.

"An awful scene last night; it made me dream. Rotten, isn't it?—V."

She pushed it between the folds of the brown paper and rang the bell.

In her excited frame of mind, it seemed an eternity before Hoon-Kit shuffled to the door and knocked.

"Give this to one of the *Tuan-Hakim's* men and tell him to take it immediately to the *Tuan* Moberly's house. It is the parcel that should have gone earlier this morning. He need say nothing to the *Tuan-Hakim. Tahu?*"

The man grinned and withdrew.

In five minutes he was back again.

He found his mistress fully dressed, standing at the open door that led to the verandah.

"The man has gone," he reported.

She heaved a deep sigh of relief.

"Very well." She produced a silver dollar and held it out to him. "Give this to the soldier when he returns."

The coin passed into the doubtful security of a pocket of a pair of Battiscombe's discarded trousers.

"The man was very glad," resumed Hoon-Kit, looking down at his feet. "The *Tuan-Hakim* gave him the packet last night—and this morning he could not find it. He feared that the *Tuan* would be angry."

"*Baik-lah*, Hoon-Kit," and she dismissed him.

She remained, a hand on either door-post, staring through the opening between the blinds. The colour had come back to her cheeks and there was a triumphant light in her eyes.

Things had turned out better than she had dared to expect. Moberly's presents had gone back to him, there was no danger he would return the Crimson Butterfly, and Jim would never know the parcel had been delayed.

She started violently. Through that opening at the head of the stairs where the sun threw a rectangle of yellow light across the boarded floor there fluttered an enormous crimson butterfly. It encircled for a moment in the sunlight, beat against the blinds, then settled on the table by her chair.

She stood there, rooted to the spot, her eyes drawn to it by a strange fascination.

The insect was formed like a butterfly and yet the familiar delicacy of the wings was absent. It appeared to her as a coarse, unlovely creature, with a corrugated surface like a rubber sponge, the countless pores of which seemed to open and close as she looked. Had she encountered it in the jungle, settling on the bark of a forest-monarch, she would probably have mistaken it for a poisonous fungus.

It swooped into the air again and flew straight toward her.

She uttered a wild scream and Hoon-Kit, who had been laying the table for the mid-day meal, hurried on to the verandah.

"The *mem* is ill?" he inquired blankly.

She waved her arms frantically.

"Drive it away," she cried. "Quickly!—that cushion!—anything!—It's horrible—horrible!"

Hoon-Kit reached behind him for a table-napkin and hit at the thing as it passed.

He missed it by inches and stood staring after it as it wheeled into the open again and was gone.

"The Crimson Butterfly!" she exclaimed in a voice that was barely a whisper.

The Chinaman nodded.

"*Yah*—a butterfly; that is all!"

He folded the table-napkin carefully, shaking his head all the while. It was evident in every line of his brown, wrinkled face that he was at a loss to discover the cause of his mistress's panic. Suddenly he brightened and grinned broadly.

"The *mem* does not like red butterflies?" he suggested.

She endeavoured to conjure up a smile.

"Thank you, Hoon-Kit," she said. "It was very stupid of me. I did not see it was a butterfly. I thought it was something else. Bring in a bottle of lager for your master; he will be here very soon now."

As soon as he had gone, she sank into a chair.

"It had green eyes," she muttered to herself, "I saw them."

CHAPTER VIII

THE PROFESSOR TURNS NATURALIST

"HULLO, YOUNG PEOPLE! Sorry I'm late for tiffin."

The professor came up the stairs, breathing heavily. His face was very red and glistened with moisture, his tunic was open and he was mudded up to his knees.

Joyce sprang to her feet and ran to meet him.

"Father! Where on earth have you been?"

He kissed the top of her head and waved a peculiar object over her back at Armourer.

"What d'you think of that?"

The magistrate removed his pipe from between his teeth and observed it curiously.

"A butterfly net," he suggested.

"Exactly—and if I'd had it half an hour ago, I'd have saved myself a lot of unnecessary exertion."

His daughter took it from him.

"Where did you get it?"

The professor mopped his forehead.

"A most intelligent Sikh, whom I encountered in my travels, constructed it in less than twenty minutes. He happened to have the materials handy. You see, it's quite simple. Just a couple of feet of bent cane, a little binding and some mosquito netting. He's made a first-class job of it, don't you think so, Armourer?"

The younger man took it from the girl and made a wild swipe in the empty air.

"Quite an efficient sort of implement."

Joyce laughed.

"It's very nice, of course," she conceded; "but I don't see what use it is."

"No," said her father, "I don't for one moment suppose you do. I shouldn't myself, if I hadn't caught sight of the butterfly. It was a unique specimen—large and red and particularly clumsy in flight, and it managed to inspire me with the enthusiasm of a boy. I remembered, too, that Baines's last words to me were—'If you do happen to find any rare bugs, try and get me them.' " He blinked over his glasses at Armourer. "He has a wonderful collection. I don't suppose there's another like it in the world. Well, I saw this butterfly and followed it for about a couple of miles. I had nothing with me except my helmet, so I dipped my handkerchief in a stream and knotted it over my head. The creature flew low and a dozen times I was within an ace of catching it—and then my spectacles got misted somehow and I lost sight of it altogether."

The D.O. nodded sympathetically.

"Where was this?"

"Quite near that bungalow you showed us in the trees."

"Moberly's place!"

"I think that was the name you told us. I was prompted to call and ask if anything like it had been seen there before, but I remembered it was lunch-time. The first human being I met was this Sikh—a picturesque fellow with curling beard and an elaborate turban. He told me his name was Gholam-Singh. He had witnessed my wild career after the butterfly and knew exactly what I wanted."

His daughter smiled.

"He must have thought you a priceless sort of lunatic! What a ridiculous exhibition! An elderly gentleman, with a hanky knotted over his head, chasing butterflies!"

"In the heat of the day," added the magistrate. "Rather a risky thing to do, professor, with nothing to cover the nape of your neck."

Standen snorted.

"Rubbish! I was in the shade of Mr. Moberly's rubber trees most of the time. Chasing butterflies is no more ridiculous in a native's eye than hitting a white ball into space—and calmly proceeding to walk after it! I'm sorry I missed that fellow, though. Quite apart from my promise to Baines, I became interested in it myself. It was a butterfly—and yet it wasn't, if you can understand me." He stared from one to the other. "A butterfly is an airy, dainty thing, but this—although it was correctly formed—looked more like a piece of raw meat furnished with legs and antennae."

Joyce gasped.

"But how disgusting!"

The professor sat down somewhat heavily.

"Disgusting, eh?—Well, in some respects, I suppose it was." He shook his head sadly. "Ten years ago, net or no net, I shouldn't have muffed a thing like that."

She indicated the implement which now reposed on the table.

"And now perhaps you will tell us why you want that."

He drummed with his fingers on his knees.

"To go after it again, of course. Butterflies breed quickly and where there is one there should be others." He glanced sharply at Armourer. "Have you ever seen one?"

The D.O. shook his head.

"I don't remember ever noticing anything that answers to your description; but then, you see, I'm not a naturalist."

"But you couldn't miss a thing like that," the other insisted, "nobody could."

"And you are quite determined to get one of them before you leave Borneo?"

"Most certainly. I owe Baines a good many debts of gratitude."

Armourer rubbed his hands together.

"Then that settles it. There's only one thing for it. You'll have to tell the people at Jesselton to send your *barang* up here, and give me the pleasure of your company for another week at least. Miss Standen, I am counting on you to be a sport and back me up."

A smooth-haired terrier with a patch over one eye raised itself on its hind paws and thrust a nose confidingly between her fingers.

"It certainly sounds very tempting," she admitted. "Doesn't it, daddy?"

The professor removed his glasses and wiped them. Presently he replaced them and, clasping his hands behind his back, faced his host.

"If there's one thing in this world I endeavour to avoid, it's overstaying my welcome. Ever since we left the boat we've had nothing but hospitality thrust upon us with both hands. Now, you wouldn't believe it, I know, Armourer, but in some respects I'm particularly sensitive. I should hate to think I'd left an unpleasant impression behind me in Borneo. To put it bluntly, I don't want to be regarded as a *sticker*."

Joyce looked at Armourer.

"What he really means to say is that he knows jolly well we oughtn't to bother you any further and that our obvious duty is to get back to Jesselton this afternoon, but he does so want to use that butterfly-net!"

"Good enough," laughed the magistrate. "We'll call that a bargain, shall we, professor? You'll stop here—both of you—until you get your butterfly, and I'll guarantee to have your kit fetched up here by dinner-time this evening. Suppose we have some lunch?"

"It's a conspiracy," declared the professor, and left it at that.

At the conclusion of the meal Professor Standen retired to his room to change his suit for one Armourer had lent him.

Joyce stirred her coffee thoughtfully.

"Do you really want us to stop, Mr. Armourer?"

The D.O. looked up.

"Rather!"

"Honestly?"

"Of course. To tell you the truth, Miss Standen, I'm so grimly determined to keep you here that I'm issuing instructions to the natives to *swat* every red butterfly in the neighbourhood and so dispose of their corpses that your father'll never find 'em."

She looked down at the cloth.

"That wouldn't be very fair, would it?"

"No, but it'd be frightfully effective."

"We couldn't stay here for ever, you know. Father counted on being in Borneo for a month and then going on to the Philippines. We've been here more than a week already."

Armourer filled his pipe.

"I suppose it's really rather selfish of me to try and keep you anchored in one spot. You see, Miss Standen, when one is forced to move in a restricted area one forgets that visitors, with a limited number of days at their disposal, want to move around and see everything there is to be seen. You're pretty fed up with me, aren't you, for using the crimson butterfly as a lever to persuade your father to stop?"

The girl flushed.

"Oh no. I wanted him to stay. I hate just rushing about, getting glimpses of hundreds of places. It reduces one to the level of the ordinary tourist. Whenever I look back on this one real big adventure of ours, I want to remember that I lived, for a while at least, exactly as the people do who have to be here all their lives. I shall always remember Jelandang and your thatched bungalow—and the dogs. I shall never forget that ridiculous trolly accident, the glorious view from the railway and your ride to Mrs. Battiscombe's for clothes. I must try and go over one day soon and thank her."

A shadow crossed Armourer's face. There were some things he would never forget either—that mad dance at Rembakut the night before, those cursed lips of hers and the unexpected arrival of her husband. Somehow or other, he didn't want Joyce to meet Vera Battiscombe. It would be like the meeting of something pure with something decidedly impure.

"I have every reason to be grateful for that trolly accident," he said. "It scarcely seems possible that it could only have happened yesterday. Just fancy, we have only had one look at the bay together, one walk up the slope and one sunset— and yet, to me at least, it seems as if we have never been doing anything else. Twenty-four hours ago I was feeling unutterably lonely. I was bored with myself, bored with my job, fed to the teeth with everything—"

Their eyes met.

"Were you really? You poor thing! Then we were actually doing you a good turn in coming to stay with you?"

He pushed back his chair.

"I should just think you were! I hadn't seen a decent-looking white woman for heaven knows how many months."

"Except Mrs. Battiscombe," she retorted wickedly. "Oh, you can't deny she's very beautiful and frightfully attractive. Anybody will tell you that. Even I know it, and I've only been in Jesselton a week! And I heard you ride back last night, you know."

He was staring at her awkwardly, endeavouring to frame some form of defence, when a figure appeared suddenly at the doorway. It was Vance—Moberly's first assistant.

"Sorry to butt in on you like this, Armourer, but rather a terrible thing's happened."

The magistrate started.

"What's the trouble?"

Vance rubbed his chin and looked from Armourer to Joyce.

"You'd better come outside and I'll tell you."

"I'll come now. You'll excuse me, Miss Standen?"

"Certainly."

He followed the other on to the verandah.

"Well?"

"Moberly's dead!"

"What!"

"He's dead," said Vance again. "Trevor found him just after lunch. He was doubled up in his chair on the verandah. Trevor sent for me."

Armourer glanced at his watch.

"I'll ride over with you. Any idea of the cause?"

Vance pursed up his lips.

"He was poisoned, of course. There's not the least doubt about that. He'd gone a ghastly colour. It's a queer business altogether. There was a piece of paper between his fingers and an opened packet on the table at his side." He lowered his voice. "You know, of course, that Mrs. Battiscombe used to run over there pretty frequently. Well, the paper appeared to be a note from her and the packet contained some brooches and things he'd given her."

The magistrate picked up his hat.

"She'd turned him down?"

"It looks like it."

"And you suggest he poisoned himself?"

The planter frowned.

"I don't know what to think. There's a horrible crimson mark right across his left check, like a ghastly birth-mark, and shaped like a butterfly."

CHAPTER IX

THE TRAGEDY AT BUKIT-SERANG

As they rode up the slope towards Moberly's bungalow a short dark man came down the steps to meet them.

"Hello, Armourer! Glad you've rolled up. Rotten business, isn't it?"

Armourer had caught sight of the huddled form in the chair.

"I'm frightfully sorry. Poor old Dick! Has the doctor been?"

Trevor shook his head.

"I sent for him right away, but the messenger came back with the information that he had run over to Kudat and was not expected back before Tuesday. The estate apothecary has had a look at him. He says it's poison right enough. I've collared his cook-boy—he's down in the watchman's quarters now. He's been with Moberly a long time, and I don't suppose he had anything to do with it; but Vance thought it better to be on the safe side."

"Good! You haven't moved anything"

"No. Everything's just as I found it."

They mounted the steps.

It was some moments before Armourer approached the dead planter. He stood with his hands in his pockets and an unpleasant, choking sensation in his throat. Three fit, live men gazing at a fourth who had passed out so quickly that it shocked them! Moberly had been so active, so intensely masculine, that this sudden snapping of the thread had knocked them completely off their balance.

Vance was the first to break the silence.

"There's that mark I told you about," he said huskily.

The magistrate went forward.

Controlling his nerves with an effort, he took the dead man's shoulders and pushed him gently from his huddled position until he lay outstretched. Right across his left cheek, from the fringe of his hair to the base of the jawbone, extended a vivid crimson rash where the skin had come up in lumps, as if stung by a nettle.

There was a letter between the fingers of the right hand, and from the diminutive parcel on the table dangled the Butterfly pendant, suspended from its chain of gold filigree.

Armourer started.

It was an unusual type of chain, peculiarly wrought, and it dawned upon him that he had seen one exactly like it quite recently. Mrs. Battiscombe! It came upon him in a flash. He remembered now that when she had ignited her cigarette from the end of his cigar he had noticed that she wore a chain—and that he had seen it again when they were dancing. The letter poor Moberly held was from her. She had been wearing the pendant when he left Battiscombe's house—and here it was on the planter's table. There must have been an unholy row at Rembakut during the past dozen hours or so. Battiscombe must have suspected Moberly or— He rubbed his forehead with the tips of his fingers. The only man who had any cause to quarrel with Moberly was James Battiscombe. It was all very perplexing.

He turned to Vance.

"Anybody called here this morning?"

"No."

"You're quite certain about this? How, for example, did this packet get here?"

"A black soldier brought it to the kitchen-quarters just before lunch. I particularly asked the *boy* about that."

"Moberly was out all the morning," added Trevor. "I met him over on the far side at about eleven. He seemed unusually fit then."

Armourer glanced at the packet again and a sudden thought struck him. He withdrew the remaining few links of the chain and dangled the pendant in front of Moberly's left cheek.

He looked back at the others.

"Anything strike you?" he asked.

Vance started.

"Yes, by Gad! It's practically the same thing in miniature."

Trevor bent forward excitedly.

"A most extraordinary coincidence. It was the first thing I noticed—the mark on the chief's face and that weird ornament hanging there. I had intended mentioning it to Vance, but in the excitement of the moment I forgot. You don't attach any importance to it, do you?"

The magistrate found an old envelope and tucked the ornament into it.

"I don't know what to think," he admitted, "but I'm going to take charge of this until I'm satisfied it has no bearing on the cause of Dick's sudden death. It's a confounded nuisance the doctor's away."

"How about that black fellow?" suggested Vance.

Armourer rubbed his chin.

"Abu-Samar? Is he any good?"

Trevor smiled.

"He says he is. After all, it's hardly a doctor we want—except as a matter of form. We know the chief's dead and any fool can see he's been poisoned. I'm open to bet anybody that old Macnally when he comes won't be able to tell us if the poison was vegetable, animal, or mineral."

The magistrate snapped his fingers.

"Lord! I must be daft! Here, Trevor, send somebody over to my place at once and ask Professor Standen to come across. You can get your black fellow too, if you like."

Trevor shot down the steps and called to a tall Sikh who was coming up the slope.

"Gholam-Singh! Come here. I want you."

Armourer gripped Vance's arm.

The sound of the watchman's name brought him back to the professor's story of a chase after a red butterfly.

"Vance, did you ever notice a large crimson butterfly any-where around here?"

The other shook his head.

"Never," he answered firmly.

"Nor did I, and yet Professor Standen—who happens to be my guest at the moment—saw one here to-day and tried to catch it. He followed it almost to this house. If he hadn't been afraid of butting in on Dick's lunch-hour, he'd have called. What an extraordinary thing life is! A less scrupulous man would have altered the entire aspect of the case. Standen could have told us perhaps just how Moberly died; he might even have prevented a catastrophe."

"But," protested Vance, sitting down heavily, "nobody's ever heard of a poisonous butterfly. Supposing there were such a thing in existence, it's difficult to imagine it would leave a mark like that."

Armourer nodded gravely.

"I know that," he said; "but we can't get away from facts. Moberly was poisoned. He has a rash on his face shaped like a butterfly—and Standen saw a strange insect fluttering in this neighbourhood just about the time the ghastly tragedy occurred."

"And then there's the brooch," Vance reminded him. "Have you read Mrs. Battiscombe's note?"

The magistrate shook his head.

He possessed himself of the paper and scanned it hastily.

"Jim has come to his senses at last . . . we must put an end to everything . . . Keep everything you find here . . . Some day I hope to . . . explain. An awful scene last night; it made me dream . . . Rotten, isn't it?"

Their eyes met.

"It beats me," said Vance. "Er—Armourer!"

"Well?"

"I don't know exactly how you're inclined to regard this business, but I think we can safely leave Jimmie Battiscombe out of it. It's unfortunate there should have been a row between Mrs. Battiscombe and himself over the chief, but, knowing Jimmie as we do, we can hardly look upon him as a man likely to indulge in homicide—however justifiable. Trevor hit the right nail on the head when he referred to the presence of the butterfly ornament as a remarkable coincidence. It couldn't be anything else. Everybody liked Moberly. He had his weaknesses, I admit, but he was a damn' good fellow all the same. Can't we keep our mouths shut about that letter?"

Armourer was sucking at the stem of an empty pipe.

"Yes," he said at length; "why not? If Standen is satisfied that Dick died from the sting of an insect of some sort, I should be the last to publish anything which would add to a scandal that's already had too much circulation."

Their hands gripped.

"I'm glad you think that," said Vance brokenly.

His face dropped into his hands.

"Where's young Trevor gone?" asked Armourer presently.

The planter withdrew his fingers and stared round him.

"Don't know. Gone to find Abu-Samar, I should imagine." A sound broke upon his ears and he sat perfectly still, listening. "What's that?"

The magistrate had gone to the rail.

"Somebody coming through the trees on horse-back— riding like the devil." He caught Vance's arm and pulled him up. "Here, quickly!"

"What's the matter?"

"I don't know." He threw open the first door he found and drew the other through it. "Don't utter a sound."

They stood in the shadow with the door ajar.

Almost before Vance could collect himself, the rider had dismounted. He heard a voice—a woman's voice—calling.

"Dick!—Dick!—Are you up there?"

It was Vera Battiscombe.

Armourer gripped the other's arm warningly.

She came slowly up the steps into view.

They saw her stand for a moment, irresolute, between the still form in the chair and the entrance.

Suddenly she laughed.

"Why, he's asleep!" she murmured, and went forward as if to shake him.

An almost irresistible desire swept over Vance to shout out something, to do something to break the shock of the inevitable discovery. He shuddered and gripped hard at the corner of a dressing-table to steady himself.

A piercing shriek sent his ears singing.

A second—and she was backing towards the rail in horror, her beautiful face a deathly white, her eyes wide open in terror.

"It was true then! They have killed him! He told me—! *The Crimson Butterfly!*"

Her hands clasped to her ears, she ran, panic-stricken, to the stair-head.

Vance was half-way through the door when Armourer caught him roughly and threw him back.

She turned suddenly, controlling her nerves with a stupendous effort, and walked deliberately to the packet on the table. Her trembling fingers tore at the paper, scattering the contents broadcast.

"Gone!" she muttered hoarsely. "They have found it!"

She reeled, one arm bent over her forehead, and fell heavily to the floor.

CHAPTER X

THE MYSTERY DEEPENS

THERE WERE FOUR PEOPLE in the garden when Armourer left the bedroom—the Sikh, with Professor Standen, Trevor and Abu-Samar.

He went out to meet them.

"Hullo, professor! I'm afraid I've rather an unpleasant job for you." He turned to the black doctor. "Are you Abu-Samar?"

Samar bowed.

"Well, you'd better go straight into that room where you see the door open. You will find Mr. Vance there with an English lady who has fainted. I want you to do all you can for her."

He waited until the other had gone up, then drew Standen into the shade.

"There's a dead man up there," he began. "It's Moberly—the planter about whom I spoke to you yesterday. You remember your red butterfly? Well, I fancy you have reason to be thankful that you didn't catch it. I believe it killed Dick Moberly."

The professor blinked at him.

"Killed Mr. Moberly!" he ejaculated. "Surely you're not in earnest?"

"Very much so, I'm afraid. If you hadn't told me about that butterfly, I shouldn't have known what to think. But both the time when you saw it and the peculiar mark on the poor chap's face seem to point to the fact that Moberly was stung by it and died from the poison it exuded."

"There's a mark, eh? What sort of mark?"

The magistrate led the way to the verandah.

"Come up and see for yourself, The doctor's away and I've no alternative than to place the matter entirely in your hands."

As the professor bent over the chair, Armourer swept the trinkets from the table and passed them over to Trevor. The letter he had already tucked away in a pocket.

"That is Moberly's property," he said in a low voice; "you'd better take charge of it and put it with the rest of his effects. If you miss anything," he added meaningly, "talk to Vance about it—afterwards?

The first assistant came out at that moment.

"Mrs. Battiscombe's come round all right," he announced, "but she seems in a pretty bad way. We'd better get Jimmie over here."

Armourer set his jaw firmly.

"No. We'll have her carried to my place and advise him from there. Miss Standen can look after her and I'll get the professor to certify she's too ill to be moved. There are one or two questions I want to ask her as soon as she's fit to answer them. Get some men and a *pikul*, and, if you can spare him, I'd like Trevor to see her safely over. You're a medical man, of course, professor?"

Standen glanced over his shoulder.

"What's that?"

The magistrate repeated his question.

"Oh, yes; I'm a doctor right enough."

He stripped off his jacket, rolled up his sleeves and ripped open the dead man's tunic.

"I tell you what, Armourer, I'm not leaving Borneo until I have secured a specimen of that particular type of insect. It's most providential I was on the spot when this occurred. We are undoubtedly on the verge of a great discovery. A poisonous butterfly! People at home would laugh at us, wouldn't they? But a venomous, vindictive insect, charged with poison-cells from wing-tip to wing-tip! It sounds incredible, impossible—and yet we have undeniable evidence."

The little man was becoming quite excited, and with every fresh exertion his face became a deeper red. His experienced fingers travelled all over the corpse, now pressing a muscle, now lifting an eye-lid. Peculiar little grunts escaped him at intervals, until in a grim sort of way he reminded Armourer of one of his terriers out after rats. Moberly, whom they had all known and liked, had, as far as the professor was concerned, become an interesting subject.

The magistrate could hardly have expected it to be otherwise, but it struck him as a ghoulish sort of performance all the same. He saw Abu-Samar in the doorway.

"Well, doctor, and how's your patient?"

"She is delirious," he replied. "She keeps asking for a certain article of jewellery which, it appears, she has lost. It might help matters to give it her."

Armourer looked hard at Trevor.

"Oh, yes!" he returned easily. "What sort of ornament, Dr. Samar?"

"A ruby ornament on a gold chain—with emerald eyes," said Samar without turning a hair. "Have either of you gentlemen seen it?"

Armourer shook his head.

"Not I."

"Nor I," added Vance quickly.

Trevor glanced from one to the other before replying.

"A ruby ornament with emerald eyes! Good Lord, no. I haven't got it."

He felt inordinately guilty as he spoke, but Samar did not appear to notice. He looked at his watch.

"I am going away now. I propose looking back this evening to see if there is any improvement. She will be all right until then."

Armourer smiled pleasantly.

"You needn't bother, Dr. Samar. Mr. Battiscombe will be over shortly and I expect he will want to send for his own medical man. I'm afraid I was responsible for troubling you in this case and you'd better apply to me for your fee."

"Not at all," interrupted the first assistant. "This is an estate affair, and we'll settle it."

"On second thoughts," corrected Armourer, "it seems to me that it's outside Bukit-Serang altogether, and the person who's primarily responsible for his wife's health is Mr. James Battiscombe. Good afternoon, Dr. Samar. Thanks very much. You'll send that *chit* to me, won't you?"

They carried the planter between them to his own room, and Trevor accompanied Mrs. Battiscombe to the magistrate's bungalow.

It was five o'clock when the three remaining Englishmen sat in consultation round the table upon which the trinkets had once reposed.

"Poisoned by some insect—the exact nature of which is unknown," said the professor suddenly, as if he had been turning the phrase over in his mind for some time.

The magistrate looked up.

"You would give a certificate to that effect?"

Standen spread out his hands.

"Most certainly. What else could one say?"

"Nothing, of course. I was only interested to learn how you would put it."

Armourer caught Vance's eye.

"Well, that's settled. I'm awfully obliged to you, professor. Vance, old son, you can't do any good moping about here. Come over and have dinner with us. We'll meet Trevor and make him join us."

The planter pressed a moist hand to his forehead.

"I don't like the idea of leaving the place."

Armourer dropped a hand on to his shoulder.

"It'll do you all the good in the world to get away from things. Stick a couple of watchmen on guard outside."

"All right," said the other gloomily. "I'll come."

They rode through the trees, the professor mounted on Mrs. Battiscombe's pony. They were within a quarter of a mile of Armourer's house when Standen wheeled round on the path.

"What's the matter?" asked the magistrate.

The professor frowned deeply.

"If you young men will excuse me, I'll go back and have another look at Mr. Moberly. I don't expect to be more than half an hour."

"I'll come with you," suggested Vance.

Standen shook his head.

"I'd rather not, if you don't mind."

"Just as you like, of course. You'd better explain to Gholam-Singh that you have my permission to go in."

They were sitting on the verandah when the professor returned.

Joyce had just come from her room, where Mrs. Battiscombe now lay, and Trevor was talking to her.

The professor beckoned to Vance.

"Are you quite sure of your men?" he demanded.

The planter started.

"Yes, I suppose so. Why?"

"Because I feel convinced that somebody had been in Moberly's room between the time that we left and when I got back there. The body was not in the same position, there was a peculiar pungent odour hanging everywhere—and the mark on the face had entirely vanished!"

CHAPTER XI

JOYCE DISPLAYS CURIOSITY

ARMOURER felt Joyce at his side.

"I'm thirsting for information," she explained softly. "Whenever I approach father—he just glares at me and carries on a conversation with somebody else. I've tried Mr. Trevor, but he only colours up and looks uncomfortable—and Mr. Vance seems so utterly miserable that I haven't the heart to tackle him."

The magistrate smiled down at her.

"What do you want to know?"

"Oh, heaps of things. Why Mr. Vance came for you in such a hurry after tiffin; why you sent for daddy; why Mrs. Battiscombe fell ill so suddenly—and why you all persist in indulging in whispered conversations? Is somebody dead?"

Armourer started.

"Yes," he felt bound to confess. "The planter who owned that nice bungalow in the trees died this afternoon—very suddenly. There was no doctor handy, so we sent for Professor Standen. Mrs. Battiscombe rode over to see Mr. Moberly, and—well, the sudden news that he had pegged out upset her."

"She fainted?"

"That's right."

"At Mr. Moberly's house?"

The magistrate nodded.

"Then, if you wanted to move her at all, why didn't you send her to her husband's bungalow?"

Armourer glanced nervously over the rail at the group of men talking together below.

"Because, Miss Standen, this was a good deal nearer and there happened to be another white woman here who could look after her. We've sent for Mr. Battiscombe, but he happened to be out when our messenger called. He'll come over as soon as the news reaches him."

The girl appeared to be thinking deeply.

"Is Mr. Battiscombe a nice man?"

"Rather; one of the best."

"She's frightfully pretty, isn't she?"

"Oh, yes."

"He won't be angry when he learns that her illness was caused by the news of Mr. Moberly's death? She is dreadfully ill, you know."

Armourer was not feeling any too comfortable at that moment. He was aware that Vera Battiscombe was in a high fever and a little afraid to what extremes her delirium might carry her. Above all, he had no desire for Joyce to glean from her ravings exactly what happened at Rembakut on the previous evening. In his keenness to solve the mystery of the Crimson Butterfly, he had forgotten until that moment that Battiscombe had surprised them on the verandah and would be inclined to regard the presence of Vera—ill and at Armourer's house—with suspicion. Battiscombe had been blind for so long that it was difficult to make allowances for what he would think now that his eyes were opened.

"I expect we shall have to approach her husband very tactfully," he said, "and, in case we decide to frame some ingenious little story to meet the emergency, you had better know nothing. She talks a good deal, I suppose?"

"Yes."

"About anybody in particular?"

She leaned back against the table.

"She doesn't talk sensibly, of course. Sometimes she rambles on for minutes at a time; then there are long periods of silence, broken perhaps by little incoherent remarks. I can only remember hearing 'Dick' and 'Jim,' and once she murmured something about a butterfly. I nursed a man once who apparently saw the most beautiful butterflies in his dreams.

He used to tell me about them. He had been hit in the head. Mrs. Battiscombe didn't strike her head when she fell?"

"I don't think so."

There ensued a long pause, at the end of which Joyce said:

"I must go back to her now."

She was on the point of entering the room when the magistrate called to her softly:

"Miss Standen!"

"What is it?"

"I want you to pay particular attention to anything further she says about that butterfly. Make some sort of note of her remarks, if you can."

She smiled wistfully.

"All right; I will. More secrets?"

"I'm afraid so. I'll tell you all about it one of these days."

She turned the handle and pushed open the door.

"It's been quite a day of butterflies, hasn't it? Daddy chased a red one for quite a while this morning."

"By Jove!" ejaculated Armourer with well-simulated surprise. "So he did!"

He went down the steps and joined the others.

The professor was leaning against a post; Vance, looking particularly dejected, stood with his hands in his pockets a couple of yards away; Trevor was sitting on the ground. It was the hour of sunset again—and so much had happened since Joyce and Michael witnessed the last one together twenty-four hours ago! Dick had been alive then, and Armourer had waved to him as he passed his house on the way to the estate store for a tooth-brush. Vera Battiscombe—who now lay, fragile and fever-racked, babbling incoherencies—had been a desirable vampire-thing, woefully in possession of all her faculties.

"Have you still got that ornament on you?" demanded Trevor, as Armourer came up.

The magistrate felt in his pocket.

"Yes. Why?"

"Professor Standen would like to have a look at it."

He passed the envelope to the professor, who withdrew the pendant and held it to the light.

He glanced presently from one to the other.

"Astounding! And you say it was on the table when the poor chap died?"

Vance nodded.

"We are taking Standen into our confidence," he explained to Armourer. "It won't go any further. You don't mind, do you?"

"Not in the very least. It's quite on the cards he may be able to help us out." He turned to the professor. "You'd better hear the whole of the yarn, anyway. I went to Rembakut—that's Battiscombe's place—last night, if you remember, to get some things for your daughter. Battiscombe was out, and his wife, pleading loneliness, begged me to stay with her until he returned. I didn't see the Butterfly then, but I clearly recollect noticing that chain round her neck. It next appeared, with the pendant attached, on the table by Dick's elbow this afternoon. We all remarked on the coincidence, the similarity to the mark on Dick's face; but we could only regard it as a coincidence and nothing else."

"Naturally. Well—?"

"Then Mrs. Battiscombe rode over and something prompted me to drag Vance into an adjoining room and watch what she did. I feel pretty rotten about it now, because the discovery has proved more of a shock to her system than I believed possible at the time. But there was that letter to be considered, stating that she and Jim had had a row over Moberly, and I wanted to prove conclusively that neither Jim nor she knew anything about the tragedy. I was so keen on my job that I actually jotted down what she said the moment she realised that Dick was dead." He glanced at the back of an envelope. " 'It was true then! . . . They have killed him! . . . He told me . . . The Crimson Butterfly!' "

" 'They have killed him,' " repeated Standen. "You are quite sure she said that?"

"Quite. You heard it too, Vance."

The planter inclined his head.

"Quite clearly."

The professor was still examining the pendant.

"And then—?"

"And then she began foraging among the various articles of jewellery on the table, apparently searching for that. She couldn't find it, because I had it already—in my pocket. Her next remark was: 'Gone! . . . They have found it!'—and then she fell."

"But," put in Trevor, "the interesting fact remains that the chief was stung by a butterfly—or some similar insect, because we all saw the mark and the professor noticed a strange-looking creature in the neighbourhood of the bungalow just before lunch. You can't get away from that."

"We all know that," agreed Vance, "but what's puzzling all of us at the moment is who told Mrs. Battiscombe that Dick was going to be killed. There's another thing too: we've all of us been out East a good spell and not one of us can remember having heard of a poisonous butterfly—and yet she referred to *The Crimson Butterfly* as if she'd known it all her life. I'm not inclined to be superstitious, and I take any native yarn I hear with a pinch of salt, but I've got an idea at the back of my skull that that damned ornament had everything to do with Moberly's death."

"You're getting morbid," declared the second assistant.

"Very likely—but I defy anyone to think deeply about an affair like this without getting morbid. Look at the facts: Mrs. Battiscombe sent that ornament to Dick, and about the first thing she did when she found he was dead was to try and get it back. It wasn't the tragedy that knocked her out—it was the knowledge that somebody had found that pendant. Isn't that so, Armourer?"

Armourer sucked thoughtfully at his pipe.

"It looks like it."

"If it were merely one of Dick's presents to her, why should she want it back? Who was the accomplice who, fearing that the resemblance between the ornament and the mark would be noticed, slipped into Moberly's bungalow and employed some mysterious chemical preparation to remove the mark?"

In the weird half-light his long face looked more than usually sallow.

"Don't you think," he continued, levelling a finger at Armourer, "that, in the light of recent developments, the butterfly Professor Standen thought he saw is our one stumbling-block to the solution of the mystery? Without that, it seems pretty clear sailing. Dick and Mrs. Battiscombe were about a good deal together. It's possible he may have offended some vindictive native and that she heard him threaten the chief. More likely still, Dick might have taken that ornament from some obscure sanctuary to give to her. You know these queer religions. The guardian of the shrine, or whatever you like to call him, could have poisoned Dick, made that mark with some corrosive fluid and—"

"It won't work," broke in the magistrate gravely. "You see, Vance, the ornament was left behind. He would hardly have forgotten that."

The professor coughed.

"And," he insisted, "I didn't merely think I saw a red butterfly. I did visualise it—and gave a very sound description to Armourer when I got back. Moreover, so anxious was I to make another attempt to catch it, that I got your very excellent Gholam-Singh to make me a net; and all this before anyone had heard that Mr. Moberly was dead. Personally, I adhere to the opinion that that particular insect—a four-winged monstrosity masquerading as a butterfly—was responsible for the tragedy we are now discussing. With regard to the fresh complications that have since arisen—I confess myself mystified. It is within the bounds of possibility that these will be found to have quite simple explanations as soon as Mrs. Battiscombe is well enough to tell us about them. You know, Vance, the longer I live the less anxious I am to jump to obvious conclusions. Whenever there are two sides to a question, I like to probe both very thoroughly. I don't know the lady in question, of course. I've been on this island only a matter of days. But I have it on excellent authority that Mrs. Battiscombe was celebrated for her beauty, her easy-going disposition—if one may call it so—and her quick-wittedness. She came up the steps to Mr. Moberly's verandah, saw the dead man and the scar on his face, and uttered a perfectly natural exclamation—*'The Crimson Butterfly!'* It was a crimson butterfly; it was shaped like one and it was crimson in colour. At that point she remembered the trinket and, recognising that its unfortunate resemblance to the mark would be bound to attract notice, decided to conceal it. It came as a shock to her to discover that the resemblance had been noticed and the ornament removed. The other purely hysterical ejaculations I should be disposed to wash out altogether. What does a delightful, butterfly creature like Mrs. Battiscombe know about *killing!*"

Darkness fell suddenly and they found their way one by one to the verandah.

Standen found himself next to Armourer.

"How does that strike you?" he demanded.

The magistrate wrinkled his forehead.

"I've listened attentively to both sides," he announced. "I'm always doing it; it's my job!—I've nothing to find fault with in your earnestness or your eloquence; but neither of your solutions is in the least bit watertight. What do you say to a drink?"

CHAPTER XII

COLLEAGUES CONFER

ARMOURER had just emerged from the bathroom, wrapped in a long towel, when Trevor put his head round the door.

"Battiscombe's here."

The magistrate sat down heavily on the bed.

"The devil he is!—That makes six to dinner!—I wonder how the grub'll spin out!"

Trevor came right in and closed the door after him.

"He hasn't been home since lunch. Says he had an urgent message to meet the Commissioner at Ketatan. We thought you'd better tell him about Mrs. Battiscombe."

Armourer rubbed a damp spot on his leg with a corner of the towel.

"Oh, all right. Send him in here—Oh, just a minute, Trevor. We might as well let him down as lightly as we can. Tell Vance the yarn is that Mrs. B. was picked up in the trees on your estate—better say *near* your estate—and that you brought her here, as you'd heard there was an English girl staying with me. I'll fit in poor Dick's affair as best I can."

The assistant rubbed the back of his head.

"He's bound to find out in the long run."

"It's just possible he will; but we don't want to risk his going off the deep end at the moment. It won't suit my purpose to have him worrying about his wife and poor Dick. I want him to concentrate on the Crimson Butterfly business."

"All right."

He was about to go in search of Battiscombe, when the huge form of the magistrate from Rembakut filled the doorway.

"Hullo, Trevor! You here, too? Quite a considerable gathering."

Trevor laughed weakly.

"I'm just off to tell Armourer's *boy* that there'll be another to *makan*. See you later."

The door closed.

Armourer passed over the cigarette tin and indicated a chair with his bare foot.

"Well, Jim! You think me a howling outsider, don't you?"

Battiscombe frowned and then laughed.

"Oh, you're thinking of last night! I thought quite a lot of things then, but fortunately for everybody concerned I've reconsidered them. We'll forget that, if you don't mind."

The younger man looked at his toes.

"Thanks. I was afraid you'd want me to explain—and there isn't any explanation. I was just a damn' fool, that's all there is to it."

He struck a match and held it out to the other.

"The awkward thing is that Mrs. Battiscombe's here now—ill."

"What!"

The match flickered out and Battiscombe stared round the room as if expecting—in a world of fresh surprises—to find his wife secreted somewhere within those four walls.

"Yes, old son. Trevor found her and brought her over. Miss Standen happened to be staying here with her father, and she very kindly consented to nurse her. We sent for you immediately."

"I haven't been back. Is she bad?"

"Just a touch of fever. I don't think there's the slightest cause for alarm. Luckily we have a doctor in the house— Miss Standen's father—and he'll pull her through all right. She mustn't be moved just yet."

Battiscombe came slowly to his feet.

"She would ride out in the heat of the day," he muttered. "I'd better go and see her."

"I shouldn't, if I were you. It might upset her."

The other groaned.

"She must have had it coming on last night. I found her

walking in her sleep. When d'you think I'll be able to see her?"

"We'll talk to Standen about that in a minute. All you've got to do is to sit down quietly and try not to get rattled. After all, everybody out here gets fever sooner or later."

Battiscombe flopped down again and the chair creaked ominously beneath his weight.

"What's Vance doing here?"

"I was just going to tell you. Vance and I have been having a pretty tough afternoon. Dick Moberly pegged out just about lunch-time."

Battiscombe stared at him in blank amazement.

"Pegged out!—Died, you mean?"

Armourer nodded.

"I'm afraid so. Macnally was away at the time and Professor Standen acted for him. It appears he was poisoned by some bug or other, apparently while he was dozing in his chair after the morning's work. Standen's an authority on poisons and I'm going to persuade the Commissioner to get him to investigate the matter officially."

"Sure it wasn't snake-bite?"

"I don't think so. It's a most peculiar case. Everything seems to point to his being stung by a thing that looked like a red butterfly, but, as Standen puts it, was charged with poison-cells from wing-tip to wing-tip. You've been out here longer than most of us. I was wondering if you could help us."

Battiscombe shook his head.

"Butterflies don't sting," he insisted.

"That's one of the queer points about it. Dick had a great crimson patch right across one cheek—exactly like a butterfly."

"A native *ju-ju*," suggested the other.

Armourer flicked the ash from his cigarette.

"Vance thinks that now; but *ju-ju*—or their Bornese equivalent—belong to the realm of fairy-tales."

Battiscombe moved awkwardly in his chair.

"Afraid I really don't know enough about 'em to express

an opinion. A fellow I knew once believed in 'em though—and he'd explored the jungle from end to end. A queer, long chap named Russell. You won't remember him, I expect; he was a trifle before your time. So Dick's dead! Doesn't seem possible, does it?"

"No. It's a ghastly business, and it's hit Vance pretty hard. He thought no end of Dick. Er—this *ju-ju*, butterfly, or whatever you like to call it, that caused the trouble was crimson—a crimson butterfly. Does that help at all? Have you ever heard of a native religion that employed one as its symbol?"

He observed the other keenly.

Battiscombe's great head swung to and fro like a pendulum.

"Never," he declared, and then frowned heavily. "A crimson butterfly! D'you mean a live butterfly—or something resembling one?"

Armourer grabbed up a pile of underclothes and began scrambling into them.

"Either."

"I've never encountered any cult in which a butterfly bore the slightest significance, but I saw a crimson butterfly on a chain last night. Vera had it and, between ourselves, I made her send it back to Dick."

"Oh, yes? Dick gave it her?"

"Apparently. It was a pretty thing, with emeralds for eyes. There was something uncanny about it, now you remind me, and for some reason or other I didn't care about holding it too long."

"Where did he dig it up?"

"In a bazaar in Colombo or Singapore. Vera didn't appear certain about it. By Jove, Michael! Dick would have got that this morning!"

"He did," said Armourer, his head coming out of the top of his vest at that moment; "it was on his table when we discovered him. Queer, wasn't it?"

"Hell!" remarked the larger man. "I don't like the look of this. Do I understand you to say that Dick had a mark on him like that butterfly?"

"We all noticed the resemblance."

"All! What d'you mean by all?"

"Professor Standen, Vance and myself—and Trevor when he came along after accompanying your wife here."

Battiscombe got up and paced the room for some seconds, a performance which seemed to stimulate his reasoning faculties.

"Moberly dead—and Vera sick! Where did young Trevor pick her up?"

Armourer was brushing his hair vigorously and did not turn his head.

"I don't know exactly."

Battiscombe caught his shoulders and forced him round.

"I'm not quite such a blithering idiot as you people persist in imagining. Tell us the whole truth, Michael."

"Good Lord, man! I'm telling you it as fast as I can."

The other held his head on one side and screwed up his eyes.

"There's a conspiracy going on somewhere. I can smell it. Trevor looked as guilty as a schoolboy caught stealing apples. Vance kept hopping first on one foot and then on the other—and I couldn't get an ounce of sense out of him. You found Vera at Dick's place, didn't you? She was just itching to ride over and explain exactly why she returned those confounded trinkets. I'll wager a thousand dollars with anybody that she hopped into riding kit as soon as I'd left the house. I can see through your little game, Michael, and I admire you all the more for it. You didn't want my feelings to be hurt. But they've been hurt a good deal lately, and one more kick won't make much odds."

A sudden thought struck him.

"She didn't make a fool of herself and—and shoot him?"

For the first time Armourer laughed.

"Nothing of that sort, old son. You can make your mind quite easy about that." He regarded his friend steadily. "The story of Dick's death was a true bill right enough. The mark was on his face and that extraordinary pendant was on the table; but Mrs. Battiscombe didn't show up until Vance had fetched me. She fainted soon after the awful truth dawned on her and she's been pretty queer ever since. I've still another kick for these poor old feelings of yours, Jim! She seemed to know Dick was going to be killed and that the Crimson Butterfly would have something to do with it."

"You don't mean that?"

"I do, Jim. That's the real reason why I told Trevor to bring her here. I thought that, in her delirium, she might say something that would give us a clue. Listen: Professor Standen saw the insect that might have caused Dick's death; he chased it almost up to his bungalow this morning. It was a horrible-looking thing, as far as I could make out. He described it rather graphically as a piece of raw meat that had grown legs and antennae."

"When was this?"

"Somewhere between noon and lunch. The tragedy must have happened shortly after."

Battiscombe was tapping his thumbnail on his teeth.

"Now that's really extraordinary!"

"What makes you say that?"

"Why, Hoon-Kit came to me with a yarn that Vera had been scared to death by a huge red butterfly that flew on to the verandah and off again. This would have been before your friend saw it, because I came up from the court-house with my usual abnormal thirst at ten minutes to twelve. Vera was in her room when Hoon-Kit trotted the beer along. He murmured something to the effect that the *mem* was afraid of red butterflies. It was such a fat-headed sort of remark to make that I made him explain himself. What d'you make of *that?*"

"It's positively uncanny. It's almost as if the butterfly and its image were connected somehow. Nobody had ever seen the ornament before except, perhaps, Mrs. Battiscombe. As far as we are concerned, it first showed up at your place and then went, almost immediately after, to Moberly's. Bang on top of this comes the actual butterfly. It floats in at Rembakut, following the trail of the pendant, and, finding it gone, flies across to Dick's house—and kills the person found in possession of it. Sounds tolerably good nonsense, doesn't it? But that's precisely how a superstitious person might be expected to look at it."

"You've a nasty mind, Michael!" declared Battiscombe, and his large frame shuddered.

"But," persisted the other, "there is a lot more in this than meets the eye. Leaving the pendant out of the question altogether, there's one great outstanding feature that raises the affair from one of simple insect-bite. While we were on our way here, some person unknown raided Dick's bungalow and in some mysterious manner erased the mark from his face. If we could discover who that was, we should be a deal nearer the solution."

Battiscombe shook himself.

"Hurry up with your dressing, for the love of Mike! I'm beginning to want a good stiff tot! Your harrowing narrative has almost made me forget that you and I have got to arrest Mr. Abu-Samar. That's why the Commissioner was in such a blinking hurry to see me."

"Arrest Abu-Samar. Whatever for?"

"For being an impostor, incendiary, and the Lord knows what. He's wanted in Sarawak, Sumatra, the Federated Malay States—and possibly in Timbuctu! Wherever he goes he stirs up trouble—and trouble is the last thing we want here."

Armourer grinned.

"As far as I can see, we've quite enough to go on with, as it is. Arrest Abu-Samar, eh? That's about the last thing I expected."

"And I kicked him out of the court-house yesterday for suggesting I should put him up for membership of the club! If I'd known then what I do now—it'd have saved an ocean of trouble!"

Armourer whistled.

"You kicked Abu-Samar, did you? Well, Jim, all I can say is—you must have had intense provocation!"

"I did," returned Battiscombe.

"Now, what about that drink?"

CHAPTER XIII

A NOCTURNAL EXPEDITION

PROFESSOR STANDEN came out of Mrs. Battiscombe's room, closing the door after him.

"Well?" inquired her husband anxiously.

The professor looked down at his hands.

"I think she's nice and comfortable now. Her temperature's not normal yet; but there's been an appreciable drop since this afternoon. I'm hoping she'll sleep till the morning. Armourer's very kindly given up his own bed to my daughter and had it fixed up in the room. Joyce has had a good deal of nursing experience—and there's nothing for you to worry about at all."

He rubbed his hands together.

"Now, what about this expedition?"

Battiscombe indicated Armourer.

"Better consult the magistrate in whose area we now are. He's in charge."

"Oh, no," protested his colleague. "*Seniores priores*—and all that sort of thing, you know. I cheerfully waive all territorial rights in favour of seniority—and weight!"

"That be hanged for a tale! The Commissioner said—"

"Damn the Commissioner!" remarked Armourer cheerfully. "Abu-Samar's your bird—not mine. My men—and my own valuable assistance—are entirely at your disposal. Professor Standen would like to join us."

"Good enough! How about you, Vance? Any stomach for nocturnal adventuring?"

The first assistant, who had been staring gloomily into the night, shifted his position on the rail.

"Oh, I'll come. I'm not in a mood for standing about and doing nothing. Trevor'd better stop with Miss Standen. One of us must be here, in any case."

Battiscombe began searching for his hat.

"Then that's settled. We'll push off now and get it off our chests. Anybody seen my topee?"

Armourer smiled.

"You can't have lost it, Jim. It's the biggest thing in hats ever made!"

The other dived behind a table and presently drew himself to his full height, a smile of triumph illuminating his features. By way of reply, he dropped it unconcernedly over Armourer's head, thereby extinguishing his fellow-magistrate completely.

They filed out into the clearing.

"How far have we got to go?" demanded Vance.

Battiscombe reflected.

"About two and a half miles. I suggest we walk it. What do you say, professor?"

"I'm game."

"I suppose you others are agreeable? My corporal knows the way and, as far as I can gather, the track's badly overgrown."

Vance looked up.

"You don't anticipate any trouble?"

Battiscombe shook his head.

"There ought not to be any bother at all. I don't fancy he's been here long enough to have any native backing. You're all armed, I imagine?"

Standen patted a side-pocket.

"I am for one."

"Armourer's lent me a gun," added the first assistant. "Mine's over on the estate."

A shadowy form appeared round the corner of the house, carrying a lamp and followed by three or four others.

Joyce looked over the rail.

"Look after daddy, Mr. Armourer, won't you? He's inclined to be reckless!"

Armourer laughed.

"All right," he called back. "We'll impose any form of restraint we think necessary."

The procession moved off. There was a stiff breeze blowing from the sea and the night air was pleasantly cool. The inimitable Kuraman—short and thickset—went on ahead with the lamp; Battiscombe and Armourer came next, while Vance followed with the professor. A short distance behind, three of Armourer's men and two of his colleagues tumbled along with their rifles slung, smoking and chattering in an undertone.

The path led them westward, turning presently south in the direction of the Ayer River.

Battiscombe tripped over a root, swore and regained his balance.

"Hope Vera'll be better in the morning," he said suddenly. "Thank heaven she's as strong as a horse. Have you got that Butterfly affair with you?"

Armourer started and began searching all his pockets in turn.

"Damn!"

"What's the matter?"

"I believe I've left it in my other clothes. I suppose it'll be all right?"

He peered through the gloom at his companion.

"Is your servant honest?"

"As honest as most. The chances are he won't have finished cleaning up in the kitchen by the time we get back. In which case he won't have been in my room. Appear to have left my pipe too. Give me a cigarette, will you!"

"You can have a cigar, if you prefer it."

He held out his case and Armourer lit up.

Battiscombe looked back at the others, but found they were already smoking.

He glanced thoughtfully at the overhanging trees.

"About another ten minutes of this and we ought to be in the open for a spell. Hope we don't strike any leeches. I hate 'em."

"Tell me about Abu-Samar," said Armourer.

"You've met him?"

He was going to add that he had sent him in to attend Vera that afternoon, but wisely refrained.

"Unpleasant looking chap, isn't he?—I took a rooted dislike to him from the very first. I didn't like his eyes."

"They are queer," admitted Armourer. "As far as my information goes, he's no earthly right to any of the letters he sticks after his name. He began life somewhere about here as a sort of medicine-man and made such a good thing at it that he saved enough money to get him to Ceylon. There he took to snake-charming and eventually got in tow with a native conjurer, who produced the usual programme of hypnotic illusions. This feller disappeared after a while and the mystery of his disappearance has never been satisfactorily cleared up. Anyhow, Samar took over his stock-in-trade and blossomed forth into a fully-fledged magician on his own account. There's a gap in the records extending over about three years, when Abu crops up again in Anam. He seems to have dropped hypnotism and gone in extensively for drugs. It appears that in this instance he employed forged certificates to endeavour to obtain a job in the French colonial service as an apothecary. The forgery was detected and Abu-Samar sent to gaol for a long term. He escaped, however, and the three principal officials responsible for his detection and imprisonment died in a mysterious manner at about the same time."

"Poison, eh?"

"That is the general belief, but no trace of any poison was discovered at the post-mortem. It is assumed that either a peculiar, self-effacing drug was used, or that—and what I imagine is more likely—the physicians who officiated weren't particularly smart at their job. How Abu left Anam nobody knows. He appeared a little later in Singapore, stirred up native trouble there, skipped by the skin of his teeth to Dutch territory—Sumatra, organised a band of freebooters that fairly terrorised the island—and, finding the place too warm for him, decided to transfer his attentions to Sarawak. Then he came here."

"Where did you unearth all this?"

"The Commissioner gave me a whole screed; it runs into about ten pages. I'll let you have a copy. It's worth framing!"

There followed a long silence.

"Jim," said Armourer suddenly, "your wife has never met Abu?"

"Good Lord, no—never. Why?"

"Don't know. I was only thinking. The bridge is just in front of us. We'd better put out all lights."

He signalled back to the other two; while Battiscombe went forward to Corporal Kuraman.

They took the track Vera had followed the day before.

It was the professor who noticed it first.

"Vance, you didn't put your pipe in your pocket while it was still alight?"

The planter dived in a hand and produced it.

"No," he returned; "not guilty!" He sniffed.

"There is a smell of burning somewhere, though, isn't there?"

"I certainly thought so. There!—Do you see that light through the trees?—Ah! it's gone again. No, there it is!"

Vance whistled softly and the two district officers halted.

"What's up?" demanded Battiscombe. "Anyone hurt?"

"The professor has just noticed a fire of some sort or other right ahead of us. No, not where you're looking; further to the left. There! Got it?"

Battiscombe called Kuraman.

"Kuraman, what's that light?"

The brown corporal shifted his round hat to the back of his head and stared in the direction his master was pointing. After a few seconds he sidestepped into the trees and looked again.

"It is the house of Abu-Samar, *Tuan*," he announced presently. "I think it is burning."

Their faces were close together now and each looked at his immediate neighbour for enlightenment.

"Better get there at the double," said Armourer; "he's got wind of this."

"Don't believe it," asserted Battiscombe. "The Commissioner arranged it off his own bat—and not a soul knew of it, barring myself. Kuraman may be mistaken. Perhaps it's a fire just this side of the place."

"We'll soon see," said Vance, and strode off into the darkness.

At the bend in the path they broke into a sharp trot. As the trees thinned out, the truth of the corporal's statement revealed itself. Driven low by the breeze, columns of smoke swept over them, setting them coughing. Between the gusts, they caught glimpses of a blazing inferno, where reed wall and sago roof were enveloped in a sea of flame that soared roaring to the skies.

"Spread out," shouted Battiscombe at the top of his voice. "Vance, you nip round to the right and take a couple of men with you; professor, d'you mind being responsible for the left? You can have Kuraman and one other. That leaves one each for us, Michael. I want you to get on the far side. Stop anybody you find. If there's any serious difficulty or you see Samar, fire a couple of rounds in the air and we'll concentrate on that spot."

"I fancy we're too late," said Armourer between his teeth—and selected his man. "Cheerio, everybody!"

Suddenly, as they stole to their posts through smoke that enveloped them like a choking fog, two shots rang out.

The professor, his eyes streaming, charged into Armourer. Both sat down heavily.

The magistrate was on his feet in an instant.

"Who the devil was that?"

"Me," responded the professor blandly. "Don't do anything rash. I've lost my fellows already in the confounded smoke. Give me a hand."

The other groped for his arm and pulled him up.

"Did you fire?" asked Standen.

"No. I fancy it was Battiscombe. It seemed to come from that direction. Come on!"

The pall shifted, and at that moment every object in the tiny clearing stood out as in the light of day.

Battiscombe was standing quite close to the house, with his man a bare yard behind him. Vance had just appeared from the trees. A figure, that had lain hidden behind a fallen portion of the structure, started suddenly to its feet and—in that fleeting second—Armourer recognised Abu-Samar. He carried a large basket, held together by a strap, and a portion of it appeared to be smouldering. He drew himself very erect and stood, immobile as an ebony statue, against a background of living flame. An arm shot upward as if in splendid defiance—and the smoke descended again, blotting out everything.

Battiscombe fired again—three rounds in quick succession—and Kuraman, dropping to one knee, emptied his magazine into the darkness.

There followed a wild, chaotic stampede, a pause for breath in the immediate vicinity of the furnace—and a scattered sortie into the night-shrouded forest.

An hour or so later they collected round Kuraman's lamp.

"That fellow bears a charmed life," declared Battiscombe, gasping for breath.

"A very amusing evening," conceded Vance; "but, from your point of view, a decided wash-out."

Armourer counted the shadowy figures that constituted the group carefully.

"One missing," he declared. "Who is it?"

"The professor," said the planter again. "I saw him a minute ago, grubbing at something in the ruins."

Standen joined them at that moment. His face, when they could get a glimpse at it, was blacker than Kuraman's, and he smiled the engaging smile of a self-satisfied nigger minstrel.

He thrust a charred bundle up to Armourer's nose.

"Smell that!"

The D.O. sniffed.

"Unpleasant," was his immediate verdict, "very!"

"Well," announced Standen, depositing it on the ground and feeling for his handkerchief, "that's precisely the same smell as I noticed in Moberly's room this afternoon when I went back. This is the basket Abu-Samar was trying to take with him. There was a good deal of blood on it when I picked it up and it had been badly trampled. It looks as if one of you fired pretty accurately. The basket contained a jumbled mass of crushed glass receptacles and—this."

He bent over the charred mess and presently extracted from its shapeless interior something wrapped in a piece of sacking.

"Bring the lamp closer," shouted Battiscombe.

A moment later they stood in a ragged circle, staring down at an enormous chrysalis. The professor touched it with his spectacle case—and the thing moved.

"You see—it's alive."

"Yes," muttered Vance, "it's alive all right, but—"

Standen surveyed them all in turn.

"I have every reason to believe, gentlemen," he declared, as if delivering a lecture to a crowd of interested students, "that this is our friend the crimson butterfly—in embryo!"

CHAPTER XIV

AT VANCE'S PLACE

VANCE'S BUNGALOW being the nearest, the party repaired there for a clean-up.

The planter was reaching down the decanter when Armourer spoke.

"What made you ferret out that basket, professor?"

Standen, who had been carrying the bundle with him all over the house, as if chary of trusting it with anybody, raised his eyes.

"I happen to be blessed with a peculiarly keen sense of smell," he declared. "When that black fellow passed me this afternoon, I caught a faint suggestion of something sickly and unpleasant. I did not pay serious attention to it at the time, but a recurrence of apparently the same odour in Moberly's bedroom set me thinking. It would hardly be true to say that I suspected Abu-Samar from that moment, but there was just a shadowy notion at the back of my mind that he might in some way be connected with the mystery. He seemed peculiarly anxious, if you remember, to obtain possession of the butterfly ornament about which he said Mrs. Battiscombe was raving."

Battiscombe started.

"What's that?" he demanded sharply.

Armourer flushed.

"You must recollect, Jim, that we all imagined Abu-Samar was genuinely a doctor. Macnally was away. Standen was at my place. We had a dead man and a sick woman and a devil of a mystery confronting us. Trevor suggested Samar. In the end we sent for both of them—and Samar attended Mrs. Battiscombe."

"You don't mean to tell me you sent that man in to my wife—alone?"

"No," jerked out Vance. "I was there too—trying to bring her round."

"You were there all the time?"

The planter looked at the ceiling.

"Most of it. I certainly came out for a bit to tell the others how she was; but I was never far away from the door."

Battiscombe bit his thumb.

"Go on, professor. Tell us a little more about your line of reasoning."

Standen adjusted his spectacles.

"Samar was the only person outside the charmed circle who knew Mr. Moberly was dead, the only one of whom we knew. There might have been others whom we didn't know, but I was not prepared to take that into account. You see, I couldn't take my mind from that smell. Then we embarked upon our little expedition. Abu-Samar, surprised by the swiftness of our approach and fully aware that the odds were against him, emerged from the burning building clinging desperately to that basket. I judged it to be of vital importance to him, or he would have relinquished it in his flight. Anxious to put my theory to the test, I concentrated on the basket. It had been discarded almost immediately after we all saw it and a heavy beam had fallen right across it, so that I had great difficulty in extricating it. I found traces of there having been other chrysalids—or *pupae*, each apparently enclosed in little bamboo cages, which were unfortunately crushed beyond recognition. How this particular specimen managed to survive I am unable to explain. I discovered it fully a yard from the basket itself, and my attention was called to it by its writhing, spasmodic movement. I hadn't even been looking for a chrysalis; but it was merely a matter of seconds before I had realised the possible importance of my discovery."

Battiscombe stared at him aghast.

"But you don't suggest he breeds the damn' things?"

"I don't suggest anything. Chrysalids vary considerably in their duration of quiescence, and we may have to be patient for quite a long while before the actual butterfly breaks through its shell. If indeed it does prove to be the Crimson Butterfly, we shall be faced with another problem. We shall have to consider how it is that Abu-Samar happens to be the sole possessor of specimens of this sort."

Vance rested his elbows on the table. Now that the excitement of the chase had worn off, he was once more a victim of acute depression.

"And the pendant?" he asked. "How do you fit that in?"

The professor shrugged his shoulders.

"I must frankly confess that this particular point baffles me completely. You must not yet lose sight of the fact that the presence of the ornament on Moberly's table may be sheer coincidence."

"I'm not losing sight of one thing: that Abu-Samar killed Dick Moberly—and if ever he falls into my hands I pity him!"

Standen shook his head slowly from side to side.

"At the present stage, everything is conjecture. If, for example, a perfectly harmless insect emerges from this *pupa*—the whole structure upon which my theory is based falls to the ground. If indeed Samar poisoned Moberly, can anybody suggest a motive?"

Battiscombe smiled grimly.

"If he'd poisoned *me*, it'd be far more easily understood. I kicked him out of my place yesterday—literally, I mean, and he went off swearing blue murder."

"I'm wondering," said Armourer, "if he meant to kill Dick at all."

All eyes turned in his direction.

"What d'you mean?" asked Vance.

"Wait a bit and I'll tell you. Did Dick know Samar?"

"Yes—a bit."

"To what extent?"

"He used to drop in at the chief's place sometimes, principally, I imagine, to try and persuade him to employ him for the coolies."

"Which, of course, Dick declined to do?"

"Yes; but," Vance added hastily, "there was never any row about it. The chief could be very diplomatic when he chose. He explained that he was the manager only and had to take his instructions from London. He also pointed out, I believe, that Macnally was the official doctor and would naturally resent any such appointment, even if it were in Dick's power to make it."

Armourer shot a side glance at his colleague.

"I may have to ask a couple of questions about Mrs. Battiscombe. Do you mind?"

A look of pain crossed Battiscombe's face.

"All right. Carry on."

"Was Mrs. Battiscombe ever at Dick's place when any of these interviews took place?"

"It's not unlikely. She was there fairly often."

"You can't say for certain?"

"No."

The magistrate drummed on the table with his fingers.

"About that pendant. You've never set eyes on it before yesterday, Jim?"

Battiscombe shook his head.

"Never; but you mustn't lay too much stress on that, because Vera tells me I never notice anything!"

"A common feminine delusion with regard to their male associates," murmured the professor.

"I'm wondering," pursued Armourer, "whether it could be possible that Samar, wanting to get a dig in at Battiscombe, gave the pendant to Moberly, knowing that he would send it to Mrs. Battiscombe."

"Meaning the intended victim to be *me*," chimed in his senior.

"That's what I was trying to get at. You see, professor, I've learnt this evening that Abu-Samar has been suspected of poisoning a good many people, and always, it appears, in a distinctly mysterious manner. Battiscombe can give you the details in full, if you want them. I don't know how you scientists regard Oriental magic, but we just ordinary folk cling fondly to the notion that there's possibly something in it. Probably we're wrong, but there remains just a sporting chance that we're not. Abu-Samar is well versed in all these spectacular tricks in which hypnotism plays a very important part. It sounds pretty feeble, I admit, but it looks as if the actual butterfly *followed* that image!"

Vance passed a hand across his forehead and yawned.

"How?" he inquired wearily.

"Ask me another!—We've had to swallow a good deal during the past few hours, so much in fact that we ought to be in a mood to tackle almost any possibility."

Battiscombe pushed himself out of his chair.

"We'd better be getting back. Michael, you seem destined to occupy one of your long chairs to-night; I'd better curl up in another. A great deal hangs on what Vera has to tell us to-morrow."

The professor blinked.

"If your suggestion is in any way correct," he remarked, "the next victim—provided there is to be a next—should be yourself. You've still got that Butterfly, haven't you?"

Armourer laughed.

"Many thanks for your cheery suggestion, professor! As a matter of fact, I happen to have left it at home."

Standen emptied his glass.

He jerked himself suddenly as if to shift a heavy weight from his mind.

"It's all the purest nonsense imaginable," he asserted testily, "and I must be in my dotage to have allowed you even to harbour such a ridiculous notion; *but* I shall feel a great deal easier in mind when we get back."

"I hope everything's all right," said the planter gloomily, with an inflection that suggested that everything might not be.

"Don't be a damn' fool!" said the professor, and stamped his way down into the garden. "Good-night, Mr. Vance," he called back more pleasantly. "I didn't want to be rude, but you echoed something I was imbecile enough to think myself!—Good night!"

CHAPTER XV

A SECOND VICTIM

ARNOLD TREVOR—left to his own devices at Jelandang—remained leaning over the verandah-rail, staring at that black patch in the trees through which his companions had vanished.

He who had played an important role in the first and second acts of the drama at Bukit-Serang had been dropped out of the third act altogether—and he was feeling pretty miserable about it. One of the least pleasant points of his character—and one which Moberly had tried vainly to eradicate—was a brooding sense of injustice, and as he gazed now into the blackness that sense came uppermost.

After all, he argued to himself, it was he who had discovered the body of the dead planter, noticed the similarity between the mark on Moberly's face and the pendant, and accompanied Mrs. Battiscombe to Armourer's house. And now, just because he came next below Vance on the estate pay-roll, he was expected to knuckle under and remain as a sort of moral support to a couple of women! Vance, who had done comparatively nothing, was pandered to by everybody. Because he was gloomy and depressed they had taken him out to dinner and included him in the expedition against Abu-Samar; though for the life of him Trevor could not see what Vance had to be gloomy about at all. Moberly was dead. From a purely sentimental point of view, it was a rotten business; but, looking facts in the face, it was an extraordinarily good thing for Vance. He would be manager now, with a substantial increase in salary and sundry fat bonuses tacked on to it, while he—Trevor—was by no means certain of being promoted to first assistant. He had seen fellows skipped over before.

He dropped his last cigarette-end into space and turned in search of one from Armourer's store. There was a table under the swinging oil-lamp, and on it, arranged there by the magistrate's servant, all the after-dinner comforts the bungalow could offer. In the immediate vicinity, piled with faded cushions, reposed a long cane chair, and curled up at ease on the cushions were Armourer's two terriers.

Trevor stood for some moments, looking down at them, and gradually the frown vanished from his forehead. Even the dogs appeared to realise that he was only second assistant at Bukit-Serang and therefore didn't count for much! In spite of himself, he laughed aloud. He was still smiling when Joyce came from her room.

"I was so sorry to have to leave you all alone," she said, "but my patient was restless. She seems quieter now. Why don't you sit down?"

He pointed to the chair.

"They won't let me!"

She ran past him and fell on her knees.

"The darlings! Aren't they just adorable!—And you hadn't the heart to turn them out?"

Trevor shook his head.

"They looked so jolly comfortable. What's he call them?"

"Mac and Mick," returned Joyce promptly. "The one that's looking out of the corners of his eyes is Mick. He knows he oughtn't to be there."

Trevor rested his hands on his hips.

"What are we going to do about it?"

She glanced to the far end of the verandah.

"There are other chairs, you know."

He fetched a couple and arranged on one of them all the cushions that were not in actual occupation.

"I don't think I want all these," said Joyce.

The man laughed.

"Well, I'm sure I don't. D'you mind if I have a whisky?"

"Not in the least."

She noticed the condition of the decanter.

"You don't mean to tell me this is your first?"

"Absolutely."

"Isn't that rather remarkable?"

"It is; but I was feeling fed to the teeth and didn't notice it was there."

Joyce sat down.

"I knew there must be some explanation," she declared.

He passed over the tin.

"Do you smoke?"

"Sometimes; but I won't have one now, thank you. I wonder when they'll be back."

"Heaven only knows. If they find their quarry at home they might be here any time now; if they have to go and look for him they may be hours. I don't know what to make of this Samar business. He seemed harmless enough in all conscience; but I suppose Battiscombe knows what he's doing."

Joyce was stroking Mick's ear.

"It's been an exciting day."

"It has. That confounded butterfly appears to have been responsible for an entire upheaval of everything. I suppose we *shall* settle down into a normal way of living again! D'you know, I just loathed being left behind here."

"What a compliment to me!"

"Oh, I didn't mean it in that way. Besides, you were occupied with Mrs. Battiscombe and it looked as if I should have to muck about out here alone. I felt as if somebody had taken me to the top of a big hill, and then deliberately pushed me over. There were all sorts of queer things in the air and I had to be content with disconnected fragments of news and half-baked theories. But until they dumped me here I was in the picture. Now the fun's all shifted to Abu's place—and I'm bang out of it."

She picked up the nearest terrier bodily and dropped it into her lap.

"I don't see that you've anything to grumble about," she retorted. "I like adventure too—and I'm left to tend the sick and wounded! You've had half-truths told you—while I

know nothing. Mr. Trevor, would you be guilty of a very serious indiscretion if you told Mickie and me about the butterfly?"

Trevor grinned.

"I'll tell Mickie after you've turned in for the night, and he
can use his own doggy discretion as to how much he di-
vulges in the morning."

She pouted.

"Meaning that you don't think I can keep a secret."

He sat down.

"I don't know that there's very much to be secret about.
How much do you know already?"

She uttered a deep sigh.

"I know that daddy chased a big red butterfly across Mr.
Moberly's estate this morning—"

"Anything else?"

"And that Mr. Moberly's dead and that Mr. Armourer is
anxious to learn what Mrs. Battiscombe may say in her delirium about butterflies—"

"Has she said anything?"

"Nothing very important. Sometimes she feels her throat
and murmurs something about a crimson butterfly. Once she
caught my hand while I was bending over her and held it
hard. I had had fever patients before and so the look in her
eyes didn't startle me. 'I am a goddess,' she said—'and my
kiss is death!' The poor dear hadn't the least notion what she
was talking about."

He stared at her so hard that she felt embarrassed.

"You are sure she said that?"

"Oh, yes. Mr. Armourer asked me to put down everything
in writing—and I did."

He shook his head.

"Her kiss was death, all right!" he muttered. "Lord! I wonder how much she really knows!"

A hand fell on his sleeve.

"Mr. Trevor, you are not suggesting that she had anything
to do with Mr. Moberly's death?"

He moved uncomfortably.

Joyce Standen was a singularly attractive woman, and he found it difficult to refuse her the information she sought. It occurred to him that if Armourer had wanted her to know he would have told her himself. Perhaps, he decided, it would be better to wait until he had seen either the magistrate or Vance. The thought of these two men brought back the old grievance. They hadn't troubled to consider him—either of them.

"Look here," he announced presently, "I'll tell you as much as there is to tell, but you must promise not to breathe a word of it to anybody. The butterfly your father saw wasn't a proper butterfly. It was a poisonous bug of some sort and it killed Moberly. It left a mark on him—as if the creature was all sting, like a jelly-fish. Mrs. Battiscombe had been a great friend of Dick Moberly's and had sent him back a ruby ornament on a chain. We found this ornament near Dick when he died. It was a butterfly and was shaped so like the mark on Moberly's face that it did set us wondering. Mrs. Battiscombe rode over, saw the mark on his cheek, murmured something about a crimson butterfly and fainted. Ever since then a lot of idiots in a much clearer state of mind than Mrs. Battiscombe have been babbling nonsense about butterflies and native charms and heaven knows what. It's getting quite a disease—like malaria; just when you think you've cured yourself of it—it crops up again. When you appeared just now I'd decided once and for all that the *ju-ju* business was bunkum; and then you set the old idea working again by mentioning Mrs. Battiscombe's remark about goddesses and death. It is rubbish, of course, but there's a rotten under-current beneath all this that I neither understand nor like. I shall be glad when it's morning again and we have some clean, fresh air to inhale."

He emptied his glass.

"Thank you," she said quietly. "It was rotten of me to make you tell me; but I did so want to know. And this expedition to-night is merely a side-issue; it has really nothing to do with the affair of this afternoon?"

"Nothing whatever, as far as I know. If you lived out here long you'd get used to this sort of business. Nothing happens for months on end and then we may have half-a-dozen exciting incidents in a week. I expect the Commissioner's had his eye on Abu-Samar for a long time."

She started.

"What was that?"

He looked back over his shoulder.

"Only Mai-Heng moving about in Armourer's room. He's late to-night, but we were six at dinner, you know, and I imagine he's had his work cut out to get through."

He remained for some moments, listening.

"Mai-Heng!" he called.

For answer there came from the magistrate's bedroom a peculiar gurgling noise and something crashed heavily to the floor.

They came to their feet together.

"Stop where you are, Miss Standen. I don't suppose it's anything."

He threw open the door.

As he did so, something as large as a bat brushed his ear and flew past him on to the verandah.

The room was in darkness and, feeling his way across it, his toe kicked against something soft. He struck a match and dropped on his knees beside the lifeless form of Armourer's cook-boy.

Mai-Heng lay on his back, a hurricane-lamp with a broken chimney at his side. His arms were above his head, his singlet open at the top, and across his dark chest was the sign of the Crimson Butterfly.

The match burned out, and Trevor, with trembling fingers, fumbled for another.

A second inspection of the dead servant revealed that he held the pendant in his left hand, its chain of gold filigree trailing across the floor.

CHAPTER XVI

THE BUTTERFLY RETURNS

TREVOR ROSE FROM HIS KNEES to find Joyce at the doorway.

He could see that she was pale and trembling.

"Is anything the matter?" she asked.

He controlled himself with an effort.

"Nothing much," he declared firmly. "Mai-Heng's met with an accident. D'you mind just slipping down the passage to the back entrance and calling for an orderly."

She hesitated.

"Where is Mai-Heng?—I don't see him."

Trevor bit his lip.

"Of course you can't see him," he returned with some irritation. "I've got him here—on the floor behind the table·— and the lamp's gone *phut*."

"I'll bring you a light."

"Don't bother now, please. I'll fix that while you're away."

She came a step towards him, peering fearfully into the darkness.

"Mr. Trevor, if there's been an accident, surely I can do something for the poor fellow. I'm used to nursing, you know."

He took her by both arms and pushed her gently from the room on to the verandah, closing the door after him.

"I hate to seem to order you about, Miss Standen; but I want one of Armourer's men at once."

"Is he unconscious?"

"Yes."

She stood for some seconds regarding him steadily, then went slowly towards the head of the passage. She turned suddenly, a faint smile hovering on her lips.

"You'll have to go," she declared. "I can't speak a word of Malay."

He made a noise with his tongue against the roof of his mouth.

"I hadn't thought of that. All right, you stop here—and mind, I don't want you to go into that room. Mai-Heng was never an over-clean specimen of humanity—and as he is now he might easily frighten you. Will you promise?"

"Very well."

He could see that she gave her consent reluctantly, and feared, from the troubled look behind her dark eyes, that she had already her suspicions as to the actual state of affairs.

He was on his way back from the men's quarters when a piercing scream broke upon the stillness of the Eastern night.

He completed the rest of the distance at break-neck speed.

In the passage-way he cursed himself for an abject idiot. One of a score of ghastly things might have occurred in his absence, and his only sane line of action under the circumstances should have been to have taken her with him.

He was considerably relieved to discover her half fainting in a chair, staring as if hypnotised at something on the wall beyond the lamplight.

He bent over her.

"It was you who screamed?"

She nodded.

"You opened that door."

She began talking rapidly, excitedly.

"No, no, I didn't even go near the room. I stood quite still just where you had left me, trying to regain my nerve. I was frightened, horribly frightened; the shadows frightened me . . . the awful silence . . . everything. Presently I gritted my teeth and forced myself to do something. I remembered that the others should be on their way back and walked to the rail to look for them. The moon had gone in, and there was nothing there but blackness. You can *feel* the blackness out here. I heard a voice—your voice, shouting something, and decided to go and meet you. As I passed the lamp an enormous insect fluttered down from the ceiling and circled round it. There had been scores of things flying there before, but they all vanished when *it* came. Something made me stop. I saw its outline at first and thought it was a huge moth; and then I realised it was a butterfly—and saw that it was red! I just flopped back into the first chair I could find and screamed at the top of my voice."

He turned his head sharply.

"A red butterfly!" he muttered hoarsely. "You must be mistaken. They don't fly at night, you know, even out here."

She pointed at the wall.

"I tell you I saw it quite plainly. It was the creature you told me about—the one my father described this afternoon. It's over there now—don't you see it?"

She clutched at his arm and a cold sensation passed down his spine.

He had never quite understood until that moment how peculiarly contagious fear was. With Mai-Heng lying there and the memory of something unpleasant brushing his cheek, Armourer's bungalow had suddenly become a house of horrors. For a matter of moments he remained rooted to the spot, an invisible—yet impassable—barrier between him and the far wall.

The approach of the magistrate's men brought him to his senses and he cast a sidelong glance at Joyce, praying that this momentary lapse had passed unnoticed.

The two black soldiers shuffled on to the verandah buttoning up their coats and looking profoundly uncomfortable. One of them carried a lamp.

"Go into the *Tuan-Hakim's* room," Trevor commanded. "You will find Mai-Heng there. Carry him out by the other door and put him in any shed that happens to be empty. Cover him up with a blanket or something."

The fact that Joyce did not understand Malay had its advantages.

The men saluted and passed into the darkness, leaving the door ajar.

Trevor shut it deliberately.

He heard them moving about inside, a volley of startled exclamations and fragments of a prolonged consultation that ensued almost immediately after. One of them said something about a blanket and a door opened somewhere.

A remark from the girl roused him to action.

"It's crawling up the wall," she cried. "Look!"

His glance fell upon the butterfly net that Gholam-Singh had made for the professor. He plucked it from the shelf upon which it lay and hooked a small chair through the living-room doorway.

Joyce was on her feet now.

"Do be careful," she implored.

"I mean to be," he said between his teeth; "but, in case I miss, hadn't you better go in to Mrs. Battiscombe? You'd be safer there."

The colour had come back to her cheeks, and in the light from the lamp she looked infinitely beautiful.

"I'm not afraid—now," she told him, "and I want to be of use, if I can. Don't send me away."

Trevor reflected.

"All right," he said at length. "There's Armourer's tennis racquet over there in the corner. Swipe at it with that if it flies towards you."

He placed the chair a couple of feet from the wall and mounted it.

Joyce possessed herself of the racquet and watched breathlessly.

The insect had crawled into the angle the ceiling made with the wall, a position that presented difficulties. She removed the shade from the lamp and the creature showed up clearly against the woodwork. She could plainly discern the thin black body, the fat fleshy wings and the long antennae that moved restlessly.

It was the green eyes of the thing, however, that were disconcerting Trevor. They seemed to be surveying his every movement with an interest that was at once almost human and distinctly inhuman. He was aware of a sense of fear, a feeling of acute nausea and an unpleasant, pungent odour.

To the girl it seemed countless ages before he brought back his arm and the net with it, remained motionless, as if taking careful aim, and brought the frame of the contrivance against the boarding.

The uppermost edge of the frame scraped against the ceiling and Trevor hit a couple of inches too low on the wall. A fraction of the body remained imprisoned for a fleeting second, and before he could make the necessary movement to ensure his capture the insect had struggled free and fluttered off into the night.

"Damn!"

Not knowing why, Joyce laughed.

"Rotten luck!" she commented.

He stepped from the chair, regarding the net ruefully.

"A jolly bad shot," he insisted. "I might have known the ceiling would baulk me. Where's it gone now?"

She pointed into the darkness.

"Out there." She contrived to speak easily. "Anyhow, you've driven it away."

He put the chair back in its place and threw the net on to the table.

"There is that consolation, I suppose; but I was a blithering idiot to miss, all the same. Must have lost my nerve at the critical moment."

He unstoppered the decanter.

"Ugh! The thing smelt horribly?"

"Smelt?"

"Yes—worse than a stink-bug, if you'll excuse the expression. Won't you have something to drink? I'm sure you want it."

She shook her head.

"No, thank you very much. I'm afraid the smell of the whisky would upset me more than that of the butterfly."

He poured out three fingers and looked up.

"There's some wine knocking about somewhere."

"Don't bother to look for it, please. I really don't want it. The only thing I ask is not to be left alone. Look at the dogs. When you went into the bedroom I put Mick back in the chair—and neither of them has moved a hair. Do sit down. I want to talk to you."

Trevor smiled.

"The Oracle is ready," he said, "and there is absolutely no charge!"

Joyce frowned.

"That was the crimson butterfly," she declared.

"I believe so."

She bent forward.

"Was it that that caused Mai-Heng's *accident*?"

Trevor emptied his glass. When he looked up at her again his face was flushed.

"You ought to go in for law," he said; "you'd make a charming and efficient barrister!"

"But you haven't answered my question."

He racked his brains for an evasive reply.

"I don't think it wise for any of us to jump to conclusions until we've had a look at Mai-Heng in the morning."

"You didn't send for a doctor."

"No, because there isn't one available at the moment."

She looked straight into his eyes.

"Mr. Trevor, why take such elaborate precautions to try and deceive me? Why didn't you let me help you with Mr. Armourer's servant?—why were you so anxious to keep me from that room? I have all my senses, you know, and a woman's intuition thrown in. I know that Mai-Heng is dead—and that he died as Mr. Moberly died this afternoon. It's true, isn't it?"

The assistant rubbed his chin.

"Mai-Heng is dead," he admitted, "but as to how he met his end—that's a doctor's affair, not mine. D'you mind if we discuss something else."

"Not in the least; but I should like to say just one thing. I'm out for the defence of my sex now, Trevor. When you told me about the other affair you seemed inclined to associate Mrs. Battiscombe with the crimson butterfly."

"Did I?"

"Well, you did, didn't you? You told me that the *ju-ju* theory was all nonsense, but the male in you wouldn't allow you to exonerate Mrs. Battiscombe entirely from blame. Now this second tragedy proves her innocence conclusively. Her ornament—which you found near Mr. Moberly when he died—could not possibly have been near that wretched Chinaman."

Trevor was conscious of a tremendous inward struggle.

"No," he conceded lamely, "it couldn't, could it?"

At that moment one of Armourer's men appeared at the opening and stood, his hands clasped behind him, waiting for someone to notice him.

"What is it?" demanded Trevor.

The native came forward.

"It is this, *Tuan*," he stammered. "When we carried Mai-Heng away we did not see it; but we felt it as we put him down. It was fixed between the fingers."

Joyce, bending forward excitedly, saw a ruby ornament on a gold chain pass from the soldier's grubby brown hand to Trevor's palm.

CHAPTER XVII

A Strange Phenomenon

Trevor looked at Joyce and there was a wealth of meaning in his eyes.

He waved his hand to indicate to the orderly that the interview was at an end and remained silent until he was out of hearing.

"How does the counsel for the defence feel now?"

The girl winced.

"Rotten!" she returned; "decidedly rotten. You might have told me."

He shook his head.

"Looking back a bit, I fancy I've already told you more than I ought; certainly more than is good for you. Now you can realise something of the nature of the shock I suffered when I tumbled across Mai-Heng—and *that*."

His fingers touched the Butterfly pendant.

"It must have been terrible."

"It was pretty ghastly."

"You can't complain you've been left out of the excitement now. I don't suppose the others have encountered anything half so thrilling."

Trevor grunted.

"I've had enough thrills for one evening, thank you!—A little of this sort of thing goes a long way. Armourer'll be mighty sick when he hears about Mai-Heng."

"Do you think he meant to steal the pendant?"

He shrugged his shoulders.

"I scarcely know what to think. Armourer's discarded clothing was lying all over the floor, and it's just possible he left the Butterfly in a pocket and Mai-Heng had only that moment discovered it. Whichever way it was, his luck was badly out."

He rested his elbows on the table and buried his head in his hands.

"I haven't the remotest idea what it all means," he announced suddenly; "have you?"

"How should I?"

"No, that's just it. How should anybody? This cursed charm appears to be at the bottom of the trouble."

She glanced at it apprehensively.

"We're back to where we started—back to the *ju-ju* business again. It is like the real butterfly, you know, only much smaller and, of course, more transparent. I simply adore that chain."

"It's pretty enough."

He picked it up and examined the workmanship minutely.

The girl's eyes sparkled.

"You can't imagine any sensible woman refusing a gift like that."

Trevor blinked.

"How d'you know it was a gift. She might have bought it."

Joyce smiled.

"Women like Mrs. Battiscombe don't have to buy pretty things; there is always somebody ready to buy them for them."

"Why only women like Mrs. Battiscombe?"

The girl coloured slightly.

"Oh, I don't know. She's just a type. The majority of women won't accept presents of that sort from just any man."

"And you suggest that she does?"

"I suppose that was rather a catty thing to say, and not at all consistent with my defence-of-the-sex idea; but I don't claim to be any more consistent than most other women. Everybody in Jesselton was talking about her when we arrived."

Trevor allowed the links of the filigree chain to fall from one hand to the other.

"There are only about three topics of conversation out here at the moment—and one of them's Vera Battiscombe. Between ourselves, Miss Standen, you're perfectly right. We were all of us pretty sick at the hold she was getting over Dick Moberly and the way she was letting Battiscombe down. She carried Dick off, so to speak, under the nose of Mrs. Moberly, and the latter, apparently unable to talk Dick back into a sensible frame of mind, cleared out altogether. Poor old Dick!"

"I suppose there was a little jealousy too?"

"Not so far as we were concerned," he hastened to inform her. "Speaking personally, I'm not inclined to be any too keen on a woman who makes all the running herself. That's where Moberly was weak. A pretty woman had only to take notice of him and he'd go bang off the deep end."

"And you think Mr. Moberly gave her this pendant?"

"She sent it back to him with a lot of other things, so I suppose he did."

"Then why and where did the real butterfly come in?"

Trevor threw up his hands.

"Ask me another!" He glanced at his watch. "Jove! they're late! I wonder if they've struck any snags."

Joyce was not to be thrown off the main topic of conversation so easily.

"Oughtn't we to do something to prevent the butterfly coming back?"

Trevor wrinkled his forehead.

"I don't suppose it'll want to after that swipe I gave it."

"There may be others."

He shuddered.

"Don't let's get too morbid. I was just lulling myself to sleep with the thought that our friend was a rare and unique specimen."

"Can't we do something with it?"

She was looking at the pendant.

"We'll have to keep it until Armourer comes back, otherwise I should suggest burying it as far away from any human habitation as possible."

Joyce nestled back in the cushions and sighed.

"Doesn't it seem a pity?—to have to bury a beautiful creation like that? It's so wonderful, so utterly unusual. I know a dozen women at home who would cheerfully risk the trail of tragedy it seems to drag after it only to possess it. And it's got to be stuck in the ground and have nasty damp earth stamped all over it!"

A perfectly obvious retort occurred to Trevor, but he refrained from expressing it.

"It's an uncomfortable possession," he said instead, and tossed the thing deliberately into the farthest corner of the verandah. "I don't know that even that is a safe precaution against following in the footsteps of Moberly and Mai-Heng; but I feel a great deal more happy with it at a distance."

"It happens to be outside my door," she reminded him.

"I don't think that matters very much. It's closed—and the others are bound to want to look at it again when they hear what's happened."

He stared into the night.

"Hello! there's a light at last. They'll be here in a few minutes."

Both the terriers pricked up their ears, shook themselves and plunged, barking, down the stairs.

Trevor rubbed his hands together and smiled queerly.

"Wonderful thing, a crowd, Miss Standen! It's difficult to imagine what any or all of 'em could do if the butterfly rolled up again; but the arrival of a bunch like that undoubtedly promotes a sense of security!"

He crossed to the stair-head and Joyce joined him there.

Making a megaphone of his hands, he called:

"Hullo, there!—Are you all right?"

A faint cry floated back to them.

The girl glanced at her companion.

"Who was that?"

"Armourer, I fancy."

"What did he say?"

"I didn't catch; but the tone sounded cheery. I wonder if they've brought the black gentleman with them. Judging from the time they've been away, they ought to have arrested an entire village!"

Something made her turn her head. She clutched at Trevor's arm with both hands.

"What is it?"

His eyes followed the direction of her gaze.

"An arm," she whispered fearfully, "a white arm came through the doorway and went back again."

He laughed uneasily.

"Which doorway?"

"The far one—my room, you know—and the pendant's gone!"

He went a couple of paces and bent down, staring at the floor.

"So it has, by Jove!"

She clung to the rail for support.

"What do you think it was?"

"Mrs. Battiscombe walking in her sleep."

"But why did she take the Butterfly? She couldn't possibly have known it was there."

"One wouldn't imagine so."

She leaned back, gasping for breath.

"It's horrible! I'm so glad the others are here."

"Here, pull yourself together," said Trevor sternly. "You've got to go into that room and find out what's happened."

"I daren't."

"I'm coming with you. It's no use waiting about for the rest. If it was Mrs. Battiscombe, so much the better. She has had the thing before—and nothing killed *her*. There's just the faintest chance it might be somebody else—and I rather hope it is. It'd help to clear up a lot of things."

He tip-toed across the verandah and opened the door to its fullest extent. The lamp was still burning within, and, on a bed at the far end, he could just make out the outline of a slumbering woman behind mosquito-curtains.

He beckoned to Joyce.

"Come on. There's nobody here. I want you to draw back those curtains."

She looked past him, like a frightened child peering into a dark cupboard and fearful of bogies, then walked towards the bed.

They stood presently side by side, gazing down at the sleeping form of Vera Battiscombe.

There was not a sign that she had stirred.

She was breathing regularly, there was a healthy colour on her cheeks, and the soft fair curls encircled her head like a wondrous halo.

Joyce uttered a little cry and pointed to her throat.

The filigree chain was clasped securely round her neck and the Crimson Butterfly nestled in the gossamer folds above a gently heaving bosom.

CHAPTER XVIII

The Professor Changes His Views

The Verandah was empty when the three men came clattering up the steps in their heavy boots with the terriers yapping excitedly at their heels.

Battiscombe dropped into a chair.

He caught Michael's eye.

"Well, the place is still here!"

Armourer stretched his weary limbs.

"Yes, it's here right enough, as you say. How do you feel, professor?"

The professor was peering round him anxiously.

"Pretty fit, thanks. I don't think I shall be altogether sorry when I'm in bed."

Battiscombe looked at his feet.

"Lord! we're in an unholy mess! That was your precious short cut from Vance's, Michael! Kuraman warned you there might be swamps at that end of the valley."

His colleague laughed.

"I was badly out there," he admitted. "Well, I suppose it's a quick drink and bed. Wonder where Trevor is."

Joyce appeared suddenly at the doorway of her room, followed by the second assistant.

She ran to her father.

"I'm so glad you've all got back safely. We were beginning to wonder what had happened. We've had a perfectly ghastly time since you left."

She bent down and kissed his forehead.

"What's been the matter?" he asked.

She looked back at Trevor.

"You'd better tell them, hadn't you?"

Trevor walked up to Armourer.

"I've a piece of bad news for you," he said. "Your servant—Mai-Heng—has been killed by the crimson butterfly."

All three started and Battiscombe sprang to his feet.

"What's that?"

The planter passed a weary hand across his forehead.

"Mai-Heng is dead. I found him in there"—he pointed to Armourer's room. "He had unearthed that confounded ornament from somewhere and I found it between his fingers."

Armourer shot a glance at Battiscombe.

"I told you I'd left it in my clothes."

"When I opened the door," pursued Trevor, "the butterfly flew past me and frightened Miss Standen. I tried to kill it, but missed—and it flew away. The pendant didn't seem to be a pleasant sort of thing to carry about with one, so I chucked it into a corner. The next thing that happened was a white arm groping through a doorway for it. This fresh development rather staggered us. By the time we'd gathered our wits together, the chain had somehow found its way round Mrs. Battiscombe's neck—and the queer thing is that she looks as fit as a fiddle."

The professor was fidgeting with his glasses.

"It's really very remarkable," he murmured to himself. "You're quite certain in your own mind that you actually saw the insect? You'll pardon my asking an apparently foolish question, but quite a number of queer bugs fly about on a tropic night—and it would be perfectly simple to make a mistake."

Joyce shook her head.

"We weren't mistaken, daddy. It crawled up the wall and stayed there for some time."

"And Mai-Heng died with the Butterfly pendant in his hand?"

"Yes," said Trevor, "and the same peculiar mark was across his chest."

Battiscombe, who had been pondering deeply, asked the next question.

"And you say that my wife got up from her bed and picked the thing from the floor?"

"I don't," retorted Trevor. "I can only tell you the facts exactly as they happened. Miss Standen saw the arm and we both found the Butterfly at Mrs. Battiscombe's throat. She was lying much as Miss Standen had left her, the curtains were tucked in all round the bed; there was nothing in fact to indicate that she had moved."

"It couldn't get there by itself."

"I know that."

"If my wife did take it, how did she know it was there on the floor close by the door of her room?"

"How did she know it was in the house at all?" interposed Armourer.

"She couldn't have known, unless she had listened; and she couldn't very well have listened because she was ill. Anyhow, the thing's round her neck and any of you who want to can see it for yourselves."

Battiscombe emitted a deep sigh.

"And to think that we let Abu-Samar slip through our fingers!"

Trevor stared.

"What the dickens has Abu-Samar to do with it?"

Armourer tapped out his pipe.

"Everything, apparently."

"But he hasn't been near the place."

Battiscombe reached over the decanter.

"Trevor hasn't heard about the latest developments," he said slowly. "Heaven knows only what Dr. Abu-Samar has up his sleeve. Among other things he's a conjurer—a sort of native magician—and the professor's theory is that he breeds those butterflies."

Trevor found his hat.

"This is getting too deep for me," he complained. "I'm paid by a lot of niggardly directors in London to plant rubber and there's a clause in my contract which says I'm not to interest myself in any other business. Does anybody know where they put my pony?"

Armourer stepped between him and the exit.

"You're not going back to-night?"

"You can bet your life I am. It's close on one now—and I have to be down in the coolie-lines at five-thirty. Besides, your house isn't elastic."

"I could fix you up somehow."

Trevor shook his head.

"It isn't worth the bother; thanks all the same. There's a good moon again now and I can be back at my place in under three-quarters of an hour. If you take my advice, you'll leave the pendant where it is, and sleep with your doors and windows closed."

"What about Mrs. Battiscombe?"

Trevor paused on the top step.

"As I was saying just before you came in, Mrs. Battiscombe's worn the charm before—and it didn't hurt *her*. If that idea doesn't appeal to you, you'd better go out and bury it. Good night, everybody!"

Armourer went down after him.

"A nice young fellow that!" commented the professor.

He looked round to see that Joyce had fallen asleep in her chair.

"She's had a rough time," said Battiscombe softly. "You'd better get her back to Jesselton to-morrow."

"She won't go until Mrs. Battiscombe is better," declared her father.

"Then as soon as my wife is fit to be moved we'll pack them both off to the coast. This is no place for women at the moment."

"The extraordinary thing is," said the professor, "that until Armourer brought that wretched talisman here it was one of the most charming spots it had ever been my good fortune to encounter. I am contriving now to keep quite an open mind with regard to this peculiar sequence of events. Until an hour or so ago I must confess I was bigoted. It seemed so utterly absurd that an inanimate red stone on a gold chain could have the remotest connection with a poisonous and highly vicious insect. Mind you, I am not yet prepared to admit that

any such connection exists; but, with this further development fresh in our minds, it would be the sheerest folly to ignore the apparent significance of the presence of that ornament in any given place."

Battiscombe's red face bore a troubled expression.

"And so—?"

"And so, before we retire to-night, we must follow
Trevor's second suggestion and bury it somewhere, marking
the spot so that we may be able to find it again."

"Why not sling it into a swamp? The thing's unclean."

Standen stroked his beard.

"No, I shouldn't suggest that. We may want it again."

"I shan't—for one, and I'm willing to wager that the others
will be glad to see the back of it."

The professor suddenly tightened the skin at the back of his
left hand, thus imprisoning a mosquito in the act of stinging
him, and dispatched it smartly with the other.

"Until the entire mystery is satisfactorily cleared up," he
declared, "it would be a pity to lose sight of so important a
clue."

He kicked the charred basket which now reposed at his
feet.

"You forget that an actual specimen of the crimson butterfly has not yet come into my hands. My chrysalis may produce something quite harmless, in which case we shall not
only be farther from our goal than ever, but we shall have
lost a great deal of valuable time. I must get a crimson butterfly before I can hope to embark upon my investigations."

"We hope to catch Abu-Samar before long—and my wife
may be able to tell us something in the morning."

The older man shook his head sadly.

"I shouldn't bank too much on Mrs. Battiscombe's knowledge, if I were you. Samar has taken to the backwoods—and
Borneo is a big place. Possibly he has countless friends in
the interior who will shield him. No, Battiscombe, it's the
butterfly we want, and if the ornament can be employed as a
bait for these things, I'm going to use it for all I'm worth."

"It'll be devilish risky."

"Of course. Scientific research is usually dangerous. In the unearthing of new secrets investigators play with forces concerning the limits of which they have often not the remotest idea. Still, in the interests of science and humanity, these risks have to be taken. If, indeed, Samar breeds these insects, he may one day let them loose in their thousands, to pick off humanity as the locusts pick off grain. Without a known antidote we shall be in a terrible position; and to discover an antidote one must know one's poison first. I shall get Armourer to build me a hut in the forest, which I shall endeavour to equip as a rough laboratory. I shall keep the charm hanging there, cover the windows with netting and smear the outer walls with what is commonly known to naturalists as *treacle*. If there is something about the talisman which attracts this form of insect-life, the crimson butterfly should obviously be attracted to that spot."

Armourer came up the steps.

"Well, you two conspirators, what about bed?—Professor, you've yours waiting for you. Jimmy and I are going to fix up temporary quarters in the living-room. It's a confounded nuisance my man's gone west, but I know where I can rope in another in the morning."

The professor came to his feet, dusting cigarette ash from the folds of his tunic.

"Battiscombe," he said, "do you mind getting me that pendant before we wake Joyce? I shall be obliged, Armourer, if you can show me where to find a spade."

Armourer laughed.

"You're not going out again."

"I am," Standen assured him. "I'm going to bury the charm before I turn in."

Armourer threw out his arms.

"Behold!" he cried, "the conversion of an unbeliever!"

CHAPTER XIX

AN IMPORTANT CAPTURE

JAMES BATTISCOMBE stretched himself and yawned. He sat up presently to find the bright light of early morning shining in through an open shutter and Armourer's chair untenanted.

He looked at his watch.

It was ten minutes past seven.

He groped for his tunic, and, slipping it on over the pyjama jacket his host had provided, padded in bare feet out on to the verandah.

Armourer—in a somewhat faded bath-gown—had forestalled him and was leaning on the rail gazing down at the absurd antics of Mick and Mac. He turned to greet his colleague.

"Hullo, old son! Feel rested?"

Battiscombe rubbed his eyes.

"Don't know yet. I hope this was an old suit of yours, because I'm feeling a draught somewhere and I've a shrewd suspicion the jacket's split down the back."

Armourer laughed.

"You needn't worry yourself about that. It's as old as the hills. Wonderful morning, isn't it?"

"Top-hole!"

He cast an appreciative eye over a rolling and varied landscape. Beyond the belt of trees through which they had passed the night before, he caught the vivid green of young paddy, stretching to the spot where the virgin jungle began. Away over to the right, where new wire glinted in the sun, he recognised the newly planted rubber of an estate which had yesterday been under Moberly's management. To the right again, placid and incredibly blue, he saw the sea. A group of natives gesticulated below, a Chinese trader, with his wife as a beast of burden behind, sauntered stolidly along the path which led eastward, and a big brown hawk hovered in the heavens.

"No more tragedies, I suppose," he added presently.

Armourer shook his head.

"No, thank goodness. I looked in on the professor five minutes back, and tapped on Miss Standen's door until I got an answer. I've taken the liberty, by the way, of sending one of your men across for your clothes and shaving kit. Kuraman found a chap who could ride a bit, so you oughtn't to have to wait very long."

The other beamed.

"That's extremely thoughtful of you, Michael, my boy. I was just wondering what sort of figure I should cut at breakfast. Lord! What a strenuous day we had yesterday! It makes me ache all over to think of it. Wonder what the Commissioner will say when he hears about Abu-Samar!"

"He'll have a deal more to say when he learns of the crimson butterfly business."

Battiscombe groaned.

"I can see a devil of a lot of strenuous work in the offing. He'll be popping up all over the place at the most unexpected and inconvenient moments. We shall be required to send in reports every five minutes. In short there'll never be a moment of peace for either of us until Dr. Abu-Samar has been captured and handed over."

An orderly, with tea and green bananas on a tray, came from the back of the house and set down his burden on the table.

"Get some biscuits," ordered Armourer. "You'll find them in a tin on the second shelf in the living-room. Yes," he said to his companion, "Stewart's all right when you understand him; and he takes a lot of understanding."

"He's so beastly energetic," complained the other. "He ought to have a little weight to carry about with him. It'd give him a better idea what tropic life means to some of us!"

The professor's door opened and the occupant of the room emerged, clad in a yellow dressing-gown that had seen much wear and slippers trampled down at the back.

"Aha!" he cried; "up with the lark!"

Armourer was pouring out tea.

"No, I'm afraid the lark had the better of us this morning. Still, considering the hour at which we retired, we've nothing much to be ashamed of—Let's see, professor, you don't take sugar?"

"No—and no milk, if you don't mind."

"There's lemon here."

"Thank you, just one slice. That's excellent! Has anybody heard how Mrs. Battiscombe is?"

Battiscombe looked up.

"We were waiting for you to go in and find out."

Standen placed his cup carefully on the table and shuffled to the door. He rapped on it with his knuckles and a muffled feminine voice answered.

"Hullo? what is it?"

"It is I," said the professor. "How are you this morning, my dear?"

"Me? Oh, I'm all right. I slept like a top."

"I'm glad to hear that. No unpleasant dreams?"

"I don't remember any. I think I was too tired even to dream."

"How's your patient?"

There was a long pause, which appeared to indicate that Joyce had slept since Armourer first roused her and had to make certain of her patient's condition before replying. Presently the handle turned and the door opened for a couple of inches.

"Come in," said Miss Standen through the crack; "I'd like you to look at her."

The other two men exchanged glances as the professor, a tasselled cord trailing behind him, disappeared.

"Not so well," suggested Battiscombe suddenly.

Armourer sipped his tea.

"I don't suppose she's very bad. She was fairly fit last night, and it looked as if the fever had burnt itself out. It's no use worrying yourself; Standen'll tell us all the news in a couple of shakes."

Battiscombe sat down and stared gloomily at some ants that had found their way into the sugar-basin.

"Somehow I can't get used to the fact that Vera's ill; she's always kept so fit. If anyone's down at our place, it's I. D'you know, Michael, as soon as she's well enough to travel, I'm going to send her home. Lord only knows how I'm going to run to two establishments, but it's got to be done. It'll be an awful wrench, of course, and I shall be as miserable as *Hades*, but it's simply got to be. Between ourselves, old son, the East's no place for some women."

"I understand," said his friend quietly. "Our climate doesn't suit all temperaments."

He was endeavouring to agree with Battiscombe in blaming the climate, but was not altogether certain in his own mind how Vera Battiscombe would figure even in England. From the bottom of his heart he pitied her husband. Vera and he were so opposite, and it was probably because of this that they had succeeded in hanging together for so long. And, apart from the intricacies of the problem which confronted them both, here was Jim Battiscombe genuinely worried over the health of a woman who had fallen sick because of the death of another man. Even the blindness of love had its compensations!

He caught Battiscombe looking at him.

"Wouldn't you send her home, if you were in my shoes?"

"Yes," he felt bound to confess, "I fancy I should."

"We'll have to find out all she knows about that confounded Butterfly first. It's that that worries me more than anything. She was wearing a thing round her neck that I didn't care to touch. Michael, do you honestly believe Dick gave it her?"

Armourer felt distinctly uncomfortable.

"I'm scarcely in a position to judge."

"But do you?"

The other looked at his hands.

"It scarcely seems feasible, does it? If it were ever in Dick's possession, why wasn't he killed *before* he got rid of it?"

"That's precisely what's been puzzling me."

"Here's the professor," said Armourer with intense relief. "Now perhaps we shall learn something."

Standen came towards them, blinking through his spectacles like an owl.

"Your tea'll be cold by now," declared his host. "I'll throw it away and pour out a fresh cup. How is Mrs. Battiscombe?"

"I'm afraid she's not quite so well this morning. There's nothing about her condition that gives cause for anxiety; but her temperature is up again, and we shall have to keep her quiet for longer than I had expected."

Battiscombe's face fell.

"We're giving you a lot of trouble, professor."

"Trouble? Nothing of the sort. I'm delighted to be of the least service to any of you. You won't forget my temporary laboratory, Armourer. I am really quite serious about that."

"I'll get something fixed up at the earliest possible moment. It'll probably take us a couple of days."

"I suppose it will. I must try and run into Jesselton to-morrow and see if the hospital can lend me some appliances."

"It'll mean spending the night there," said Armourer.

"I must put up with that. Your own medical man should be here by then, and I know my daughter is in good hands. It's an extraordinary world altogether. Which of us would have imagined, when Joyce and I fell off that trolly the day before yesterday, that we should all be involved in a problem like this within a few hours!"

Armourer laughed.

"I believe you're thoroughly enjoying yourself, professor!"

Standen replaced his cup on its saucer and stared from one to the other, an amused expression on his bearded, wrinkled face.

"In some respects I suppose that is the case. My small share in the task which confronts us is one after my own heart, and I was just beginning to find a long period out of harness a little irksome. If I actually lacked incentive, a moment's reflection on the enormous issues at stake could not fail to provide me with it. In a queer sort of way, I'm engaged in a grim duel with a hidden and unscrupulous enemy. It remains to be seen if the wisdom of the West can succeed in laying bare the oft-times perplexing secrets of the mysterious East."

Battiscombe extracted a splinter from a bare toe.

"I'm prepared to wager that it can and will. It's about the most providential thing that ever happened—your being on the spot at such a crisis. I can't tell you how grateful we are."

Joyce's voice came shrilly from the far side of the wooden partition.

"Will some kind person bring me a cup of tea?"

"Oh, Lord!" apologised Armourer, "I'm so sorry!"

As soon as his clothes arrived, Battiscombe breakfasted and rode back to Rembakut. Armourer descended a few moments after his departure and took up his duties in a sweltering and somewhat primitive court of justice. The professor fidgeted upon the verandah for a matter of three-quarters of an hour, then stuck the butterfly-net under one arm and sauntered out into the brilliant sunshine.

He said little at lunch and disappeared again shortly after the meal was finished.

At a quarter to four he came slowly up the steps, and Joyce and Armourer, who dozed in long chairs at separate extremes of the verandah, glanced up simultaneously.

Standen set one foot on the floor, looking for all the world like a conquering commander arriving on the quarter-deck of a vanquished rival. The net was still under one arm, and he held the other awkwardly, with the air of a guilty schoolboy endeavouring to conceal a bulging pocket.

"For the first time in my whole existence," he announced, "I find the secrets of the Orient worthy of attention. What magnificent conjurers these fellows are! It would almost seem as if their normal audiences had grown so critical that it was necessary to constantly increase the wrappings of mystery around their artifices to enable them to continue to deceive. Because," he added defiantly, "they are only tricks, you know, picturesque, elaborate tricks! However improbable it may seem to you, there is a satisfactory, rational reason for everything."

Joyce gave vent to a chuckle that was lacking in respect towards an elderly and distinguished parent.

"Daddy's been forced to change his mind about something," she told Armourer, "and is endeavouring to justify his first opinion! He does so hate being wrong!"

Even this attack—from within his own walls, so to speak—could not shatter the professor's air of determined good-humour.

"What is one to do with a daughter like that?" he demanded.

"The question of the moment is," declared the magistrate, "what is this wonderful secret that you persist in keeping from us?"

The professor tapped his pocket significantly.

"The crimson butterfly flies to its image like a common or garden moth to a flame." He found a chair and leaned back in it, fanning himself with his hand. "I've really had a most successful afternoon. I've proved conclusively that the ornament and the insect, as we more than half suspected last night, act in concert. Whenever it is free to do so, the animate flies in search of the inanimate."

"It sounds frightfully impressive," broke in Joyce, "but what does it really mean?"

Before the professor could embark upon his explanation, Armourer spoke.

"You say, whenever it is *free*. Do you suggest then that there are times when the creature is not free?"

"Yes, most decidedly. I hope I shall never be forced to admit that an insect can discriminate between man and woman. Since this extraordinary sequence of events began, there have been two victims—and both of them males. Mrs. Battiscombe wore the pendant with apparent impunity. The custodian of the butterfly, the man who discovered the partiality of the insect for that particular type of stone, must obviously assure himself as to the approximate position of the pendant before he releases the butterfly on its mission of vengeance."

"Abu-Samar."

Standen nodded.

"But how do you know all this?" inquired his daughter.

"Because," said the professor," a crimson butterfly in a rather battered condition found its way to the spot where I buried the ornament. I imagine it to be the one Trevor injured."

Armourer sprang from his chair.

"You actually saw it?"

"I actually caught it," laughed the professor. "I have a living specimen of the crimson butterfly here with me now!"

CHAPTER XX

Joyce Goes to Jesselton

During the week following the discovery of the butterfly Professor Standen found it necessary to go down to Jesselton twice—and on the second occasion he took Joyce.

Armourer had pressed him to do this, because he felt certain she desired a change, if only for a few hours.

Mrs. Battiscombe's illness, prolonged as it had been, had taken a decided turn for the better, and in the case of an unexpected relapse Dr. Macnally was now within easy call.

The magistrate saw them off.

"Have a good time," he said to Joyce, "and don't let your father drag you around with him."

"I shan't," declared the girl. "I shall call on Mrs. Anderson and stop at her house until he chooses to fetch me. I know what father is when he gets with medical men."

Standen patted her arm affectionately.

"You shall do just as you like, my dear, and if you care to stop behind until I've finished my task you're quite at liberty to do so."

He strode to the far end of the coach to blow an obstruction from his cigarette-holder.

"Why don't you?" asked Armourer.

"Why don't I what?"

"Stop in Jesselton until the affair is cleared up."

She wrinkled her forehead.

"I don't think I want to. You see, I've only acquaintances in town."

"And we've become more than acquaintances."

She looked away.

"Rather! I'm almost beginning to look upon Jelandang as a second home. Besides, I shouldn't care to leave Mrs. Battiscombe until she was quite recovered. In spite of all the unpleasant things people say about her, I like her immensely."

"And so you're coming back because of Mrs. Battiscombe?"

"Not altogether. I like the house and the dogs, and our evening game of cards is becoming quite an institution. Why don't you want me to come back?"

She looked up suddenly and he felt himself crimsoning to the roots of his hair.

"I do," he said earnestly. "It'll be rotten up there without you. I only suggested you might stay away for a bit because I was afraid you would have a breakdown. You've been dancing attendance on Mrs. Battiscombe for days and your system can't possibly have had time to accustom itself to our climate."

The train jolted forward and Armourer swung himself off.

"Good-bye," he shouted, keeping pace for some yards with it. "I'd like to come with you, only I daren't show my face in Jesselton until I've achieved something definite."

Joyce leaned out of the window.

"Good-bye. Mind you look after yourself—and Mrs. Battiscombe!"

He stared after the jolting line of white coaches until they were lost to view amid jungle-clad banks.

He tucked his malacca under one arm and turned to regain the path.

"Now what on earth did she mean by that?" he demanded of his inner—and presumably wiser—self.

He was becoming desperately infatuated with Joyce Standen and her thrust had found its way home with an accuracy that was astonishing. Nobody realised more than he did what an uncomfortable guest Mrs. Battiscombe was to a man in his position, and the fact that Joyce had reminded him of this, *hurt*. For more than a week he had been trying to live down that other incident on the verandah at Rembakut, when Vera Battiscombe had somehow bewitched him into kissing

her—and Jim had surprised them *in flagrante delicto*. Unless
Vera had told her in an outburst of confidence, Joyce could
not possibly know anything about that. Lord! how contrary
this wicked world was! He had tried to keep Vera and Joyce
apart and, following upon the heels of this desire, Fate had
landed them in a proximity that was too close to be pleasant.
When Joyce had been in danger at his bungalow an unkind
fortune had decreed that it should be Trevor, not he, who
should be there to protect her. And now, with the professor
spending hours at a time in his remote laboratory, when by
every reasonable law they should have scores of opportuni-
ties to be alone altogether here was this same Mrs. Battiscombe constantly butting in with petulant demands for nour-
ishment, water, or being read to.

He thanked his stars, as he strode through the undergrowth,
that Battiscombe was coming over to sleep. To spend a night
with only the bewitching Vera under his roof would be tan-
tamount to provoking a scandal that would electrify the island!

He was beginning to wish he had never brought her there
at all. When she fainted on Moberly's bungalow he should
have dispatched her instantly to her husband's house and left
it for Jimmy to cross-question her as to her knowledge of the
Crimson Butterfly. As it was, he had gained nothing by having her there; for Standen had stated that she was not to be
worried and that any questions concerning Moberly's death
must be left until a complete recovery was definitely assured.

As for the redoubtable Abu-Samar, he had vanished as
completely as if the earth had swallowed him up.

A coroner's jury, hastily scraped together, had disposed of
both cases under the vague heading of *Death by Misadven-
ture* and had followed this swiftly decided verdict by drinking Vance's cellar nearly dry. The Commissioner had put
into circulation a typewritten order advising all settlers to
take special precautions to protect themselves against *a new
and poisonous type of butterfly* and requesting an immediate
report in the event of a further specimen being seen. A reward of $250 was, moreover, offered for information which

might lead to the apprehension of Mr. Abu-Samar—a reward which, in view of Samar's former escapades (and with dollars rating at 2s. 4d.), was pronounced by the indignant Battiscombe as grossly inadequate.

In an interview with Professor Standen the Commissioner had declared that, while he was instructed by the Governor to sanction and assist his researches for such a time as he should deem reasonable, he was by no means satisfied that the absconding pseudo-doctor was in any way responsible for the recent tragedies. He looked to the professor to supply information, if possible, as to the habits and breeding-places of the new insect, the nature of the poison it exuded and the type of antidote to be employed—and suggested that a month or, at the most, six weeks would be ample time in which to furnish the required data. The task of hunting down Abu-Samar he relegated to his local magistrates and a sort of flying squadron of native infantry under a fresh-comer from England named Lindsay. It should, perhaps, be recorded here that Lindsay's handful of brown-skinned soldiers certainly *flew* but, beyond that, achieved nothing—a fact which, considering their leader's limited experience of Borneo, was scarcely to be wondered at. Armourer was greeted on his arrival at the bungalow by a short missive from Battiscombe.

"DEAR MICHAEL," it ran, "I had intended to be with you this evening, but Fate—and the Commissioner—willed it otherwise. I am embarking forthwith upon the ninety-and-ninth wild-goose chase into the interior. Some optimistic village headman, with an eye to the main chance, believes he has located our friend Abu. Of course he hasn't, but that's neither here nor there! The interesting fact remains that I've to go—and I've a devil of a liver!

"Explain things to Vera.

"Heaven knows when I shall be back, but at some point or other I shall get covered in leeches; I feel it in my bones!—Yours ever, JIMMY."

Armourer read it through twice, crumpled it up between his fingers, smoothed it out again and perused it for a third time.

"Damn!" he ejaculated savagely, and wedged the letter between two volumes on the shelf.

Five minutes later he scribbled a line to Vance and handed it to an orderly. Whatever happened he was not going to be left alone with that woman. Since his experience at Rembakut he had a pious horror of Vera—even when convalescent!

He paced the verandah for some time with Mick and Mac, who, unable immediately to accustom themselves to a considerably reduced household, followed him abjectly wherever he went.

It was two hours before a reply came back.

Vance was sorry he couldn't get away, but he was sending Trevor, who would ride over some time after dinner. They were shorthanded and very busy and there was a good deal of sickness in the coolie-lines.

Armourer stared at the ceiling.

After dinner! That might mean ten o'clock—and it was now barely five. Five long hours with Vera Battiscombe; the prospect made him shudder. She would profit by her privileged position as an invalid to wear as few clothes as possible—and she would commence proceedings by calling him Michael. She would persist in talking—and he wouldn't be able to summon up sufficient rudeness to stop her. She would dwell upon all those things he most wanted to forget and finish by taunting him with a supposed affection for Joyce, which he knew he would not be able effectively to deny.

What a pleasant evening it was going to be!

The only sensible move would be to go out until dinner; but he remembered to his disgust that she was still regarded as on the sick-list and could not be left to the tender mercies of a new cook-boy.

In sheer exasperation he cursed heartily, though inwardly, Abu-Samar, the Commissioner, James Battiscombe—for having such a wife—and himself for having ever given her houseroom. He almost cursed the professor into the bargain, for having gone to Jesselton; but this would have included Joyce.

Vera did not appear at tea, an occurrence which, far from raising his hopes, merely aroused suspicions. Like a skilled general meditating a surprise attack, she was planning to commence her assault at the hour when she counted she would find him at his weakest!

He was having his first whisky of the evening and meditating a hot bath, when her door opened.

The sun had dropped—a flaming ball—into the western sea, and in those few fleeting moments of half-light the universe seemed hushed. Beyond the pall that was swiftly creeping over everything big stars were already showing. There came a timid murmuring of insect voices, working up like a distant orchestra in some frenzied Russian composition, until the atmosphere seemed full of it.

A great hour this—second only to the dawn, and Armourer saw in it Vera's zero-hour.

She appeared to sail towards him out from the gloom, pale, beautiful, ravishing . . . He could see that her cheeks were as white as marble and her lips as crimson as the fatal Butterfly . . .

He stood there trembling, aghast at the immensity of her beauty, powerless . . . She dropped suddenly at his feet and the touch of the crêpey substance of her pale blue kimono on his wrist set his teeth on edge.

"Michael," she murmured tremulously, "why have you kept me here? . . . What have you done with my beautiful Butterfly?"

CHAPTER XXI

THE SIREN SPEAKS

SHE LAY THERE, clasping at his knees, fragile as a piece of rare porcelain, with eyes as innocent in their gaze as those of a child, and it was minutes before Armourer could make up his mind to touch her.

He contrived not to look at her, staring vaguely into the night-shrouded open lands and the shadowy outlines of the forest beyond.

Strong man that he was, he felt that her presence there imperilled his soul. He saw her no longer as Vera—the wife of a cheery, fat, commonplace colleague; but as a siren from the underworld sent there to tempt him to some nameless indiscretion that would effectively shatter his earthly hopes.

The new cook-boy, shuffling in with the lamp, was the most welcome sound he ever remembered hearing.

She drew herself upright without his assistance and perched herself on the edge of the table, accomplishing each movement with an ease and grace that was remarkable in a woman in the early stages of convalescence.

The servant hung the lamp on a hook screwed into a beam and manipulated the wick until the centre portion of the broad verandah was bathed in yellow radiance.

"Hot water, Chong-Si," said the magistrate briefly, and the Chinaman withdrew.

"So it *was* your Butterfly?" he asked suddenly.

A rippling laugh escaped her lips.

"Yes, my poor Michael, and if you do not return it to me to-night, I promise you I shall conjure up every ounce of feminine spite at my command, and tell that brown-haired girl all about our romantic little dance at Rembakut."

Armourer winced. He was beginning to realise that, during her illness, a subtle change had come over her. Even before the tragedy at Bukit-Serang she had conducted her rather indiscriminate love affairs in a way that deceived nobody but her husband; but there had been, nevertheless, certain glimmerings of delicacy and reserve, which new appeared to be entirely missing. There was an added hardness to her voice, too, which puzzled him.

He placed his back firmly against a post and folded his arms.

"Why do you want it back? Considering its associations, I should have imagined it about the last thing you would ever want to see again."

She hooked a cigarette from the tin he always kept on the table, and held out a hand for matches.

"Associations!" she echoed mockingly, "what on earth are its associations to me? It's a beautiful thing and I like it."

He shook his head.

"I'm afraid it is entirely out of the question, Mrs. Battiscombe. It left my possession some days ago and will probably never come into it again."

She slipped from her perch and came right up to him, her eyes never leaving his face.

"You are lying to me," she cried hoarsely. "You have it here—in the house somewhere. I must have it, I tell you; it belongs to me."

She threw a glance round the verandah as if contemplating a thorough search for the missing ornament.

Armourer felt for his pipe.

"I tell you I haven't got it," he said.

"But you have; you can't have sent it away. You found it over there—where Dick died."

He pressed the tobacco firmly home with his forefinger. He was beginning to feel himself again and was relieved to discover that this new Vera seemed a good deal less dangerous at the outset than the old.

"That's perfectly correct. I found the Butterfly on Moberly's table and brought it here; but it's not here now and hasn't been for some days."

She clutched at his arm.

"Michael! Stop teasing me! You have locked it away in some drawer." She began pleading with him, fondling him, coaxing him with all the nauseous persistence of a confirmed drug-taker. "You don't understand what it means to me—this thing. It is essential to me for my health—for everything. Without it, I believe I shall die . . ."

This fresh attitude of hers presented too good an opportunity to be allowed to pass by. He resolved to ignore the professor's advice and endeavour to glean a little information. Considering that she had mentioned Dick first, he could not sec what harm a few questions would do.

"The pendant was in Moberly's possession when we found it and it will probably go with the rest of his effects to his wife."

A wild look flashed into her eyes.

"No, no," she cried, "they mustn't do that; you must stop them. Ann Moberly mustn't have it. It belongs to me."

Armourer nodded gravely.

"But you sent it back to Dick—and it was his property when he died," he reminded her.

She stiffened suddenly and stared into the night. Presently her head came slowly round.

"Michael," she whispered, "I want you to believe me, and to respect my confidence. That night when you rode to Rembakut—and kissed me—was a red-letter day in my life. After Dick and the others it was simply wonderful to think that a great, strong, clean man like yourself could care for me. There were Dick's presents and one other—this Butterfly pendant, I had accepted it in a moment of weakness and feared that to send it back to him would be to open up a correspondence with him again. I didn't want to do that. I felt myself standing at the gateway of a new life. I didn't want these men's presents any longer; I just wanted *you*. Jim had been drinking and kept grumbling about my friendship for

Dick, and suddenly I saw that this was my one opportunity of gracefully shutting the door on him. I declared I would return everything he had given me, and slipped the pendant into the parcel as well. After it had gone I was haunted with the thought that Dick might return it and there would be further complications with Jim. I rode over to get it back from him myself. You know the rest, don't you?"

She dropped wearily into a chair. There was no sound for some moments but the regular puffing of the magistrate at his pipe.

"Then Moberly didn't give you the Crimson Butterfly?"

Her head was buried in her hands and the answer came to him through her fingers.

"It came from a man you disliked? Then why are you so mortally anxious to have it back again?"

She withdrew her hands.

"Because," she told him steadily, "I have had letters from this man, demanding it and threatening to see Jim if it is not returned."

A broad ray of daylight filtered into his brain.

"He has been writing to you here?"

She moved impatiently.

"Why do you persist in questioning me like this. I have been ill."

"I want you to answer this because I fancy I may be able to help you."

She dropped her hands helplessly into her lap.

"Yes, he has written to me here."

"Good! That's all I wanted to know. Now, Mrs. Battiscombe, if you will bring me one of those letters and show me the address from which he writes, I think I can safely predict that your troubles will be at an end."

Chong-Si appeared at the living-room door.

"Your bath is ready, *Tuan*," he announced.

"*Baik-lah!* I will be there in a minute."

The man vanished.

Armourer looked round to find Mrs. Battiscombe in tears.

She was using every artifice to induce him to surrender the Crimson Butterfly, which was really rather pitiful in its way, because, as he had already tried to make her believe, the pendant had passed from his keeping a week ago.

"My dear woman," he protested; "it's no earthly use upsetting yourself. It doesn't matter to me one iota what this man was to you; I merely want his address."

"Give me my Butterfly," she sobbed, "and let me send it myself."

"Now, look here," he said sternly, "we've been at loggerheads over this wretched ornament for quite long enough. I haven't got it, and, for reasons which I believe you partly understand, I never want to handle it again. The best thing you can do, in your own interests and those of your husband, is to make a clean breast of the whole matter. I want you to tell me how the Butterfly pendant killed Dick Moberly."

She stared at him wildly.

"What do you mean? Why do you stare at me like that?—I didn't kill him; surely you don't think that?"

Armourer controlled his features with an effort.

"We have been waiting for you to recover," he told her, "so that you might be able to clear yourself. The Butterfly pendant has in some way been associated with the deaths of two people—and the person actually in possession of it immediately before these tragedies—was yourself. Now will you show me those letters?"

"I have burnt them."

"Will you tell me the address to which you intended sending the ornament?"

The fit of sobbing vanished as easily as it had come.

"No," she said defiantly, "never, never, never!"

"I am going to suggest that there never were any such letters."

She half rose from her chair.

"How dare you!"

She sank back again, feigning exhaustion.

"You have told me several conflicting things this evening," he continued, "and I am about to sort from them what I consider to be the actual state of affairs. You were tired of Dick Moberly and sent that charm to him with his presents, fully cognisant of what the result would be. A little later you repented and rode madly from Rembakut to Bukit-Serang, hoping to be in time to prevent a tragedy."

She sprang to her feet, her eyes blazing.

"God!" she screamed at him, "I hate you! I knew nothing of its powers. I had only had it since the afternoon. The man told me, jokingly, that it was a charm which would help me to accomplish my desires. In a stupid moment I wished Dick dead—and a superstitious feeling made me ride over to get the thing back from him. I never knew he would die—like that. I didn't want him to die. It was such a shock to me that I have been ill ever since." She fell back again and lay gazing dry-eyed at the ceiling. "And while I have been ill," she continued brokenly, "all this has been said against me! But, Michael, I am innocent; you know that I am innocent."

"I want the address of the man who gave you that charm," pursued the magistrate relentlessly.

"I lied to you," she confessed. "He has never written to me in his life. He calls to me when I am sleeping, he beckons to me and I see behind him the brazier in the wilderness and the red butterflies. On the night when I slept with the Butterfly at my throat I had no dreams. That is why I ask you to give it back to me. I am suffering all the tortures of the damned."

His pipe had gone out and he knew that the water in the little bathroom annexe was turning from luke-warm to cold. In the living-room Chong-Si moved softly, with every now and then a jingling of forks and spoons as he arranged them for the evening meal.

There floated back to Armourer a memory of a sentence Joyce had written down for him on a card: "*I am a goddess,*" Vera had said in her delirium, "*and my kiss is death!*"

In a dim sort of fashion he was beginning to understand. He shuddered to think of the risk he had run during that mad evening on Battiscombe's verandah. Her kiss might well have been death then, had a butterfly been released to fly in quest of its own image!

"The professor has the pendant," he said at length. "He is employing it for some experiment in the little laboratory we have managed to fix up for him. I am sorry, Mrs. Battiscombe, if I have upset you. None of us actually supposed that you killed Dick Moberly. I shall be able to tell them that you were merely an instrument."

She bent forward.

"Whose instrument?" she inquired fearfully, trying to discover how much he knew.

"*Abu-Samar's,*" said Armourer steadily—and Vera Battiscombe hid her face.

CHAPTER XXII

DISAPPEARANCE OF MRS. BATTISCOMBE

As ARMOURER DRESSED HIMSELF slowly for the evening meal, feeling clean and refreshed after his bath, he pondered over the various phases of his interview with Vera.

Abu-Samar had given her the Crimson Butterfly; that fact he regarded as completely established. He had given it her on the afternoon of the day preceding Moberly's death, she had worn it when he danced with her, and Jim had discovered it later. To avoid mentioning Samar, she had included this ornament with Dick's presents when she returned them, and to prevent the planter sending it back again, she had ridden over to explain her position. She had not expected a tragedy; but the discovery of the dead man and the mark on his face had immediately recalled to her memory Abu-Samar's statement that the Butterfly was a charm that would enable her to attain her desires—and her own foolish wish, expressed in a weak moment, that Moberly should die.

He tilted back the mirror so that he could see to brush his hair.

It seemed to him that this was the only sensible way of regarding her part in the affair.

The extent of her friendship with Abu-Samar was no affair of his. He was concerned with the chain of events leading up to the tragedy at Bukit-Serang and the later tragedy at his own house—and the chain, weird, fantastic, incredible as it was, was almost complete.

Abu-Samar, desiring to revenge himself upon Battiscombe for an insult, had played upon Vera's notorious love of admiration and costly gifts to ensure that the talisman that somehow attracted these poisonous insects should be taken to the magistrate's house. Following upon a peculiar sequence of events for which he could not possibly have allowed, the pendant found its way to Moberly's bungalow, and the butterfly, when released, brought about the decease of the wrong man.

Professor Standen would have to supply details that would strengthen certain of the links.

It remained to be discovered what singular attractive properties the ornament possessed, and why Mrs. Battiscombe should be immune from attack. The fact that both the victims were men he regarded as merely an accident.

Abu-Samar—that arch-criminal, hypnotist, producer of colossal illusions—had concentrated upon his art until he had succeeded in producing a masterpiece. As Standen had said, it was a trick, accomplished in the broad light of day without the aid of mirrors, traps, or any of the recognised *apparata* of the Western illusionist, but still unworthy of any more dignified title than a trick.

And, in common with his more civilised prototype, he was dependent upon an accomplice and upon certain conditions. Without Mrs. Battiscombe he could not have counted upon the Butterfly pendant being in its desired position, and with the pendant kept at a safe distance from his intended victims, he was unable to produce the trick at all.

Armourer rubbed his hands together and took a final lock at himself in the glass.

Things were beginning to simmer down. Provided that reasonable care were exerted, a repetition of the affair at Bukit-Serang was next to impossible, and all that remained to be done was to capture Abu-Samar. Unless—and the thought rendered him uneasy—the magician, driven into the backwoods and becoming desperate, were to let loose a cloud of these insects to wreak indiscriminate vengeance upon anybody who should come in their way.

Here they were dependent upon Professor Standen too. A powerful antidote would in this case be the only hope to avert a catastrophe which was too ghastly to contemplate seriously.

The Butterfly ornament on its filigree chain might, in addition to directing the movements of the real butterfly, render it more than usually vindictive; but, even without the ornament, he could not lose sight of the fact that these creatures were still saturated with venom from wing-tip to wing-tip and still at liberty to make use of their fatal powers upon the slightest provocation.

As he strolled out on to the verandah he caught himself hoping that the professor's experiments were making headway in the right direction. He hoped, too, that Jimmy Battiscombe—with his rooted aversion to leeches—had been dispatched upon a false scent. It would be particularly unpleasant to come suddenly upon the black magician and his vile collection of unclean insects without being prepared with something that could be counted upon to counteract the effects of the poison.

He found Chong-Si at the living-room doorway.

"The *mem* is tired," he informed his master; "she will not eat."

Armourer walked to the rail and, leaning his hands on it, stared into the night. He had expected this.

"Very well, Chong-Si," he said over his shoulder. "Take some food to her room and then get my dinner as quickly as possible."

The terriers stole up the stairs, Mick carrying a small rat and Mac endeavouring to relieve his companion in crime of its ownership.

"Here! Take that thing outside," recommended their lord and master—and the procession retreated by the way it had come.

He was glad he had those dogs. Until Joyce had walked into his life, he had been tolerably contented with his lot. She had been his guest for little more than a week and now, in her first absence, he was already beginning to feel unutterably lonely. Looked at from every reasonable point of view, this phenomenon appeared absurd. He had never regarded himself seriously as a marrying sort of man; he had had his work to interest him, the intricacies of native dialect, the manifold peculiarities and inconsistencies of local character. Even in the event of his screwing himself up to the point of proposing matrimony, it was far more likely than not that she would refuse him. He could scarcely see how she could do otherwise. He had lived so long alone that he flattered himself he knew his own shortcomings pretty well. He assumed that these shortcomings were patent to all the world—more particularly to a beautiful, discerning creature like Joyce. He was just an ordinary magistrate in very ordinary surroundings and dependent for his existence upon an ordinary man's pay—supplemented by a couple of hundred or so of his own. In the words of Euclid, the thing was absurd—and yet there was some obstinate kink in his nature that wouldn't let him give up hoping.

As he leaned there, gazing down towards the spot where Mick and Mac still continued their boisterous struggle for the possession of a rat, a familiar sound broke upon his ears.

He drew himself erect, listening intently.

There was no doubt about it. Somebody on horseback had already left the trees and was cantering towards the house.

Five minutes later he moistened his lips and called.

"Hullo, there! That you, Trevor?"

The planter's assistant came up the steps.

"Hullo, Armourer! Here I am and here's my kit."

He unhitched a haversack and let it fall to the floor.

"Just in time for *makan*; we're late to-night. I let my bath-water get cold and Chong-Si had to boil me some more. How are you?"

Trevor found a chair.

"First class, thanks. I got away sooner than I'd expected and took it into my head to sponge on you for a meal. Yes, I'll manage a drink, if you don't mind. That ride did me a world of good. It's a sticky sort of evening."

The magistrate concocted an *aperitif*.

"Get that inside you and we'll go and eat."

The other tested and signified his approval with a nod.

"If ever you give up this sort of thing you ought to try a hand at cocktail-shaking. It's your line all right! How's the mystery progressing?"

Armourer lowered his brows.

"Slowly."

"And Abu?"

"He's still at large. Battiscombe should have been here to-night, but he's gone up-country. That's why I sent for one of you fellows." He lowered his voice. "Jimmy doesn't seem to mind much how or where he leaves his wife; but *I* do. You follow me, don't you?"

Trevor winked.

"She's still here, then?"

"Oh, she's here, right enough; though I don't suppose we shall be favoured with her company to-night. She has signified her intention of dining in her room. The professor and his daughter are in Jesselton."

They strolled in to dinner.

"And so," murmured Trevor as Chong-Si set down the soup, "the distinguished magistrate has found it necessary to seek moral support."

"He has indeed!"

He flicked an insect from the rim of his plate with his thumb-nail.

Trevor looked thoughtful.

"Well, I can't say that I blame you. Mrs. B. would be the most delightful woman in the world—if she were a little less cosmopolitan in her tastes. But a flirtation loses half its charm when there's every possibility of it developing to something more serious. After all, there's no particular fun in attempting to conquer something that's in a constant state of surrender. Rather clever for me, what?"

"There are times," declared his host, "when you verge upon genius!—Have some more soup?"

"No, thanks. Now, if it had been Miss Standen instead of the aforesaid female, things would have been very different."

Armourer looked up sharply.

"How so?"

"You wouldn't have sent for me."

The magistrate pushed away his plate.

"I should," he replied slowly. "I should most emphatically have sent for you; but I shouldn't have grown particularly anxious if your duties had detained you until, say, eleven."

Trevor stared at him hard.

"Armourer," he announced at length, "you're bitten! You have fallen a victim to the innocent charms of your dark-eyed visitor. Now isn't that just my luck!"

"Don't be an idiot!" growled the other—and then, in an altered tone: "You're not keen on her, really?"

"No—not hopelessly; but I fancy I could have been. Lord! I see it all now! This desperate effort to preserve appearances, to preserve an hitherto untarnished reputation! It's as clear as daylight. What a cunning old devil you are!"

Armourer was crimsoning beneath the tan.

"You are jumping at conclusions."

"They don't need much jumping at. I suppose I ought to offer my congratulations!"

His glance fell upon the bottle before him.

"I say, are we supposed to celebrate an occasion like this with *beer?*"

"Trevor," said Armourer coldly, "you are not a genius; you never were, and I see no reason to suppose that you ever will be! You can have champagne if you like; but I can frankly assure you at the same time that there's no need for any celebration. Miss Standen is merely an extremely welcome guest at Jelandang; nothing more and nothing less."

He rang the bell.

"Which means," said the irrepressible Trevor, "that the lady has not yet been consulted on the subject! Nevertheless, I simply refuse to refrain from drinking your health in the only fluid worth drinking it in. Taking into consideration your undeniable dash and *élan*, I regard the forthcoming engagement as a *fait accompli*. Tell Chong-Si to make it two bottles!"

The servant shuffled in from the kitchen.

"Chong-Si," ordered Armourer, "bring me two bottles of champagne." He detached a key from a ring and tossed it to the cook-boy. "And, oh—just a minute. You'd better ask the *mem* if she would care to take wine. *Tahu?*"

Chong-Si made off.

He was back again in under two minutes, a bottle in either hand and a look of consternation on his face.

"The *mem* has gone out, *Tuan*," he stammered.

The magistrate came to his feet.

"Gone out?"

"*Yah, Tuan*. As I went to the cupboard, I saw something pass the door of the store-room. I looked down the passage— and found that it was the lady, with something white thrown over her head. She went out by the back door." He placed the bottles on the table and groped in the depths of a pocket. "There was this letter on the tray in the lady's room."

He handed Armourer a note addressed to himself.

CHAPTER XXIII

THE HUT IN THE TREES

ARMOURER READ THE MISSIVE through and handed it to Trevor.

"What d'you make of that?" he demanded.

The other scanned it.

"DEAR MICHAEL," it read, "I can bear it no longer. Whenever I close my eyes I see him. I see the rocks in the wilderness, the red light from the brazier—and him, beckoning me. This evening your pitiless catechism broke down the last rampart of my resistance. The call came again—and I could only obey. A mysterious *something* guides my pen and I have had to force myself to write even these few lines. I find it impossible to inscribe his name, but you, who have guessed so much already, will understand. The wretchedness that my follies have brought to everybody has descended at last upon myself. What ghastly fate awaits me in the beyond I know not, but if it is because of my looks that he has sought me I pray that some horrible disease may mar my features before I encounter him alone.

"Good-bye.

"Vera."

Trevor stared at his friend in amazement.

"Holy Moses! what's it all mean?"

"The *him*," said Armourer, "is Abu-Samar. It was he who gave that ornament to Mrs. Battiscombe."

"I see; and all this rigmarole about wildernesses and red lights and somebody calling, what's all that signify?"

The magistrate reached down his hat.

"Abu was never a doctor. His chief stunt is hypnotism. He has apparently taken advantage of Mrs. Battiscombe's weak state of health to impose his will upon her—from a distance. I don't understand much about this sort of thing, but I believe it's quite possible. Looks as if the champagne's *off* for the moment, doesn't it?"

Trevor made a wry face.

"Whenever I come to this confounded house of yours, there's always some excitement in the wind. A few more experiences of this sort and I shall begin to believe that our district officers constitute a particularly energetic and hard-worked body of men! I think my topee's on the verandah."

They went out together by the back way and Chong-Si watched their movements apprehensively. If any particular thought were uppermost in his mind at that minute it was probably one concerning the demise of his immediate predecessor.

Armourer's first move was to turn out his men and dispatch them with instructions to scour the neighbourhood thoroughly.

"We'll try the path through the trees first," he told Trevor, "follow it as far as your wire and come back by the professor's shack. She's only ten minutes start of us."

The other nodded.

"She can't have got far and the white thing over her head should render her fairly conspicuous in the darkness. Going to ride?"

Armourer reflected.

"No. Ponies will only be in the way if we have to leave the track. We shall be far more comfortable on foot."

They strode on in silence, filling their pipes as they went.

"I hope we find her all right," said the magistrate, suddenly. "I feel kind of responsible for this."

Trevor glanced up at his companion.

"That's pretty good nonsense, isn't it? Jim couldn't expect you to spend your time in her room."

"I know all about that; but, you see, I asked her a lot of questions about the pendant just before *makan*, and the professor had previously warned me not to do so. It might quite easily be supposed that my attitude was responsible for her flight. You remember what she said in the letter about my pitiless catechism."

Trevor struck a match and puffed furiously for some seconds.

"I shouldn't say anything about that letter. It's of no value except to show what state of mind she was in. It doesn't supply any definite clue to the direction she's taken."

"It doesn't," returned the other slowly; "but, if I have made a mistake, I can take my gruelling with the next man. I don't fancy I should care to suppress anything."

"It might be misunderstood; it struck me as being rather intimate. It started *Michael*, I mean—and finished *Vera*."

Armourer bit his lip.

"I've never written to *her*," he protested, "and I can't very well help what she chooses to write to me, can I? Besides, Jimmy always addresses me by my Christian name."

"You don't think he'll mind?"

"Not particularly. Why should he?"

"And the professor and Miss Standen? Supposing they get to hear of it?"

The magistrate hold out his hand.

"Give me the matches, Trevor. Thanks. You've a particularly irritating way of hitting the right nail on the head. I'm not going to commit myself to destroying or withholding anything, but I shall certainly think over the wisdom of divulging the contents of that confounded note. D'you know, Trevor, that woman's becoming a veritable thorn in my side."

"She evidently likes you."

Armourer uttered an exclamation of disgust.

"Then all I can say is I wish she didn't. Jimmy swears he'll send her home as soon as she's fit to travel, and I shall try and keep him up to it. She's a damned dangerous woman."

"'Amen to that!" added the other, "but we've got to find her first."

They encountered a native in the trees and Armourer questioned him.

"Where are you going?"

The man seemed frightened.

"*Sana*," he muttered, indicating with a dark forefinger the direction in which a village lay.

"Have you seen anybody on the path or in the forest?"

The creature shook his head.

"Nobody, *Tuan*."

"Nobody at all? Not a white lady, for example, with a shawl over her head?"

He shook his head again.

"I came from the *Kampong* on the far side of the hill. There were girls drawing water from a stream, but after that, nobody."

Armourer shrugged his shoulders and let him go.

He looked at Trevor.

"That's rather important," he said. "He must have followed our path for more than a mile before we met him. She can't have come this way."

The other rubbed his chin.

"She may have left the track at some point. I suggest we keep on for, say, another half-mile."

Armourer shone an electric torch on the ground at his feet.

"The worst of it is," he complained, "that the earth's as hard as nails everywhere. A regiment of soldiers could march along here without leaving a single foot-mark."

A hundred yards farther on a man with a hurricane lamp stepped suddenly from the bushes.

"Who's that?" called Armourer sharply.

"Sembilan, *Tuan*," came the startled response, and a little black private came respectfully to attention.

"Sembilan, is it? Have you found the white lady?"

"No, *Tuan-Hakim*. The *mem* is nowhere to be seen; but I have found this on a thorn-bush."

He held before them a white silk wrap with a long fringe.

Armourer recognised the scent which still clung to it long before he had time to examine the texture of the material.

"Where did you find this?"

The soldier pointed behind him.

"Just there, *Tuan*, but a few moments before you came. The grass had been trodden down and the track points this way—across the main path and into the trees on the other side."

"Carry on, Sembilan," commanded Armourer, "we will follow."

They followed their guide through dense undergrowth, parted in places as if something had recently passed that way. Mosquitoes whined everywhere, monkeys crooned sleepily overhead, and presently a patch of cool air brought them to the bed of a trickling forest stream.

Sembilan came back, holding his lamp above his head, and pointed excitedly at the ground.

"By Jove!" murmured Trevor, "we're on the right track. That's a woman's heel or I'm a Dutchman. See! There it is again."

Armourer followed the direction of his gaze.

"Thank heaven for that!" he announced presently. "We've discovered something! Don't hang about there, man, gibbering like an infernal ape! Get on with it!"

The native grinned and moved forward.

"What the dickens made her take to the jungle?" asked Trevor after a long pause.

"Don't know," responded the other. "Perhaps she's following some course dictated by that scoundrel Abu. She must be in a sort of trance, or she surely wouldn't have left this shawl behind."

Trevor was thinking.

"We'll hunt up a map when we get back," he said, "and draw a line on it from your place to this point, and on to infinity. If she's bound to steer a direct course to where he now is, we might follow that line until we find him." He dug Armourer in the ribs. "That's pretty sound reasoning, eh?"

"Marvellous! Any idea where we are now?"

"No."

"Well, how are you going to find it on the map?"

"Don't know. I was leaving that to you. Do *you* know where we are?"

The magistrate sucked at an empty pipe.

"We're about a hundred yards from the professor's laboratory, and Mrs. Battiscombe in her wanderings has covered three parts of a circle. Rather knocks your theory on the head, doesn't it?"

This sudden revelation left Trevor utterly unabashed.

"It was very stupid of me," he announced cheerfully. "I had forgotten to allow for feminine instability of character!"

Two minutes brought them to the hut.

Armourer uttered an exclamation and ran the final ten yards.

"What's up?" demanded Trevor, following suit.

"This," declared the other, and swung the door to and fro on its hinges. "The padlock's been forced off. Sembilan! bring that lamp inside."

Trevor, picking his way gingerly, was greeted by an odour of chemicals that set him coughing.

He touched his companion's arm.

"There's a bottle been knocked down here," he said. "I should be careful how you go. Some of these things burn."

Armourer held the lamp so that its rays illuminated the roof. He pointed to a few links of gold chain that still swung from a hook.

"That's what she was after, old son. She plagued me for it this evening. You see, the pendant's gone."

Trevor gasped.

"But, man alive, she didn't know where the shack was, she couldn't possibly have forced that door—"

The magistrate waved his arms in the air.

"It's no use asking or implying questions. All I can tell you is that the Crimson Butterfly has gone, that she's got it on her now—and that we've got to find her and bring her back."

CHAPTER XXIV

THE GODDESS OF THE BUTTERFLY

THEY WERE MAKING FOR THE OPEN again when, in the light of the hurricane-lamp Armourer still carried, Trevor noticed something.

"Wait a minute!"

The magistrate stopped and looked back.

"What's the matter?"

The planter pointed to the concrete floor of the professor's laboratory. The fluid from the broken bottle had formed a dark patch which had spread—like a fantastic map—halfway across the hut. Both Englishmen, warned by the pungent odour, had avoided this patch when they entered, but somebody who had preceded them had been less cautious. On either side there were vague, smudgy tracks, and at the far end, the clear imprint of bare toes.

"More than one person has been here," he said with conviction.

"Yes," conceded Armourer; "you're right there."

He stepped outside and Trevor heard him engaged in conversation with Sembilan.

The magistrate thrust his head in at the door.

"Come along, old son. This is beginning to get interesting. Sembilan says there are four distinct tracks outside. Standen, it appears, employs a good deal of water in his experiments—and slings most of it out through the doorway. The soft state of the earth outside helps us enormously. The awkward part of it is that those little half-moons made by Mrs. Battiscombe's heels peter out here altogether."

"Samar sent somebody for her," suggested Trevor, "and she was carried from here."

Armourer nodded.

"I don't think there's the least doubt about that. Wherever his hiding-place happens to be, it's sure to be at a considerable distance—and he could hardly have expected her to walk."

Trevor was stooping down, both hands on his knees.

"Can your fellow tell us the direction they've taken?"

"The devil of it is he's found two tracks, both clearly marked, and leading in different directions."

Trevor pursed up his lips.

"Sembilan must be a pretty smart chap at the game, for I can't see a damn' thing beyond a few smudgy foot-prints just where we're standing. The only conclusion I can come to is that the two paths were deliberately made so as to throw us off the scent. There were four tracks—or, rather, four sets of footmarks—you said. Those of Mrs. Battiscombe and three others. I suggest that, to ensure a smart getaway, Abu dispatched a couple of hefty men with a *pikul*—and a third to hang around and make false paths to confuse us. Possibly this third native met her close to your house and induced her to follow that queer roundabout way through the trees, rather than keep to the path. When they split up outside here, the bearers and Mrs. Battiscombe must obviously have gone in one direction—and the remaining native in the other. The larger party should naturally make the biggest track."

Armourer whistled up his man, who was standing knee-deep in fern and rank grass, staring solemnly in all directions.

"The *Tuan* Trevor thinks that three people went by one path and only one by another."

"*Yah, Tuan*, that is so. The one who was alone came first and went away alone. After a little while the white lady came with two men."

Trevor rubbed the back of his head.

"Now, how the dickens does he know that?"

Armourer smiled.

"Sembilan has a gift for this sort of thing." He turned to the soldier. "Very well, we will follow the main track."

"Why not divide?" suggested his friend. "One of us could take Sembilan—and the other go alone. For all we know, the lonely gentleman may prove an important witness. If he arrived on the scene first, it is probably he who forced the lock and pinched the pendant."

"I'll go alone," said Armourer promptly. "I know my way about here better than you do. If anybody can follow the marks left by Mrs. Battiscombe's bearers, it's Sembilan. You'll be safe enough with him. You'd better get along as fast as you can."

"But," protested Trevor, "you won't be able to follow the other route without an intelligent native to help you."

The magistrate dropped a heavy hand on his shoulder.

"Don't you bother about me. I shall get in touch with one of my men inside a quarter of an hour—and the professor's shack is a good pushing-off point. Have you got a gun?"

Trevor grinned.

"I have. Vance makes us all carry 'em now. The obvious inference is that they're for shooting butterflies! Cheerio!"

"You know what you're after," Armourer shouted after him. "You've to bring back Mrs. Battiscombe by hook or by crook. If Abu's fellows show any sign of resistance—shoot 'em! But try and keep one of them alive until I can interview him as to Abu's whereabouts."

He stood for some minutes watching the hurricane-lamp bobbing its way out of sight among the trees, then tested his torch to reassure himself as to the amount of *juice* left in the battery.

His pipe had gone out and he filled and lit it again.

He was in two minds as to what his next move should be. He was still a fair distance from his bungalow, and all his men, with the exception of an orderly on duty and the cook-boy, were presumably still scouring the district. If he decided to make his way back, he would run the risk of missing the whole bunch of them and wasting valuable time. If he endeavoured to follow the single native alone, it was ten chances to one he would lose himself and his quarry into the bargain. In a case of this sort, he was obliged to acknowledge the superiority of native intelligence.

Impatient as he was to accomplish something definite, he decided to wait where he was. Sembilan had hit upon the route Mrs. Battiscombe had taken, and, even without the evidence of the shawl on the thorn-bush, it was more than probable some of the others would follow suit.

It was dark under the trees and, accustomed as his eyes had grown to the gloom, he could only recognise objects at a few paces. The forest seemed never still. There was a constant rustling, varied at intervals by queer, crashing sounds, the piercing shriek of a night-bird, and a weird groaning as branches high above him worked upon each other, swayed by the breeze that had suddenly sprung up.

He set his back against a trunk and tried to forget that there were comfortable chairs at Jelandang, an unfinished meal and two unopened bottles of champagne.

Five minutes passed . . . ten . . . fifteen.

His pipe went out again and he did not bother to replenish it. He gazed all round him. There were no signs of his men, no footsteps, distant voices—nothing . . . Just that incessant modulated chorus of jungle sounds: nothing more.

It was beginning to get monotonous.

For want of something better to do, he sauntered back into Standen's laboratory and flashed his torch over rough shelves stocked with bottles, crucibles, lengths of glass tubing and measures. There was a heap of papers in a corner of the bench, covered with neat groupings of mysterious hieroglyphics, a tin-lid that had been used as an ashtray, and a rack of test-tubes of varying sizes. Tucked under the bench he found kerosene-tins, some empty, some filled with water, and a miniature Primus stove.

It astonished him to discover how much the professor had succeeded in raking together in the course of a few days.

He looked at his watch.

Trevor had been gone nearly half an hour. He wondered how he was getting on. He wished now that he had gone with him. It seemed so futile, waiting there—and yet he could not see what else he could have done under the circumstances.

The breeze was blowing harder now and the atmosphere was growing chill. He turned up his collar.

Another five minutes and he would go in search of his men.

He was not an habitually nervous man and yet he hated the idea of switching off that light. He tried the experiment and turned it on again.

As he did so, the pale rays were reflected in some bright object on the floor by the doorway.

He stooped and picked it up.

It was a narrow, fluted circlet of gold, the size of a bracelet, and broken to allow it to be fitted over the ankle of a native girl. He had seen many of these things before, but never wrought in so precious a metal.

The light went out again and he remained in the darkness, thinking deeply.

Even Sembilan's jungle wisdom had failed to reveal this. One of the nocturnal visitors to the hut had been a native woman.

The discovery puzzled Armourer.

Abu-Samar would not have dispatched a woman to help to carry Mrs. Battiscombe. Could it be possible that the knowledge that the pendant was kept unguarded there had got abroad, and that some brown-skinned maiden from the locality had decided to steal it for its beauty. Assuming such a possibility to be correct, it was doubly strange that she should have chosen so momentous a night for her raid. What, too, had caused the wrench that forced this mysterious female to part with her anklet?

He shone his light on the dark patch of fluid on the floor and tested it gingerly with a finger-tip. He uttered an exclamation and wiped it hastily on his coat.

She had stepped into the chemical and burnt her foot. Clutching wildly at the injured member, the anklet had been torn off and forgotten in her momentary agony.

He went to the door, slipping the torch into his pocket. Moonlight was filtering through the trees, throwing ghostly patches of jet shadow, describing a barbaric patchwork of black and gold.

He stepped quickly back, feeling for the automatic at his hip.

Some large object had passed between two trees not a score of feet from the hut.

Every nerve alert, he waited.

It was coming closer . . . he could hear it now . . . soft, padding steps in the open.

He hazarded a look.

A vague indefinite body, that might have been a man or even a giant ape, stooped and grunted almost on the threshold.

He levelled his pistol and flashed on the torch at the same time.

A shrill scream pierced his ears, two arms swept wildly heavenward, and a native woman stood erect before him, writhing and moaning in mortal terror.

She was lithe, and better-looking than the majority of her kind; there were ornaments of silver and gold at her ears and wrists and the Crimson Butterfly, the ends of its chain held together by a strip of leather, hung at her throat.

He caught her arm and threw her roughly behind him into the shack. He fixed the switch of his pocket-lamp and rested it on its side on the bench, then produced the anklet he had found.

At the sight if it she uttered a joyful cry.

"That is mine," she whispered hoarsely; "I came back to find it."

He touched the ornament at her throat with his forefinger.

"And that?" he demanded. "How came you by that?"

"That is mine, too," she told him defiantly. "It was stolen from me and given to another woman, and for a time I did nothing because I was afraid. There is a devil in this thing, O *Tuan-Hakim*, but while I wear it the devil is silent. While I

go free there is peace in the forest and in the open lands beyond the forest; but he who seeks to harm me—dies!"

The magistrate tucked his revolver out of sight.

"Who are you?" he asked.

She held herself proudly, the crimson ornament sparkling
at her neck.

"I am she who men call Dara, whose home is where no
trees grow, where there is a tall hill and a fire that never
burns out. I am the goddess of the Crimson Butterfly."

Armourer scratched his chin.

He stood for some moments looking at her, then picked up
his torch.

Presently a smile illuminated his features and a great hope
rose within him, warming his blood and surging to his head
like strong wine.

"Come with me, Dara," he said softly. "I have been seeking you for a long while."

CHAPTER XXV

OUTNUMBERED

ARNOLD TREVOR, HOT ON THE TRACK of Abu-Samar's men, found it increasingly difficult to keep up with his guide.

Sembilan had divested himself of the boots his uniform included and, knotting the laces together, carried them over one shoulder. The stiffness of military training had gone out of him and once more he was the savage, discovering passages through the dense undergrowth where none seemed to exist, crouching, leaping, swinging himself on to low branches like an ape to assist him in clearing the more formidable obstacles that came in his way.

In the soft earth by the bed of a miniature cataract, where giant fern and lush weed grew in rank profusion, he threw himself on his face and deciphered the impressions in the soil as a shortsighted student might peruse a book.

"Found anything?" demanded the Englishman breathlessly.

Sembilan drew himself into a squatting position and his dark face turned upwards.

"*Yah, Tuan*. There are signs everywhere. Here they have walked—and here; and there, on the other side of the water, there are many marks. They have taken this direction."

And he began running along the bed of the torrent, forging uphill where brown rocks showed amid a broken carpet of luxuriant moss.

Trevor struggled after him.

They came presently to the summit of a hill and stood gazing across a stretch of open country bathed in yellow moonlight, pitted with holes, tossed and denuded by some far-off volcanic shock. A hundred yards to the eastward yawned a gaping chasm and, on the far side, two figures had just emerged, carrying something swung from a pole that stretched between them.

The soldier put his hands to his mouth and let forth a wild, discordant yell that echoed and re-echoed as if a thousand demon voices had hurled it back at them in mocking derision.

The foremost of the bearers turned his head and, a second after, both began running towards the belt of trees beyond.

Before Trevor could stop him Sembilan had unslung his rifle and fired. A second shot followed the first and the nearest native stumbled forward on to his knees, dropping his end of the *pikul* to the ground.

His companion crouched low and, shouldering the rough hammock, pole and all, slid down a steep bank out of sight.

Trevor and Sembilan came to their feet together and ran for all they were worth. The brink of the chasm held them up for a couple of minutes, for its depths defied the moonlight and the path by which the others had travelled was difficult to find.

By the time they had crossed, their quarry had reached the trees.

The planter paused by the side of the man whom Sembilan had shot and marvelled at the accuracy of the soldier's firing. The native was still kneeling, his head against a boulder, and it took but a moment to discover that he was dead.

Trevor looked up to see that his dusky companion was still pressing forward, and that he was in imminent danger of losing sight of him in the forest towards which he was now heading.

He swore softly to himself, sprinted for a couple of hundred yards, tripped over a rock and fell, recovered himself, bruised and battered, and resumed the pursuit again.

Sembilan had vanished altogether, but he thought he knew the point in the leafy screen through which he had passed. At all costs he must find him. To be left alone in this ghastly wilderness would be tragedy indeed. He was entirely without provisions and might wander for days before he found his way to any civilised habitation.

The moon passed behind a cloudbank with the trees still an appreciable distance from him. He halted and stared round him blankly. Against a pall of blackness a faint light shone. Sembilan's hurricane-lamp! A feeling of intense relief surging within him, Trevor hastened towards the light.

He found it presently, just the lamp, but no Sembilan! The man's intelligence had recognised his difficulty and left the lamp there to guide him. He grabbed at the handle gratefully. Armourer had been right when he had told him he would be safe with Sembilan. The little soldier with the quaint round hat strapped under his chin was a host in himself.

The trees were taller here and the dense undergrowth of the more stunted forests had given way to a moss which, though soft to the feet, it was difficult to make progress over.

A movement to his right made him hold the lamp above his head and, to his intense horror, he saw an immense ape, standing in the fork of a tree, staring stupidly down at him. The thing gibbered at him, smiting its great chest until it resounded like a drum, and the planter, knowing well that a bad shot would produce unpleasant complications, slithered on in a panic.

If he had once pined for adventure, he was wallowing in it now to a degree far greater than he had bargained for!

Something was going on ahead of him. He could hear extraordinary grunting sounds, the noise of heavy bodies being dragged about among the dried leaves . . . a hoarse panting for breath. With the memory of that horror in the branches, it occurred to him that he might have plunged upon a colony of these creatures, and that in the event of such being the case his prospects of survival were singularly small.

He turned completely round, swinging the lamp so that it threw its light over a large area.

He saw them now—two dark figures wrestling on the ground—and one of these he recognised as Sembilan.

As he plunged with a wild cry to his assistance, something swept his check so closely that he felt the breath of it—and the lamp was dashed from his hand.

The impact of the blow set him stumbling.

Supporting himself on one hand, he wrenched his revolver free from the pocket in which he carried it, and fired into the shadowy mass that hovered over him.

The mass swayed away from him, uttering wild, unearthly yells that woke the hairy denizens of the trees and sent them screaming and whining in chorus.

He heard Sembilan calling.

"Quick, *Tuan!* The light!"

He groped around him until he found it and, lifting what remained of the glass chimney, applied a match to the wick. Presently a corner of it caught the flame and he dropped the glass.

Sembilan was kneeling over the prostrate form of a man—·and Trevor's antagonist was nowhere to be seen.

As the planter approached, the soldier rose slowly.

"Dead!" he declared grimly.

"Who is it?" asked the Englishman.

Sembilan shrugged his shoulders.

"Who shall say?—He leapt on me from a tree as I followed after the man who carried the *mem*." He rubbed his shoulder and screwed up his face. "He had the strength of a panther—that man!—And yet I killed him," he added with pride. "We wrestled for a long time—and then I tripped him and slipped from his hands. I split his skull with my rifle-butt—so! There were others in the forest."

"I know," said Trevor. "I fired at one of them myself. Which way have they taken the *mem?*"

The soldier shook his head.

"I do not know, *Tuan*. Many people have been here to-night and it is impossible to recognise one track from another. Abu-Samar has sent men to stop us. They are bigger than the natives at the coast and they carry poisoned darts and blow-pipes. We must wait for the light."

Trevor rested his back against a tree and mopped his fore-head. He was conscious of acute fatigue and an aching void within, but it went badly against the grain to give up all hope of rescuing Mrs. Battiscombe.

"How far are we from dawn?"

Sembilan consulted a patch of sky just visible through the trees.

"More than three hours, *Tuan*."

"They will have carried the white lady a long way by now?"

"A very long way."

A deep groan from somewhere close at hand attracted their attention.

Moving warily, Trevor discovered a native doubled up in a hollow beneath a giant tree. The man was lying in a pool of blood and there was a hole in his side that the planter could have put his fist in.

"There is your man, *Tuan*," said Sembilan. "I think he cannot live very long."

"Poor devil!" muttered Trevor.

A thought struck him.

"Talk to him, Sembilan; try and get him to say something. He should know which way they have gone."

The soldier addressed the man in Malay, in the Dusun dialect, and in a language Trevor could not follow.

"It is no good, *Tuan*," explained Sembilan after a while. "He does not understand. He belongs to one of those tribes that live in the heart of the island. He speaks only his own tongue—and who shall say what that is?"

The creature stiffened suddenly, clutched with both hands at the moss and lay very still.

"*Sudah habis!*" murmured the soldier. "It is finished, O *Tuan!*"

He thrust an arm through the sling of his rifle and began threading his way through the trees.

"Where are you going?" asked Trevor.

"Back to the open again. There is no good to be done here. It is not so easy to shoot a man when he hides behind a tree. If Abu-Samar's men come in search of us, there are holes out there where we can lie in ambush for them and pick them off before they find us with their blow-pipes."

The planter hesitated.

"I should like to see what is beyond the trees," he told the man doggedly.

Sembilan shrugged his shoulders.

"*Baik, Tuan!* If you go I will follow, and if you ask me to lead I will lead; but after the trees there are more trees, and after that more trees again. Also I know that the men Abu sent have not followed the other, but are waiting in the shadows."

"And the *mem?*"

The soldier shook his head sadly.

"Not even the *Tuan-Hakim*—who is wise—could bring her back to-night."

He reached over suddenly and knocked out the light.

Five minutes later, when they were in the open again, with the stars shining reassuringly down on them. Trevor turned to Sembilan.

"What did you think you saw?" he asked.

"I saw shadows," said the soldier, "long patches of shadow that were swiftly closing in on us—and the shadows had eyes!"

"There are apes in the forest," suggested Trevor.

"These were not apes," retorted Sembilan grimly.

He cast an apprehensive glance over his shoulder and, catching the planter's arm, drew him behind a boulder as a shower of tiny objects pattered to the ground like the first drops of a thunder-shower.

Without waiting for a second occurrence of this phenomenon they ran until they had placed the chasm between them and their unseen enemy.

"Apes do not use the *sumpitan!*" announced Sembilan, as they came to a halt.

They were staring back at the trees, trying to get a glimpse of the attacking party, when the soldier—who seemed to have eyes all round his head—touched his companion and pointed to two figures swinging towards them from behind.

Trevor gripped his revolver-butt tightly, thinking for a moment that the enemy had outflanked them.

A reassuring remark from Sembilan set him laughing.

"It is the *Tuan-Hakim's* men," he said. "He has sent them after us."

They ran to meet them.

The taller of the two men saluted and handed Trevor a note from Armourer:

"My Dear Old Thing,

"Use your own judgment. If you have any hope of success, take these men with you and go right ahead. I'll square things with Vance. If, on the other hand. you have come to a dead-end, come back here at your leisure. I have made an important capture. I am sending some *grub* along. I daresay you can do with it!

"M. Armourer."

The second man handed him a basket.

It contained a loaf of bread, some butter and cheese, a tin of salmon, a tin-opener, and an odd assortment of cutlery.

But the thing which amused the planter most was a glowing tribute to Armourer's thoughtfulness and sense of humour: it was a bottle of champagne, the gilded neck of which towered above all the other contents of the basket!

CHAPTER XXVI

DARA DECIDES

ARMOURER POSTED A MAN at either entrance to his house, and, by dint of patient reasoning with the brown girl, eventually succeeded in persuading her to accompany him to the verandah.

On the way from the professor's shack he had discovered a great deal concerning her character. She was suspicious, of course, obstinate as only a native can be obstinate, perfectly capable, if bullied, of maintaining a sullen silence and refusing to utter a syllable even on pain of torture or death.

He imagined that she had been employed as some sort of priestess at a shrine and had somehow got it into her head that she was a goddess and therefore entitled to respect. She walked with her head high, with an easy swing of the shoulders and a proud, half-ironic smile always playing at the corners of her mouth.

She was lissom and good-looking, even when regarded from a purely Western point of view; her hair was black and shining and drawn back from her forehead to form a long, cylindrical knot behind a particularly handsome head, and he had detected beneath this knot the handle of a knife, the long thin blade of which was cunningly concealed.

It occurred to him that an enormous amount of tact would be required to induce her to reveal the secrets that lay behind those lustrous brown eyes.

He tossed a cushion on to the floor and she squatted down on it, never for a single moment withdrawing her gaze from his face. The cigarette-tin caught his eye and he held it out to her.

She hesitated, then drew out three together. She was fumbling with two of them, trying to push them back with the others, when Armourer spoke:

"Keep them, Dara; you may have need of them. I have many things I want to say to you to-night."

"The *Tuan-Hakim* is kind," she murmured.

He lit his own and held the match until the end of her cigarette glowed hopefully.

"How do you know that I am a magistrate?" he asked.

The girl smiled.

"Because of the soldiers, *Tuan*, and because once I lived in a house not very distant from here."

"Abu-Samar's?"

She exhaled a wreath of blue smoke and nodded.

For some minutes the magistrate smoked in silence.

Dara was not quite such an enigma after all. She had lived with Abu-Samar and it was probably in his bungalow that she had learned to smoke cigarettes. Already he was beginning to see hopes of drawing her out.

"And yet you are the goddess of the Crimson Butterfly?"

She started.

"*Yah, Tuan*, that is so."

He looked at his hands.

"What was the goddess doing so far from her temple and her people?"

A startled look had crept into her eyes and she gazed round her apprehensively.

"I am the *Tuan-Hakim's* prisoner?" she suggested.

Armourer shook his head slowly from side to side.

"The goddess of the Crimson Butterfly is no man's prisoner. You are my guest, little Dara. To-night we will find you a house and a bed and my soldiers will be on watch outside in case Abu-Samar should come to steal the Butterfly again."

She leaned back on her hands.

"Abu-Samar is a strange man, *Tuan*, and very powerful. To him the weapons of the little brown men are as nothing; walls cannot keep him out. He comes and he talks and presently he goes again—and even the dogs do not move in their sleep either at his coming or his going."

Armourer laughed.

"You are afraid of Abu-Samar," he told her, "and because you are afraid you believe all these things. I, who understand, tell you that these things are not possible. Samar has two arms and two legs and a body." He threw his automatic on to the table. "I need but speak once—with this—and Abu-Samar will be no more."

She blinked at him.

"Even you—who are wise—do not understand this man."

"Tell me," said the magistrate, "all you think I do not know."

"About what, *Tuan?*"

"About Abu-Samar and the temple in the wilderness where there is always a fire burning. Tell me how you came to leave that place and go with Samar."

She set her lips obstinately.

"I cannot."

He played his trump-card.

"Listen, Dara: To-night there was a white woman in this house and Abu-Samar called to her and she went to him. Possibly she will live in his house, as you have lived; she will wear the ornaments that you have worn. He will take her to the temple and say to the people who worship there: 'See, this woman is very beautiful, more beautiful even than Dara. She is the real goddess of the Butterfly!' "

Her eyes opened wide—like saucers—and she sat staring into space as if endeavouring to visualise the possible consequences of any confession. A shudder passed through her frame.

"Great *Tuan*, I was goddess of the Crimson Butterfly. I wore the ornament at my throat and the big red butterflies flew in the light of the brazier, hovering there to protect me. There were no other butterflies anywhere; only those. Then Abu came and saw me. He came many times after that. He brought presents and presently he spoke to me. He asked me to leave the temple—to go away with him, and I was afraid because of his eyes. I told him that the kiss of the goddess was death, because the butterflies watched over her, and he went away. He was gone for many moons and suddenly the butterflies left the temple and flew away. Then Abu returned and took me."

Armourer crushed out his cigarette and felt for his pipe.

"How did he make the butterflies go?"

She shook her head.

"Who can tell, *Tuan?* Abu has a magic that is very powerful. One morning when I woke I found that the ornament was gone from my neck. I spoke to Abu and he said that he wanted it for his magic. When we were in the house in the trees that was burnt, the white lady came."

The magistrate crossed his legs.

"Oh, yes?—Many times?"

"Once only, *Tuan.* Abu made her come. He sent me away, but I watched through a hole in the wall. He took the Crimson Butterfly from a box and fastened it round her neck. She was very frightened and ran away into the trees. But she kept the Butterfly."

"Where is Abu-Samar now?"

She clasped her hands over her ears and rocked to and fro.

"Do not ask me, *Tuan.* If I were to tell you, Abu would most surely kill me."

Armourer leaned forward.

"Dara," he said earnestly, "this man Samar frightens people with his eyes; that is why you, too, are frightened. Samar has a magic. There are two kinds of magic, Dara—black magic, which is Samar's, and white magic, which is mine. The white magic laughs at the other because it understands it. In a little while you will find here an old white man with a beard who has a magic more powerful than either. We shall go to Abu together, the old man and I, and you shall take us to him. We shall take with us many men and guns. We shall take this white lady from Abu and send her across the black waters in an engine-*kapal*. Abu we shall bring back in chains. The servants of the British *Raj* will sit in judgment over him and hang him from a tall tree—and you will be goddess of the Crimson Butterfly again."

He watched her keenly, anxious to discover what impression he had made.

She squatted there, still swaying a little, gazing thoughtfully at the boards.

"Before she came," she said softly, "I was everything to Abu. He made me many promises. He swore to me that with the magic he had stolen from the butterflies he would drive the white people from my country. When they were quite gone he would be king—and I his queen. The chieftains would be grateful to him and give him gold and ivory and precious stones—and I should have wonderful things to wear."

"A king has many wives," suggested the magistrate.

She looked up at him and her face brightened.

"That is true, *Tuan*, but I was to be his first wife—always. Now she is there—and I am alone. Would that I had waited for her in the hut in the trees—and killed her!"

She rose suddenly and came across to where he sat. Dropping to her knees by his chair, she clutched at his sleeve.

"If I lead you to him, Great *Tuan*, will you swear to do all that you have promised?"

He surveyed her steadily.

"By the word of an Englishman. I swear it."

"You will send her away on a boat that moves without sails, so that she may never come back to him?"

He nodded.

"And to my people in the wilderness you will say: 'This is Dara—the real goddess—that was taken from you by the Evil One against her will. See, I have brought her back to you.' Then one of them will say to you: 'This is not so, for it is written that the kiss of the goddess is death—that he who takes her—dies.' And you will show them the body of Abu!"

Armourer suppressed a smile with difficulty. It amused him to hear this child of the forest dictating to him the line of action he should take.

"I shall take you back, Dara," he agreed without committing himself too far. "I shall take you to the temple and talk to the wise men. After I have spoken, they will keep you there. There will be rejoicing in the villages and they will light fires and beat their gongs because you have returned. It will be *hari besar*—a great day, Dara."

She stretched out an arm and gazed at the many bracelets that hung from her wrist. A dreamy look came into her eyes and her expression softened.

"Many men will desire me," she murmured.

"And the red butterflies will come back to protect you," he added, calling upon his imagination.

She sighed.

"*Hari besar!* and Abu will be dead! It is a great pity, *Tuan*. I loved that man more than all others."

Armourer recognised that they were running into dangerous waters.

"The kiss of the goddess is death," he reminded her quickly. "While he lives the wise men will not believe that you went away unwillingly. Abu has travelled far. Perhaps even he will seek out the white lady again—and forget you."

She trembled visibly.

"Abu must die!" she cried hoarsely. "I see that he must die."

The magistrate tried not to appear too eager.

"I'm afraid so, Dara. In a day or two you will lead me to where he has taken the white *mem*."

"Yah, *Tuan-Hakim*," she responded slowly, "I will lead you—and you and the other white man will protect me against him!"

Armourer promised.

He reached over and rang the bell for Chong-Si.

CHAPTER XXVII

ARMOURER PLANS AN ADVANCE

THERE WAS NO SLEEP for Armourer that night.

Besides Sembilan and the two soldiers he had dispatched with a note and provisions for Trevor, the force at his disposal consisted of a corporal and two men, and from midnight onwards he kept these fully occupied.

Immediately after his momentous interview with Dara he sent the corporal to Ketatan station with a wire for the Commissioner and instructions to await a reply before returning. The remaining two left at the same time for Vance's estate, to borrow coolies and collect all food supplies available in the district.

The task of guarding the brown girl he shared with Chong-Si; but Dara, far from seeking to escape, appeared anxious to remain in the company of the white man who had promised to protect her, displaying restlessness only on the few occasions when his duties compelled him to leave the verandah.

In company with the two terriers, Chong-Si regarded her presence there with suspicion. In his experience as a cook-boy to European masters, native women were only admitted to the living quarters when it was intended they should become permanent members of the household, and he had no desire for any black *ngi* to assist him in administering to Armourer's comforts. Apart from this, the Butterfly ornament at her throat inspired him with a sense of acute uneasiness.

He had heard a vivid and rather exaggerated account of the death of the man whose place he had taken, and the pendant that Dara wore bore a striking similarity to the one in the story. Consequently, upon the few occasions when he was left alone with her, he took care to put the entire length of the verandah between her and himself.

Mick and Mac—never quite able to forget the proximity of a stranger—interrupted their slumbers on the long chair with intermittent barkings and growlings intended to express their disapproval, and to convey to the girl that she was only there on sufferance and that at any other time, should it be their good fortune to encounter her in the open, they would cheerfully combine in a whole-hearted attempt to deprive her of her *sarong!*

Dara, on the other hand, with the Crimson Butterfly restored to her and Armourer's assurances to lend her courage, treated all these marks of disapproval with blissful unconcern. Upon the second occasion that the arrangements for the forthcoming expedition compelled the magistrate to absent himself, she rose from the floor, possessed herself of the cigarette-tin, a box of matches and the cushion Armourer had given her, and curling herself comfortably in a corner, alternately smoked and dozed.

Once only, when in a waking moment she intercepted a glance from Chong-Si charged with all the venom and contempt that a low-caste Chinee is capable of putting into his eyes, did she show signs of being conscious of his presence.

She responded to his look with interest, lowered her lids, shuffled herself into a more comfortable position, and spat on the floor.

It was Chong-Si's first duty of the day to thoroughly clean that floor, and her action, combined with the knowledge that he was powerless to call upon her to remove that mark, cause him to writhe inwardly.

By a freak of doggy psychology, however, Dara's misdemeanour was destined to gain her a valuable ally in Mick, the more disreputable of Armourer's two dogs. On account of a reprehensible habit of hiding odd bones and slaughtered vermin in corners of the verandah, Chong-Si and himself had never been the best of friends, and he could not refrain from admiring the coolness with which she had committed an offence dear to his own heart!

He cast a sidelong glance at the servant, descended from the chair and crept, with ears back, towards the woman. He gained the object of his desire in a roundabout manner, encircling in his rambling course most of the articles of furniture on the verandah, sniffed at the floor, cocked up one ear, backed growlingly from Dara's first friendly overtures, and succumbed abjectly to the second. The other terrier shortly followed suit, and the magistrate, returning by way of the stairs, found Chong-Si—ill-favoured and obviously ill at ease—hopelessly outnumbered by a majority of three to one!

Armourer, dropping into a chair, nodded to the servant. "*Baik-lah*, Chong-Si! Go and sleep."

He clasped his hands behind his head and stared at the ceiling, trying to discover whether he had forgotten anything vital.

His eye fell on the decanter and he poured himself out a generous helping, feeling that he had thoroughly earned it.

Half an hour later Trevor stumbled up the steps and sat down heavily.

"Well, old son! here we are, tired and mudded up to the ears and damn' glad to feel a decent floor beneath our feet!"

Armourer pushed over his glass.

"If you want a cigarette, that girl in the corner has them. How did you get on?"

Trevor groaned.

"We covered a deuce of a lot of ground and indulged in quite a respectable *scrap* with some nude fellows armed with blow-pipes; but, as far as Mrs. Battiscombe is concerned, we failed miserably."

He accepted a drink, lit his pipe and gave the magistrate the story.

Armourer listened in silence.

At the conclusion of the narrative, he sat bolt upright and, reaching for the other's hand, shook it hard.

"Damn' good man!" he commented.

Trevor appeared surprised.

"But we did nothing," he protested.

Armourer grinned.

"I'm glad you call it nothing! I call it a deuce of a lot. I admit you didn't pull off the main object of your expedition, but you accomplished all that could be expected of you and brought back a lot of valuable information into the bargain. Our lady friend over there has promised to guide us to Abu's headquarters, but, in the event of her failing us at the last moment, we know sufficient land-marks to enable us to make a good start. More than that, we have learnt that Abu has a considerable following, the nature of weapons likely to be employed—and we can take precautions accordingly."

The planter conjured up a twisted smile.

"It's very decent of you to put it like that, but I can assure you I don't feel in the least bit satisfied with myself. To think that a damned black scoundrel should be able to spirit a white woman from under our very noses—and get away with it! That's what gets my goat. But we were so confoundedly handicapped. There was that confusion in the beginning, with three or four people making tracks and nobody quite certain which to follow. When we did make up our minds, it was jolly rough going. To cap everything, Sembilan—who, by the way, behaved like a Trojan—was held up by a fellow dropping on him from the trees. To come down to brass tacks, I suppose you ought to have gone with Sembilan, and I should have waited by the hut until some more of your chaps came up."

Armourer shook his head.

"Not a bit of it! I shouldn't have done any better, and quite probably not so well. You came to the conclusion that any other sensible man would have arrived at; that your obvious duty, on finding your party outnumbered, was to trek back for reinforcements. Honour and glory are two very fine things, and they look uncommonly well in print, but there are times when a live man with a tongue in his head and a useful pair of eyes is a damned sight more use than all your defunct heroes! Our job is to get Mrs. Battiscombe back, and time is certainly an important factor; but, with a genius like Samar to contend with, it needs a properly organised expedition."

Trevor suppressed a yawn.

"When are you going to start?"

"As soon as ever I get official sanction from Jesselton. That ought to be here any minute now. I've asked for a few more men and I hope to get moving before the sun is well up."

The other's face fell.

"I suppose I'm out of this, as usual?"

"Don't you believe it! I'm taking the law into my own hands and Vance will have to put up with being short-handed for a few days."

"He may decide to come himself; in which case I shall have to run the estate."

Armourer shook his head.

"I'm not giving him the chance. Between ourselves, I don't think he's quite the man for this business. We're bound to encounter disappointments, and Vance is anything but a cheering companion in adversity. Also he's taken Moberly's death so badly that he'll want us to assign him the privilege of dispatching Abu-Samar. My first duty is to get Samar *alive*."

Trevor rubbed his hands together.

"D'you know," he declared, "I'm rather looking forward to this little outing. I never fancied myself very much as a nigger-driver, but I'm beginning to believe that hunting down criminals is the job I was originally intended for. I wonder if you've a hundred or so cartridges that'll fit this pistol of mine?"

The magistrate looked at it.

"It seems to be the regulation bore."

"It is."

"Well, you'll be relieved to learn that I can accommodate you. I expect you're tired."

"I am," confessed the other. "If you happen to have a spare bed anywhere, I'll curl up on it for a couple of hours."

"You can have three to choose from. I'm not using mine."

Trevor unlaced his boots.

"So that," he remarked, nodding towards Dara, "is the important witness?"

"That's it."

"Not a bad-looking girl."

Armourer smiled.

"I've seen worse!"

The planter came to his feet, boots in hand, and threw a final glance into the corner. Suddenly he started. "D'you see what she's got on?" he demanded excitedly.

"The Crimson Butterfly, you mean?"

"Good Lord, yes! I thought we'd lost sight of it for ever. Are you sure it's quite all right?"

"The Crimson Butterfly," said Armourer, "appears to be one of those things that is quite harmless when it's in its right place. It happens to be there at this moment. When you make your next appearance, I'll introduce you to Dara—the real goddess of the Crimson Butterfly!"

Trevor whistled.

"So you've snaffled *her*, eh? Well, it's some consolation to learn that somebody's done something!" He disappeared through the doorway of Armourer's room without another word.

CHAPTER XXVIII

THE ANTIDOTE

THE COMMISSIONER'S REPLY was brought to Armourer at a little before seven.

Like the greater proportion of official messages, it was at once highly satisfactory and, intensely irritating.

The magistrate was ordered to proceed on his expedition against Abu-Samar with the least delay possible; at the same time, he was on no account to leave Jelandang before a suitable substitute had arrived there to take his place. A runner had been dispatched to Lindsay—whose *flying-column* was understood to be somewhere in Armourer's area—instructing him to proceed immediately to Jelandang. Armourer was to hand over his duties to him and to take command of his men—who numbered eleven. Cases of ammunition and rations would be placed on the morning train, and the magistrate was advised to have bearers waiting at the nearest halt in readiness to receive them.

The Commissioner was endeavouring to get in touch with Battiscombe, and Armourer was enjoined to leave a suitable guide at Jelandang who would proceed to Battiscombe, as soon as his party had been located, and bring him along in support of the main body.

He folded the letter carefully and thrust it into the upper pocket of his tunic. Leaning on the verandah-rail, he watched the bustle of preparation in the clearing below.

A small army of natives, borrowed from a neighbouring village, had replaced Vance's coolies. Short, sturdy men, most of them nude from the waist upwards, who chattered and laughed amid a pyramid of cases, as if about to embark upon the greatest joyride in their experience. A sturdy corporal, with an expressionless face, was methodically obtaining order from chaos. Sembilan, as fresh as if he had slept the round of the clock, was grooming Trevor's pony, while Armourer's mount, already attended to, had wandered to where the grass appeared to offer the most nutriment. At the foot of the steps a couple of men were cleaning rifles.

Armourer was turning the contents of Stewart's letter over in his mind. It was a comprehensive document, concise and well thought out, and it gave the magistrate grim satisfaction to reflect that somebody besides himself had lost many hours of slumber over the Abu-Samar affair.

The delay irritated him. He had planned, toiled, strained every nerve to get away with the dawn, and now he found himself compelled to cool his heels until Lindsay chose to roll up. But argue with himself as he might, he could not deny the wisdom of waiting for those eleven additional men. Then there was the question of the cases to be fetched from the railway. The train was due at the halt at ten minutes past eleven. More than probably it would be late—and the goods had to be handled and brought across to the starting-point. More delay! It meant postponing their departure until after lunch, and perhaps till the evening, if Lindsay lost his way. With the knowledge that Samar had men hanging about in the trees, he intended to move in as compact a body as possible and run no risk of having his supply-column cut off.

Chong-Si brought in the tea.

Armourer poured out two cups and, opening the door of his own room, carried them to where Trevor still slept. The planter stirred as the mosquito-curtains parted, and looked up sleepily.

"Hullo, old son!"

"Hullo!" responded the magistrate. "How d'you feel?"

Trevor sat up.

"O.K. thanks. What's the time?"

"Somewhere around half-past seven."

Trevor slid his feet to the ground and took his cup. He stirred it thoughtfully.

"Suppose we'll be pushing off soon?"

Armourer shook his head.

"I don't see the slightest hope of starting before evening. Stewart wants me to wait for my relief to arrive. That in itself is damnably annoying, but he's bringing us eleven men, for which I suppose we ought to be thankful. Then there's a lot of junk to be fetched from the railway. It won't be there before eleven, and I thought, if you didn't mind, that you might take the bearers over and see they don't hang about on the way."

Trevor felt for the slippers he had brought over in his haversack. "Right you are! I'm game."

"I shall leave two of my own fellows with the new chap and a third to join Battiscombe and bring him along after us as soon as the Commissioner locates him. That leaves us fifteen men—eleven of Lindsay's and four of mine. Jimmy's probably taken half a dozen on his little jaunt, so we ought to have ample for the job."

Trevor blinked.

"Got plenty of ammunition?"

"I've a fair supply already—and there's more on the way."

"And the brown girl?"

Armourer nodded his head towards the verandah.

"She's still out there. As far as I can gather, she seems fit and shows no signs of wanting to go back on her bargain. If we can get away in the cool of the evening, we should make good progress before nightfall. I haven't the remotest idea how far we have to go, but it's going to be forced marching for everybody until we come in contact with Abu-Samar's outposts."

He took Trevor's empty cup and, having disembarrassed himself of both, perched himself on the foot of the bed.

"I've been trying to reason myself into a sensible state of mind regarding Mrs. Battiscombe's predicament," he continued. "She's in an unholy mess, of course, but I am inclined to believe she's in no immediate danger. You yourself can testify that she had no end of a rotten trip into the backwoods. From the little I know of the effects of hypnotism, I understand that it leaves people pretty weak. She was only convalescent when she bolted from here and, although Jimmy insists that she has a wonderful constitution, I'm convinced that this last experience has brought on the fever again."

"Yes," agreed Trevor, "I fancy you're right there. Even if she went away in some sort of a trance, she must have come to her senses by now, and be scared into the bargain."

The magistrate placed a hand on either knee.

"That's just how I figure it out. You see, Trevor, that all this confounded delay, although intensely annoying, means that we shall have time to collect our wits and organise. We shall move as a well-equipped, well-provisioned column, instead of straggling along in little detachments that might come to grief if suddenly surrounded and cut off by Samar's men. They'll get to work with their poisoned darts in any case, and it's quite on the cards we'll have Abu's collection of insects to contend with as well; but some of us are bound to get through. Then there's the *moral* effect of a determined punitive force. Whatever influence our friend has over the tribesmen, they're bound to get uneasy when they begin to learn that Mrs. Battiscombe's abduction has been regarded, not from the point of view of ransom, but in a far more serious light."

Trevor began spreading the contents of his haversack over the bed.

"I'll get dressed at once," he announced, "and you'd better turn in for a spell."

Armourer smiled.

"I shan't attempt to sleep before lunch," he said. "If by that time I see no prospect of an early departure, I may try and squeeze in a couple of hours. There's a deuce of a lot of spade-work to be got through yet."

The planter was surveying his mud-stained garments of the night before.

"I'm afraid I'll have to borrow some clothes. If you happen to have a suit that's shrunk in the wash so much the better! You're a good deal bigger than me."

"I'll see what Chong-Si can do for you," laughed the magistrate.

He shouted for the servant.

"There's one thing to be thankful for," declared Trevor, "and that is that Jimmy Battiscombe isn't anywhere in the neighbourhood. He's gone through a lot lately and this last bit of news would about bowl him over."

Chong-Si appeared at the door.

"The *Tuan* Trevor wants some clothes," said his master. "Bring everything you can find and let him choose for himself."

The Chinaman reflected for a moment and began pulling open drawers and diving into the inner mysteries of a zinc-lined trunk.

When Trevor met the train he found, not only the cases he had come there to collect, but the genial professor and his pretty daughter.

Standen was in great spirits.

"Morning, Trevor!" he shouted from the coach. "So you've been raked into this little affair too?"

The younger man hurried forward to assist Joyce.

As soon as both were on *terra firma*, Trevor turned to Standen.

"You know what's happened?" he suggested.

The professor nodded.

"The Commissioner sent me news last night, and I made arrangements to return immediately. It's a regrettable state of affairs, of course, and I feel extremely anxious about Mrs. Battiscombe, but the incident has brought the Samar business to a head, and I suppose that's something."

"Give me your *barang*," said Trevor; "my men can carry it up with the rest of the stuff. How d'you do, Miss Standen? You've arrived just in time to see the start of what promises to be a really interesting adventure."

A man poked his head from a window and called.

"Say, Trevor, tell Armourer that young Lindsay's on his way now and should be at his place this afternoon. He'll understand."

The planter waved an arm.

"All right, Barnes, and many thanks. He'll be glad to hear it. You keeping fit?"

"Fit as a fiddle. You look well."

The train moved on.

They were on their way up the slope, with a straggling line of bearers behind them, when the professor spoke again.

"I suppose there is such a thing as luck," he declared suddenly. "Abu-Samar's had it all on his side up to within the last couple of days—and now it's swung round to ours."

Trevor glanced up sharply, a puzzled expression on his face. "It's swung round, has it"

"Absolutely." He tapped a large water-bottle which was slung from his shoulder on a leather strap. "Everything depends on the contents of this flask. I hit on it yesterday, after countless futile experiments, and went down to Jesselton to put it to the test. Joyce and I are joining your expedition— myself because I believe my presence is essential, and my daughter because she refuses point-blank to be left behind. Whatever horrors our black magician may have in store for us, I am ready for him."

Trevor gasped.

"You don't mean to say you've found an antidote?"

Standen patted the younger man's shoulder.

"There's not the least doubt about it." He beamed all over his face. "That's puts a different complexion on affairs, doesn't it?"

"By Jove, it does!" murmured Trevor. "It ought to prove the turning-point of everything."

Joyce laughed.

"Poor old daddy!" she said. "He's *so* pleased with himself. Everybody's been praising him and trotting round after him—and he does just love being praised and trotted round after! He's tried his marvellous discovery on monkeys and native criminals, and he's so delighted with his new toy that I really believe he'd have experimented on me, if I'd let him!"

The professor shook his head delightedly.

"There's a daughter for you, Mr. Trevor! Her sole object in existence is to hold her poor old father up to ridicule—but we've found the antidote, my boy, and that's all that really matters."

Lindsay reached Jelandang at four and at five-thirty Armourer rode out, at the head of his column, with a fierce sun on its downward course and a pleasant breeze shaking the topmost leaves of the palms.

Joyce rode between her father and Trevor, and Lindsay, leaning over the verandah-rail with two rebellious terriers tethered beside him, watched them off.

CHAPTER XXIX

IN THE CLUTCHES OF ABU-SAMAR

WHEN VERA BATTISCOMBE came to her senses, she found herself lying on a sort of hammock made from the entire skin of some animal and fastened at either end to a wooden frame by means of leathern thongs. A blanket had been thrown over her, and as soon as she was conscious of the touch of its rough surface against her neck, she pushed it off in disgust.

She felt hot and sticky, her limbs ached, and there was an acute pain behind her eyes, so that she was forced to close them continually, opening them only at intervals to gaze in bewilderment upon her new surroundings.

Presently she raised herself on her arms and endeavoured, from a mingling of memories, thoughts and fears, to discover something that might account for her presence in so primitive a dwelling.

The room was approximately ten feet square and, except for a heap of miscellaneous articles ranged along the far wall and partially covered with a length of sacking, there was scarcely anything in the nature of furniture. There was a square of coloured matting on the floor, a roughly carved stool, some odd sacks, which might have contained grain, and a large earthenware water-jar.

At the foot of her bed, a strip of matting concealed what she surmised to be the only door; there were no windows and the light filtered in through great chinks in the walls and gaps in the thatching above.

The watch at her wrist registered a quarter to one, but she discovered upon a closer examination that it had stopped.

The atmosphere was one of intense heat and from somewhere close at hand came the incessant buzzing of flies.

She sank back again, one hand pressed to her forehead, and tried to think.

The throbbing was easier now. Gradually, as she groped for a starting-point, the picture of Joyce's room in Armourer's bungalow built itself up before her. How had she come to leave it? At some time or other in her life—it seemed countless ages distant—she had quarrelled with Michael about something. However her thoughts rambled, they always came back to that. She had cried, she remembered now, and gone back to her room. A Chinaman had brought her food—that would be Chong-Si. She had found a pencil and written, and presently she had gone out. She remembered that it was dark and that there were stars. She remembered being frightened under the trees when she found that she had lost her way, and a queer house with an open door. Something had made her enter. Queer, disjointed fragments kept coming back to her. She had been looking for something—something which persisted in eluding her.

"The Crimson Butterfly!" she exclaimed aloud—and then laughed at her own folly in voicing what must have been an absurd hallucination—a dream phantom.

She thought again.

Perhaps this, too, was a dream? In a little while these unfamiliar surroundings would vanish, and the walls of the sick-room—in which she must actually be—would take their place. She remembered quite well that she had been ill— very ill. Joyce had been there, sleeping in another bed, and the professor, with his scrubby beard and serious owl-like expression, had hovered over her. She seemed to recollect that Jim had been there too; she had heard his voice on the verandah.

A lizard, creeping suddenly into a lozenge of sunshine on the wall at her side, screamed shrilly and she sat bolt upright.

She rubbed her eyes, fingered the leathern thongs curiously, reached over and pulled at the nearest sack—and a shower of rice pattered to the floor.

Her clenched fists pressed against her temples. It was real then—all real! Merciful heaven! What did it all mean?

She looked at her clothes. They were stained, crumpled and torn, and, except for her shoes, she was in outdoor attire. Becoming curiously scrupulous as to details, she stared round in search of those shoes. She looked at the stool. There was something lying on it that she had not noticed before. She leaned forward. It appeared to be a hat—a red hat with a black tassel. She wanted to go over to it and examine it, but her initial attempts to gain her feet sent her staggering stupidly back on to the couch.

She laughed weakly and suddenly dissolved into tears, her face buried in her hands.

Presently she choked down her sobs, summoned all the strength at her command and made a further effort. This time she stumbled on to her hands, pushed herself up again and finally fell in a heap to the floor, setting the entire building rocking.

She crawled the remainder of the distance and was within an ace of touching the hat when horror seized her and she shrank from it as from some ghastly apparition.

It was a red *fez!*

Abu-Samar! Where had she heard that name before? Her lips formed the syllables glibly, as if the name were one which she had voiced repeatedly. Abu-Samar! A tall man, in a blue suit and that same hat, standing by a white bridge! A coloured man! It was all coming back to her now, overwhelming her in great waves.

She had gone to his house; but not this house. There were orange-coloured curtains and a cedar-wood box brimming over with precious ornaments that glinted and sparkled in the light. He had given her a Crimson Butterfly—a ruby thing with emerald eyes, on a chain of gold filigree. He had clasped it round her neck—and she had run away, leading her pony after her. There was a blank here which she strove to fill. She had lost that ornament somehow, found it, then lost it again. That was why she had wandered out that night into the trees. She went into the hut because she thought it was there. Somebody had told her it would be there.

She had wandered from the hut again into the open and shrunk back into the shelter of a big tree. She had been very tired, had sunk to the ground exhausted. After that she remembered little, save a sensation of being whirled into the air by some mysterious force—and rocked into a deep sleep. This slumber had continued apparently for centuries, interrupted at intervals by wild nightmares, dreams of falling from great heights, strange noises and the rushing of waters.

A sense of unutterable loneliness gripped her, and, creeping over on all fours, she drew back the matting from the opening. The scene that met her eyes startled her.

The hut in which she was revealed itself as a tree-dwelling, a crazy crow's-nest nestling among the branches, with a flimsy ladder leading down to the ground, twenty or more feet below. Beneath her was the long thatched roof of another building, to her right a few more trees—and then, stretching to the horizon, a wilderness of moss-clad boulders, over the whole expanse of which no living thing was visible.

The mystery was deepening. The landscape was entirely strange to her. How had she crossed that cheerless desert— and why? What was the significance of her presence in this lonely, ramshackle dwelling on an oasis in the midst of utter desolation?

She thrust her head and shoulders forward cautiously, trying to see what was at the foot of the ladder—and drew herself quickly out of sight again.

She had seen a colossal native, immobile as an ebony statue, with a *parang* sheathed at his side and a spear-shaft nestling in the crook of his arm!

She was a prisoner; Abu-Samar's prisoner; for there on the stool was irrefutable evidence.

She clasped her hands over her knees and rocked to and fro in the agony of her terror.

And presently, as she crouched there, starting at every sound that came from the earth below, the house itself or the tree-tops above her, the jig-saw pieces that had defied her when she sought them crept into the picture of their own accord and silently filled themselves in.

As he had prophesied at their first meeting, she had walked from her own people—and come to him, apparently of her own accord, but in reality in obedience to an insistent command that he had somehow succeeded in transmitting through space. He had plagued her, tormented her, haunted her sleeping and her waking hours until all the barriers of her resistance had been broken down.

Contrite now and immeasurably sorry for herself, she saw the Gehenna that her own follies had wrought, stretched out her arms to the cruel flames, recognising them, acknowledging their right to envelop her. She had been faithless·—faithless to Jim, faithless in a more limited degree to Dick Moberly, who had paid bitterly for his infatuation. Her thirst for conquest, her recklessness, her mad desire to employ her beauty to ensnare every decent man who came in her way, had brought her to this.

She beat her forehead with her clenched fists in her misery. If there were indeed a kind fate of any sort watching over her, she promised it that, in the unlikely event of being snatched from the horror that threatened her, she would act squarely with Jim for as long as she lived.

And then she fell the victim to another mood.

After all, a voice within her argued, there must have been countless women more culpable than she who had never been called upon to face the consequence of their misdeeds like this. The instincts that had impelled her to embark upon the course she had followed were inherited ones, her looks had been given her at birth, the climate that gave men fever had been her inspiration. This Samar, this primeval savage masquerading in civilised attire, had planted himself deliberately in her path, shaking her limited world from its very foundations.

The thought of him made her shudder. She remembered the loathsome touch of his fingers when he gave her the crimson pendant. And she was in his power!

She gazed round her helplessly.

She must do something, feign sickness, madness, anything! She ran her fingers madly through her hair, dishevelling it until she imagined it encircled her head like an unkempt mop.

She must disfigure herself, make herself so distasteful to him that he would recoil from her.

She wondered if anywhere among that pile under the sacking there were a mirror.

She was about to make for it when the sound of voices below brought her to a standstill. Her heart beating a devil's tattoo, she listened.

Abu-Samar! The softer tones were surely his and the queer guttural utterances those of the sentry outside. Somebody was coming up the ladder.

For seconds she remained there, rooted to the spot. Suddenly, with a great effort, she threw off the *incubus* that held her there, and creeping back to her couch, drew the blanket over her.

Frightened—horribly, genuinely frightened—she watched through half-closed lids as the strip of matting swung inwards, revealing a triangle of bright light across which extended an arm in a blue serge sleeve.

Abu-Samar, bending almost double, came into the room and the matting dropped back into place.

CHAPTER XXX

ABU EXPLAINS

SHE LAY THERE, on that rude native couch, delirious with fear, not daring to glance through her lashes at the man who now bent over her.

An icy chill ran down her spine as his fingers touched her wrist.

"Better," she heard him murmur in English, "decidedly better. The pulse is still too rapid. To-morrow, perhaps."

To-morrow! Grasping in her ocean of trouble at a floating spar, this word gave her immeasurable consolation. Michael, Jim, all of them perhaps would be searching for her, and this postponement of her fate gave them still a few more hours in which to accomplish her rescue.

He was moving about the room now, muttering to himself in a dialect that was new to her. Presently he dipped a bottle in the water-jar and she heard the bubbling as the fluid replaced the air.

She hazarded a glance.

He had drawn a gourd from under the sacking and was pouring water into it from the bottle. He rinsed it and threw the drops to the floor.

As he turned to approach her, she closed her eyes again.

He set both bottle and gourd at her side and retreated to the far end of the hut.

Presently he came back again, slipped an arm under her and, supporting her firmly in a sitting position, forced some liquid between her teeth. It was cold and bitter and she swallowed some of it knowing that it would not be poison.

He withdrew his arm and she fell back limply on to the bed. A new life seemed to be coming to her and she was aware of a sensation of comfort, of inward warmth.

She felt that his eyes were upon her.

"Sit up, Mrs. Battiscombe," he commanded softly—and, in spite of herself, she obeyed.

"Open your eyes."

She opened them wide.

Abu-Samar, cool and perfectly attired even to his soft collar and tie, was staring down at her.

He drew forward the stool and sat down on it.

"And so, Mrs. Battiscombe," he purred, "you have come to me at last."

She compressed her lips. She knew that she must humour this man, stifle her feelings, strain every nerve to avoid uttering some ill-considered retort that would be calculated to goad him into fury.

"Where am I?" she inquired weakly.

His features twisted into an expression that was at once scornful and mockingly apologetic.

"You have come to the humble quarters of Abu-Samar, the refuge in the wilderness to which your own people have driven me. Presently, when the hue and cry has died down, when they have given up all hope of tracing you, we will build ourselves a palace." He indicated the jumbled heap along the far wall. "From the smoking ruins of my house at Bukit-Serang we succeeded in saving a few of my treasures. In a little while we shall have more. The native vessels will bring carpets and curtains and furniture from the coast and men will wait by the river to transport them here. We shall have comfort such as the white man does not understand, and the tribesmen, who are afraid of me, shall be our servants."

He produced a cigarette and, lighting it, puffed thoughtfully. The blue smoke hung in the still air above him as he exhaled it through his nostrils. The fierce light had gone out of his eyes, his whole expression had softened, and he appeared to her at that moment, not as the fierce, vindictive Anglophobe she had always pictured him, but rather a languid, luxury-loving Oriental, basking like a lizard in the heat. Now that he had allowed himself to relax, she could better appreciate the fine outline of his dusky profile and the ease with which he managed to pose elegantly without apparent effort.

"I have sent that other girl away," he continued presently.

She simulated interest.

"Oh? What other girl?"

"Dara—the brown woman you saw at my house when we first met. She grew jealous when she learnt that you were coming—and so I turned her out. She told me I was mad to bring you here, that the white men would come with their soldiers and guns and take you back; but we have waited five whole days—and still they are not here."

He threw back his head and laughed.

"I am not afraid of your people; their guns are nothing to me. They have all tried to take me—the Frenchmen in Anam, the Dutch, the English in Sarawak—and now it is the English again. Every time I have beaten them. For I have harnessed forces they do not know, I can shoot out my tongue like a chameleon—and kill—and draw it back so that none know whence it came. I can whisper across a continent—and those to whom I wish to speak can hear me."

He laughed again, and he reminded her strangely of a hawk.

"I frightened them with the Crimson Butterfly. That is the greatest of all my secrets, Vera. I discovered it not far from here, where there is a temple among the rocks and men worship these creatures. Dara was there then, guarding the shrine—and I saw that the butterflies did not harm her. There had always been a woman in the temple—and the insects had grown used to her; but they fell in swarms upon any man who sought to steal the emblem at her throat or spirit her away—and stung him to death. I found a man who had once worshipped the Crimson Butterfly—and he told me many things. It appeared that the priests destroyed the caterpillars when they came to life, only sparing so many, and that they smeared themselves in a preparation, so that they should not be stung. Sometimes, however, a priest was poisoned by a butterfly; the mark appeared on his skin, and was removed by a certain process in order that the worshippers should not know why he had died and still continue to believe in their immunity. I went away for a long while and thought. I wanted to discover how I could best make this secret of use to me. There was a legend that there had once been a white goddess at the shrine and that after a certain time had elapsed she would come there again. Presently a plan occurred to me. I wanted to exploit their secret and to induce the worshippers to help me in my campaign against the white man. I made them a promise. I told them that one day Dara would disappear and then the white goddess would return. I went to a place they did not know and made an enormous red butterfly and hung it in the trees. I found that the butterflies left the temple and came to it. I smeared myself in the preparation that I had managed to procure, and, after a few hours, I destroyed the thing I had made—and the insects left me and flew back. I made another and they returned, and I caught them as they hovered over it. Then I took Dara."

The ash from his cigarette had fallen in a heap into a crease in his coat and he paused to brush it off.

Vera, her head supported on one arm, regarded him steadily.

"And after that—?" she asked.

"After that I saw you and realised that I had found my white goddess. I went to your husband. I wanted an excuse to see you again. He insulted me and I decided to destroy him. I decoyed you to my house and gave you the ornament. For some reason you sent it to Moberly—and he died instead. When you found him you fainted and they sent for me, believing me to be a doctor. The Butterfly pendant had vanished and I wanted to get it back. I believed the magistrate Armourer had it and sent out another butterfly to poison him. I was beginning to understand the power of my secret, you see. I have heard since that his servant found the ornament and perished. The priests of the temple came to see me, demanding that the white goddess should appear, and I knew it was time to compel you to come to me and bring the sacred emblem with you. Believing that you knew where it was hidden, I willed you to leave the house and find it, and sent out men to follow you and bring you here."

He spread out his hands and dropped them, palm downwards, to his knees.

"You came, my white goddess, but the Butterfly is missing."

"I remember now," said the girl. "I looked for it everywhere but could not find it."

His eyes sought hers and again she saw that queer light that frightened her.

"Where did you think it was?"

"In a hut in the trees. Mr. Armourer told me that Professor Standen had it there. Somehow I found my way to it through the forest. When I reached it the door was open and there was no Butterfly."

The ease with which the words came to her lips astonished her.

He bit his lip.

"We shall find it again," he declared confidently. "Until then you shall remain with me. When the ornament returns, I shall clasp it round your neck and take you to the temple. For a little while you will remain there, so that these people shall still have confidence in me and help me. As soon as I have accomplished my end, I shall take you away again and we will go to another part of the island. Where I was born. There will be no white people here then. I shall have destroyed them all. I shall not use the ornament again. I have insects now that have never seen the charm. One day I shall open the doors of my breeding-house and they will fly everywhere."

Vera shuddered.

"I talk to them," pursued Samar dreamily, "and they fly on to my hand. I walk among them unharmed because they know me. To some extent even I can control their flight."

The effects of the drug he had given her were wearing off and already she was feeling weaker.

"It's horrible, horrible!" she cried, and Abu-Samar rose to his feet. Before she could draw it away, he had imprisoned one of her hands and touched it with his lips.

The next moment he was gone.

Presently she fell asleep and it was evening when she woke again. The atmosphere had grown appreciably cooler and gusts of wind lifted the thatch above her head.

Suddenly she heard a sound that sent her swaying across the floor to the covered doorway. She heard shouting and what she imagined to be distant rifle-fire. The noise was coming nearer and something passed the hut with a shrill whining sound.

She peered out.

Darkness had almost fallen and the wilderness was enveloped in a faint mist through which she saw bright tongues of flame and shadowy figures running.

She sank to her knees and clasped her hands.

They had come to find her! They were coming that way! Heavens! it was wonderful!

A dark form appeared suddenly on the ladder and a muscular arm swept her into space. She was flung like a sack over the native's shoulder and borne, struggling, on the perilous descent to the ground.

She screamed aloud, hammering on the ebony back with her fists.

At the foot of the ladder, the man shifted her on to his other shoulder, skirted the trees and ran rapidly with her into the falling darkness.

CHAPTER XXXI

TRAPPED IN THE BREEDING-HOUSE

IT WAS FIVE DAYS since the punitive force had left Jelandang, and during all that time Armourer had never let the brown girl out of his sight.

Night and day they had pressed forward, halting only to ease the bearers when the sun was at its height, and, of the European members of the party, only Joyce had enjoyed more than a few moments of sleep. They had made a rough hammock for her which the magistrate's men had carried in turn.

The route chosen by Dara had been different from that which Sembilan and Trevor had followed; they had studiously avoided all native villages and settlements and, until the evening of the second day, no opposition at all had been encountered.

Battiscombe's expedition came up with them as they paused in the last belt of trees before descending in skirmishing order upon the stretch of open land in which Dara assured them Abu-Samar's hiding-place lay.

Upon learning of his approach Armourer himself went back to meet his colleague, taking the native girl with him.

He sighted Battiscombe, still red of face and decidedly thinner, marching at the head of a ragged line of troops and natives.

"Hullo, Jim!"

"Hullo, Michael! Thought we were never going to catch you up! You're in a devil of a hurry, aren't you?"

It struck Armourer at that moment that his friend knew nothing of his wife's abduction.

They shook hands.

"Tell your fellows to be careful not to leave the trees. As far as I can make out, we've out-flanked Abu's scouts. There's a useful sort of mist coming and in about ten minutes I'm going to rush the position."

Battiscombe lowered himself to the ground and mopped his forehead.

"It's all too confoundedly strenuous," he groaned. "Give me my jolly old court-house and a comfortable magisterial chair with a back to it!—Who's the girl?"

"Samar's discarded lady-love. She's bubbling over with jealousy and an earnest desire for vengeance, and has elected to act as our guide."

The larger man shuffled himself into a patch of shadow and removed his sun-helmet.

"Lord, Michael! I've covered a deuce of a lot of ground since last I saw you. I've forded rivers, scaled mountains, wallowed in swamps, lost a man with snake-bite, run short of rations and haggled with insolent native potentates over the mere necessities of life!"

In spite of the unpleasant news he sought an opportunity of conveying to the other, Armourer could not resist this:

"Did you find any leeches?"

Battiscombe grinned.

"Hundreds of 'em! So many that I've got quite used to them. I'm that hardened that I look upon a day without a leech as an uneventful period of time! How did you leave Vera?"

Armourer's face became suddenly serious.

"We didn't leave her, Jim," he said, looking the other straight in the eyes, "she left us."

Battiscombe started to his feet.

"What d'you mean, Michael?—She's gone to Rembakut?"

"No," replied Armourer steadily, "she's gone to Abu-Samar."

Battiscombe staggered back as if he had been struck.

"Gone to Abu-Samar!" he echoed, and caught the other's arm. "How did this happen? What in the name of heaven were you doing to let her go?—Good Lord, man! I left her in your charge."

"I know that. Trevor was dining with me when she went. She had decided to take dinner in her room and Chong-Si was looking after the three of us, He came in suddenly with the news that the *mem* had gone out—and brought me a note from her. We didn't stop to do anything, but dispatched every man we could lay our hands on to look for her, and joined in the hunt ourselves. She went out deliberately to join Samar, but you mustn't blame her for that. He seems to have hypnotised her. Trevor, myself and Sembilan—the chap I sent to guide you—got on her trail. There were two distinct tracks—and we split up. Trevor and Sembilan almost overtook the fellows Samar had instructed to pick her up, but were held up by a posse of natives with blow-pipes. I collared Dara—the woman I have here now. I cabled Jesselton for instructions, spent the whole night organising an expedition, and have been on the go ever since."

He could not see his friend's face—it was hidden in his hands.

"Good God!" he muttered, and then: "Poor little woman!"

He squared his shoulders and turned fiercely on Armourer.

"We must get her back; don't you understand? We must move *now*."

"I know," returned Armourer. "We're only waiting for you."

They left both bearers and horses in the forest. Joyce was to follow a little after the main body, with her father, Trevor and two of Armourer's men. The remainder spread out like a fan—Michael and the girl in the centre, Battiscombe on the right and Corporal Kuraman on the extreme left.

They had covered about three hundred yards, with Samar's retreat dimly outlined in the distance, when a large force of natives sprang suddenly into being, emerging from behind the cover of the boulders, and greeted the attacking party with wild, defiant yells, followed by a shower of darts.

"Drop!" yelled Armourer; "drop down, all of you. Don't fire wildly; pick out your men!"

He snatched a rifle from the soldier who was nearest and dropped a big native before he could draw back into cover.

The battle had opened. Shots rang out on all sides, bullets found their mark, flattened themselves against boulders or whined plaintively on into space. The natives replied vigorously, sending over showers of darts with so reckless a profusion that Armourer smiled grimly to himself. He scented that the noise and flash of the rifles was getting them rattled. Their own weapons were such that they had to expose themselves to fire with any degree of accuracy—and the uniformed troops handled their guns like veterans, with a savage delight at having some inspiring sort of target to blaze away at.

At the end of the fourth big hostile shower, he waved his handkerchief and shouted at the top of his voice:

"Fix bayonets! Up—all of you—and let 'em have it!"

There were casualties then—three of them, but they had the satisfaction as they ran, crouching low, to see big bunches of men break from cover and scuttle like rabbits, tumbling one over the other.

A hundred yards and the Government troops had flattened out again, preceding their antagonists by minutes and wreaking fearful havoc before the knots had gained time to disperse.

A couple more similar manoeuvres, and blow-pipes had been flung aside for *parangs* and *krises*. A brief determined stand, and the rot which Armourer had fervently hoped for began to set in.

He emptied his revolver, downed a big native with his fist, stunned him as he strove to rise with his weapon held like a knuckle-duster, and filled up again.

Groups of men, obviously intended as enemy reserves, bolted back behind the long buildings and vanished into the mist.

At the fall of darkness, Armourer's whistle brought together Battiscombe and twelve men, and a few moments later the professor's little rear-guard joined them.

"Six—no, seven missing," declared the younger magistrate.

Three more straggled up.

Armourer heaved a sigh of relief.

"Can anybody see any more knocking around?—We've still four to account for."

Corporal Kuraman came forward.

"Three were hit in the first attack, *Tuan*," he said.

Armourer nodded.

"All right, Kuraman. I daresay we lost another after that. I say, Jimmy! that's not too bad, is it?—With your permission, I'll send your corporal and two others to bring any wounded they find to that long hut over there. We'll make that our headquarters for the time being."

Battiscombe was thinking of Vera.

"Better see what's inside," he suggested—and they moved forward again.

They advanced warily until the clump of trees and the building which ran beneath were completely encircled.

It was a long hut, with a door at either end.

Armourer tried the nearest one without success, but Trevor, who had moved round to the far side, called out:

"I say, you fellows, we can get in here; it's propped open."

Armourer selected three men, sent them forward to reconnoitre, and joined Trevor.

"Be careful how you go; there may be a trick here."

He looked back to see Joyce and her father close behind him, and, a couple of paces distant, the brown girl, who stood watching with folded arms. He remembered suddenly that he had not noticed Battiscombe for some minutes.

"Seen Jimmy, anybody?" he asked.

"Yes," said Trevor, "I caught sight of him a short while back. He was sending one of the fellows up that ladder to see if the shack up there was inhabited."

Armourer shouted for a lamp.

As soon as one was brought, he kicked open the door and, holding it open with one hand, stepped inside.

Trevor was at his heels.

"Professor," called the magistrate, "don't come in, if you don't mind. Look after Miss Standen and see that the men keep well spread out round the building. I'll shout for you if we want any assistance."

The planter, who was staring round curiously, uttered a cry.

"Look out! There's one of those confounded butterflies!"

He made a shot at it with his hat and it fluttered past Armourer, who snatched up the piece of wood that had held the door open and knocked it to the ground. Before he could put his foot on it, it had crawled out into the darkness.

"Standen," he cried at the top of his voice, "one of Samar's insects has got loose." He held the lamp through the doorway. "I don't see it anywhere, but I know I hit it."

He stepped back into the hut and the door swung to behind him.

There was something unpleasantly definite about the way it closed that made Armourer attempt to open it again. He tried it several times, then picked up the lamp and held it close to the lock.

"What's up?" asked his companion.

Armourer looked at him.

"We're locked in, old son, like the pair of idiots we are."

The planter shrugged his shoulders.

"It's not made of cast-iron; we can soon break our way out."

Armourer made his way down the centre of the building.

"It's not that that worries me," he informed him, "but the fact that there may be a lot of unpleasant surprises in store for us before we can break out. Lord! what's all this?"

He held the lamp until its light fell upon tier upon tier of bread wooden trays, strewn with freshly-picked green leaves.

Trevor possessed himself of a leaf and, dropping it quickly, put his foot on it.

"Caterpillars," he declared. "Nasty striped things, with *horns!*"

Armourer stuck an empty pipe between his teeth.

"I tell you what, old son," he said, "we've struck an uncommonly pleasant little packet this time; we're in his breeding-house!"

The colour left Trevor's cheeks.

"What's that?"

"This is where he breeds the crimson butterflies."

The planter turned on his heel.

"In that case we'd better get out before they make nasty-looking patterns all over us. I'll see how a round or two'll influence his patent lock."

"All right," returned the magistrate, "carry on with it. I'm going to see what there is at the far end." He blundered into a wooden partition and opened the door it contained carefully. There was a light inside, and he set down his lamp on the floor behind him. His automatic and his face came into the opening together, and, as they did so, he caught sight of a figure standing erect, one hand on a wooden bar. It was Dr. Abu-Samar.

The expression on the creature's face was that of a beast of the forest driven to bay. A wild light danced in his eyes, and he crouched suddenly, putting the whole of his weight on the lever.

"Hands up, Abu!" said the Englishman coolly. "I've got you."

"Not yet, O Englishman!" came the muttered reply, and at that instant the light went out. Something dropped somewhere and Armourer felt a cool inrush of air. He tired two shots at where he imagined the secret trap in the wall to be, reached back for his own lamp, and started forward.

It was only then that he realised why Samar had waited.

The walls were lined with countless small cages, all of which were now open, and the air was alive with the flapping of wings.

He heard Trevor firing into the lock and yelled to him to close the door when he got free. The insects were everywhere, fluttering against the roof and the walls, sweeping down on him with a vicious, droning sound. He dropped the hurricane lamp and hit at them wildly. One settled on his tunic and he dashed it off. At all costs he must shut that trap. It would be the greatest calamity in the world if they found the open.

He saw it now—a hole a yard square—but a few feet to his left, with the square of boarding that had covered it lying on the floor. He stripped off his coat and swept it in all directions, beating for himself a path through the danger that descended upon him in a crimson cloud.

He plunged to his knees, and drawing himself through the aperture, thrust in an arm and pulled the boarding back into place. As he did so he felt a sharp, burning sensation at his wrist. He crushed the butterfly against the outer wall, but already the damage was done.

His shout brought a soldier to the spot, and almost immediately afterwards the professor and Joyce.

They found him pitched forward on to his arms, and in those last few seconds of consciousness he recognised them.

"They are all in there," he muttered, "the butterflies—don't open anything—Samar got out first—One of the brutes stung me."

He rolled over on to his side, and the professor felt for his hypodermic syringe.

CHAPTER XXXII

BATTISCOMBE BRINGS NEWS

ACTING ON THE PROFESSOR'S INSTRUCTIONS, they brought down the rough bed that had been Vera Battiscombe's couch such a short time before, and laid Armourer on it.

The bearers, led by a runner, had already joined the main body, and a brown canvas tent was quickly erected over the sick man.

Thereafter Trevor—in the absence of Battiscombe, who had mysteriously disappeared—took charge.

Ably instructed by the indefatigable Kuraman—who had reported three men as dead and delivered the remaining third to Standen for treatment—a breastwork of cases and boulders was run up around the encampment. Failing the return of his scouts, Trevor realised that an advance into hostile country before dawn with so small a company would be distinctly unwise.

He explained his views at some length to Dara, who merely shrugged her shoulders and spread out her hands, as if to indicate that the white lord was wiser than she and must presumably know his own business best. She thereupon threw herself on the earth outside Armourer's tent, in so awkward a position that the professor tripped over her on coming out and it was only the timely intervention of the planter that prevented him from falling headlong.

"How is he?" asked the younger man anxiously.

The professor rubbed his beard.

"Oh, we'll pull him through all right. You can't accomplish these things in a few minutes, but we got him in time. Pity that Samar fellow slipped through our ring. You saw how it happened, of course? He had dug a ditch just outside his emergency exit and cunningly covered it up. He must have wriggled through it like a snake till he passed our men, and then scuttled off into the darkness—Have you found Battiscombe?"

Trevor shook his head.

"I can't think what's happened to him. I suppose Armourer told him about his wife, and he decided to clear off with the reconnoitring party. I hope he's all right."

Standen struck a match and looked at his watch.

"Nearly nine," he announced. "What about some food?"

"I've set a couple of fellows preparing a meal. It'll be the usual tack—bread and cheese and tinned stuff, with tea to follow. We can start right away if you like. Where's Miss Standen?"

The other nodded towards the tent.

"I've left her with him. She seems to have been doing nothing but nursing lately, but I fancy she likes it."

"It's jolly good of her."

The professor chuckled.

"I may be old, Trevor, but I'm not as blind as some people like to imagine. Joyce's mother has been dead for more than fifteen years and, in spite of my studies, I've had ample time to understand my own daughter. She's infinitely happy to be of use to your little expedition, of course, but I believe she's even more glad that her patient is Michael Armourer—er— This is in strict confidence, you understand."

He wiped his glasses and replaced them.

"Now, what do you say to a meal?"

"I think," said Trevor, "that Armourer, when he comes to himself, will more than appreciate the fact that Miss Standen is his nurse."

Standen thrust his arm through that of the planter.

"So that's so, is it? Well, I'm glad to hear it. Armourer's an Englishman and a gentleman, and, as far as I can see, he has a clean record. I don't ask anything better than that. Where did you say they were preparing our repast?"

Trevor piloted him to a spot where a hurricane lamp stood on a case with a miscellany of enamelled ware and cutlery encircling it.

They were lighting their pipes when Battiscombe appeared from nowhere and grabbed at a hunk of bread.

"Jove! I'm hungry!"

Trevor raised his brows.

"Where the deuce have you been?" he demanded.

"A dickens of a way. I took charge of those three men Armourer sent out. We scoured the country pretty thoroughly and eventually got into touch with a score or so of disconsolate tribesmen, who capitulated without offering resistance. I think they imagined we had the whole British Army behind us. Lord! they were scared."

The professor blinked.

"Well?"

"Oh, we had a long palaver, conducted mostly by signs, until I discovered that their leader understood some Malay. After that we got along famously. It's queer what fat-headed notions some people get into their heads!—these chaps worship that confounded Butterfly, you know!"

He munched for some moments in silence.

"All I wanted to know was what had happened to my wife. It seems that this confounded Samar promised them a white goddess instead of the black one they already had. Vera was to be the goddess. They've taken her up there now and there's to be no end of a big ceremony to-night. My friend assured me that they didn't intend harming her. Then I got a word in. I explained that the lady in question was my wife, the child of quite ordinary human beings, and that I could vouch for the fact that she hadn't at any time dropped from the skies. That set them thinking. They gibbered away for some time and then announced that they, personally, had lost all faith in Abu-Samar and would cheerfully exert their influence on our behalf upon their fellow tribesmen. I've brought 'em back with me."

He reached over for the cheese.

Trevor perched himself on the edge of the case.

"What do you want us to do?"

Battiscombe, his cheeks bulging, regarded him solemnly.

"This is a time for tact," he declared. "We'll leave half our men here, and taking the remainder with us proceed directly to where this gigantic jamboree is being held. We'll carry arms, of course, but I don't think we shall require to use them. One of the most important points against Abu-Samar is that his new goddess isn't wearing the pendant. She can't be, because I noticed it on the brown girl this evening. Abu'll have his say, and then I'll address the meeting through an interpreter. I've had one or two experiences of this sort before—and I'm still here to tell the tale! Let's see what Armourer thinks about it."

Trevor told him the news—and his face fell.

"Poor old Michael! Now isn't that just the rottenest luck imaginable?" He stared towards the long hut. "So that's where he carried out his devilish experiments, is it? We'll have to burn that down."

Standen coughed.

"I suggested doing so when it was light. We don't want to risk any of those insects getting free."

"Of course not; but I shan't feel at all comfortable until it is burnt. Thousands of those butterflies, eh? It makes one shudder to think of it. If we hadn't tackled the affair as promptly as we did, heaven alone knows what might have happened."

"Hanging's too good for a chap like Abu-Samar," put in Trevor.

Battiscombe screwed up his face.

"I wouldn't like to tell you how I feel about it," he said. "If I hadn't had something to keep me from thinking too much, I fancy I should have gone mad."

Standen nodded gravely.

"You've taken your gruelling better than most men, and I admire you for it. I know the state your nerves are in and the effort you had to make to persuade yourself to come back here to us instead of going on after Mrs. Battiscombe. If you'll listen to the advice of an older man, and one who has had some experience, you'll stop fidgeting about and sit down."

The magistrate planted himself on the ease next to Trevor.

"And what's your next advice, professor?"

"Finish your meal slowly, take a good strong *tot*, and light your pipe.—How soon have we to start?"

"I should like to get away at once, but we've ample time if we push off in half an hour. As far as I can make out, nothing useful can be accomplished before midnight. Somebody's got to stop here and look after those chattering niggers. Who's it going to be?"

Standen looked at the planter.

"Under any other circumstances, I should have cheerfully volunteered; but my experience as a leader of men is insignificant and there may be more of the insects at the temple."

"I see," said Trevor. "You mean that the antidote may be required again?"

"Precisely. On the other hand, of course, there's Armourer and our wounded men to be considered. I could make them both comfortable before I started and leave instructions with my daughter how to act if either took a serious turn for the worse."

"I'll stop," declared Trevor promptly. "How long are you likely to be away?"

Battiscombe frowned.

"We'll be back before dawn, in any case," he decided.

"I'm sorry to disappoint you, Trevor," said the professor.

The other laughed.

"I'm not grumbling. I've had more than my share of the excitement, and—well, there's nothing else for it, is there? We can manage all right here—and it's more than likely you'll be wanted up there. Take Dara with you. She's the real goddess of the Crimson Butterfly and you can't very well deprive these people of one of them without returning them the other."

Battiscombe started.

"By Jove, Trevor!" he ejaculated; "that's the ticket! I didn't know that she was the important personage."

He rubbed his hands together.

"If some kind person'll oblige me with that *tot*, we'll get busy." He looked from one to the other. "If any harm's come to Vera," he added fiercely, "I'm not altogether certain that Mr. Abu-Samar will come back with us alive."

CHAPTER XXXIII

A MOVE IN THE RIGHT DIRECTION

JAMES BATTISCOMBE'S long experience as a magistrate in remote districts had taught him the value of stage-management where native religions were concerned.

Consequently, when he and the professor, with their handful of men, joined the tribesmen who squatted outside the breastwork, he led Dara forward, holding a lamp so that its light fell upon her face and shoulders and upon the sacred emblem that glittered at her throat.

The natives, who had risen at their approach, stared in hushed amazement at her coming and presently prostrated themselves before her.

She folded her arms and addressed them in their own tongue, and the fervour of their mingled responses inspired the magistrate with hope.

The girl turned to him.

"I have told them," she said in Malay, "that I was spirited away from them by Abu-Samar; that he is a bad man and that, before the sun rises again in the east, he must die."

Battiscombe nodded.

"And the men said," pursued Dara, "that my words were wise ones and that they would take me back to my temple and tell the others what I have already told them."

"All that is good," returned Battiscombe, "except that this man Samar should die before dawn. Very surely he will die, but there are wise men at the coast who would speak with him first. Listen, Dara: When the white lady has been given over to me and we have placed you again in the temple in the hill, then shall the chieftains deliver Abu-Samar into my hands."

She did not answer.

"You hear me, Dara?"

"I hear you, great *Tuan*, and I understand."

They moved forward presently, under a violet dome where stars hung like jewelled ornaments amid wind-blown clouds. Battiscombe and the professor walked in front, with the native girl between them; a few paces behind them came the leader of the tribesmen—a man of enormous height, clad in a leopard skin, a blow-pipe, with a spearhead attached, slung across his shoulders. He was followed by Kuraman and six soldiers, who marched in double file, while the remaining natives fell in irregularly at the rear.

The first half-mile was rough going, and then, on the far side of a gorge, they wheeled on to a recognised track, which, in spite of fragments of stone occurring at frequent intervals, offered them better foothold.

Wild and mountainous country this, broken by rare strips of sparse vegetation and occasional clumps of stunted trees.

Banks of heavy clouds hung on the horizon, and at a little after eleven the moon came up.

"Blowing up for rain," declared Standen suddenly.

"Yes," said Battiscombe. "Vance'll be glad. He wants it for his young rubber."

They relapsed into silence again.

They climbed a stiff hill and began descending into a valley where a keen wind met them, carrying to their cheeks the spray from an adjacent cataract.

The native who spoke Malay caught them up.

"We will stop at the foot of the slope, *Tuan*. On the other side of the hill is the road by which our people must pass on their way to the temple."

"*Baik*," replied Battiscombe shortly, and pressed onward.

They called a halt in the hollow and the professor selected a boulder upon which he promptly sat.

"This is all very well for you younger fellows," he laughed, "but it soon begins to tell upon a man of my age."

Dara reclined at his feet, while the magistrate strolled off to interview his guide.

"O *Tuan*," said the brown girl to Standen, "you are the man with the beard who is wiser than all other white men."

The professor, who understood enough Malay to follow her meaning, bestowed upon her the look a father might give to a very young child.

"I would hardly like to say that," he murmured in his own tongue, and then, so that she could understand him: "Who told you this, Dara?"

"The *Tuan-Hakim* who is sick."

"Armourer, eh? Well, that was really uncommonly nice of him!"

She surveyed him through half-closed eyes.

"The *Tuan-Hakim* made me a promise; he said that, when the time had arrived, you and he would explain to the priests and the headman how it was that Abu had taken me away, and that you would kill this Abu, so that the prophecy might be fulfilled."

Standen was puzzled.

"What prophecy, Dara?"

"That he who touches the goddess of the Crimson Butterfly—dies. Otherwise," she added, "men will say that I went with him willingly, and will believe that I am a goddess no longer."

The professor beckoned to Battiscombe, who was already on his way back to them.

"I say, Battiscombe! This girl has taken advantage of your absence to try and drive a hard bargain with me. As far as I can gather, she wants me to agree to have Samar killed and handed over to the natives to prove that the penalty for embracing this dusky goddess is death."

The magistrate turned to Dara.

"We are moving on in but a little while," he told her, "and there is no time to discuss this thing. But, when the white *mem* has been restored to me, I shall see that these people believe and take you back again."

She observed him doubtfully.

"If Abu does not die," she declared, "very surely they will kill me after you have gone."

Battiscombe did not answer.

"Some of their fellows have gone ahead to explain the position to any of their friends they may encounter in the road," he remarked to Standen. "If they're not back in a quarter of an hour, I'm starting without them. My interpreter thought it best to get a decent number of 'em on our side, in case our mission got misunderstood and we were attacked. On the whole I fancy he's right."

"It appears very sound to me," said the other.

"We want a good backing," continued the magistrate. "We're not going to put up much of a show, if it comes to fighting, with seven men and a bunch of others who won't know quite on whose side they are. They tell me the far side of the ridge is just teeming with the black-skinned blighters. Wouldn't some of our padres at home give their cassocks and waistcoat buttons for a congregation like this?"

"By Gad, they would!" chuckled the professor.

"And think of the collection!"

Standen blew his nose vigorously.

"I suppose they have one?"

"You bet they do. Witch doctors, *ju-ju* merchants and high-priests of native cults don't just hang around producing mysteries for nothing."

"What form do you suppose it takes? I mean they wouldn't bring money."

"No," said Battiscombe, "they probably trot along a bunch of bananas, some nuts, or a coconut or two—and the priests await an opportunity and dispose of it in bulk to the first merchant that crosses the interior. There's usually a commercial side to all these things. Nobody grumbles as long as there's a good show. Your native likes his show. That's why Dara's position presents complications. We've got to convince the priests—or whatever they style themselves—that she's the genuine article—and we've to convince them in such manner as not to arouse too many suspicions in the native mind. Their principal creed is that the butterflies protect their goddess and that no man who tampers with her survives the experiment. We can't produce a butterfly and make it sting Abu-Samar, and we haven't time to find and dispose of him and tattoo on him a fair imitation of the mark the Butterfly makes when it does sting. If we're driven to extreme measures, we may have to pick the beggar off with a rifle-bullet, just to show 'em that the man who abducted Dara did die anyway."

"It wouldn't be sufficient, I suppose," asked Standen, "to assure them that Abu-Samar will die in any case?"

Battiscombe produced a pouch and began filling his pipe.

"I'm afraid not. If I could only manage to get away with that, I'd consider I'd fulfilled my duty to the letter. Hullo! Here are some of our men back. We'll fall the fellows in and get on."

CHAPTER XXXIV

THE TEMPLE OF THE CRIMSON BUTTERFLY

THE SUMMIT OF THE NEXT HILL revealed to them a vast circular amphitheatre from the centre of which a path led up to the spot where, at the top of a huge mound, an enormous brazier was burning. Behind the brazier they could just make out the entrance to what appeared to be a cave and, standing before it, three figures.

Packed closely into this hollow, partly in the moonlight and partly in the shadow of the cliffs, was a multitude of crouching forms.

Battiscombe caught the professor's arm.

"Lord!" he exclaimed, "what a mob! Did you ever see anything like it?"

"No," said Standen, "never in my life. It puzzles me that so barren a countryside should be able to produce so many."

The magistrate unhitched a pair of binoculars and focussed them on the temple.

"Well?" asked his companion after a long pause.

"Vera's there," said Battiscombe huskily, "and Samar. There's a black chap with them with nothing much on but paint."

Their guide halted before them.

"It is time, O *Tuan*," he said.

Battiscombe gritted his teeth.

"The crucial moment has arrived, Standen. What d'you think about it?"

The professor smiled.

"I'm profoundly interested," he confessed.

They began the descent.

They came presently, by way of a winding path, to a flight of steps roughly hewn from the bare rock, and ten minutes later they embarked upon the narrow passage-way that stretched between the two sections of worshippers at the shrine of the Crimson Butterfly.

The professor, walking a couple of paces behind Battiscombe, stared blandly at an ocean of dark heads and a veritable forest of spears that extended, seemingly, from either side of them to infinity.

Battiscombe, pipe in mouth, strode along with his head held high and one hand resting lightly in his jacket-pocket. He appeared delightfully at his ease, but the hidden hand was closed over a pistol-butt and his eye was ever alert for a hostile sign in his immediate neighbourhood.

It was an eerie moment.

The slightest sign of nervousness, of hesitation, would have spelt inevitable disaster. This puny band that marched to the rescue of Vera Battiscombe would have been overwhelmed and crushed out of existence by sheer weight of numbers.

Battiscombe was within twenty yards of the shrine itself when the native who spoke Malay appeared at his side and signed to him to stop.

Just above them a man was speaking in the queer, discordant dialect these people employed. The magistrate could not hope to follow the text, but kept his eyes on the speaker, endeavouring to gather from his actions and change of expression the gist of what he was saying.

"It is the high-priest," whispered his guide.

Battiscombe nodded.

"He says that this is the night of all nights, that the prophecy has been fulfilled and there is once more a white goddess at the shrine of the Butterfly."

"Oh, he does, does he?" muttered the magistrate between his teeth, and looked round for Dara. But the black girl was nowhere to be seen.

The priest—a fantastic figure in crimson loin-cloth and headpiece like a skull-cap with wings, his body smeared with broad lines of red and yellow paint—seized the white girl by a wrist and led her forward.

Battiscombe, an ugly light in his eyes, the veins standing out on his temples, made an effort to choke down his emotion. He saw his wife mauled by this bedaubed savage—a trembling, terrified Vera, clothed in a black *sarong* spotted with gold, and with barbaric ornaments hanging at her wrists.

The gathering was on its knees now and the incantation they repeated rumbled in that vast hollow like thunder.

The murmuring ceased and, in the grim silence that followed, Battiscombe caught the guide's eye.

"Ask him where the token is—the ornament that the goddess should be wearing."

The man raised his arm and shouted.

The priest was about to respond when Abu-Samar sprang in front of him and levelled an accusing finger at Battiscombe.

"It is he who has stolen the ornament," he screamed. "The white man who has come to rob the shrine of its goddess has taken the Crimson Butterfly."

A shrieking tumult rose to the heavens, there was an ominous clash of weapons, and two walls of gesticulating humanity began to close in on them.

"This is beginning to look awkward," whispered the professor in the magistrate's ear. "Can't our black friend do something?"

"I'm pumping some good sound logic into him now," the other jerked back over his shoulder. "Tell my fellows to keep their heads and not attempt to use their rifles until I give the order."

He planted the flat of his hand on a black chest that had come too close to be pleasant, and deliberately pushed it back.

"Tell them," he shouted to the guide, "that Abu-Samar is a liar and the son of liars; that he came by stealth and stole Dara—the goddess—from the shrine; that the white woman they see up there is no goddess, but my wife, whom he took away from my house when she was ill. Tell them that I have come from the great king who dwells on the other side of the black waters and that there are many men waiting at but a little distance. Tell them that I come as a friend, to find my wife, whom Samar has taken, and go away with her in peace; that the British *Raj* has sent me to give them back Dara and take Abu-Samar down to the seashore in chains, that the prophecy may be fulfilled and the defiler of the sanctuary of the Crimson Butterfly slain. Tell them that if they receive me in peace—all is well; and if they greet me with spears, the hillsides will flash with fire and there will be many dead in the valleys."

The man in the leopard skin waved his blow-pipe above his head and presently the shouting died down.

He spoke for fully twenty minutes by the professor's watch, an eloquent, impassioned speech, and Standen mentally thanked his stars that they had stumbled upon a local orator for their advocate.

The speaker dropped his arms to his sides and there was a brief space of silence. Then, like a great tidal wave, the tumult burst upon them again. It was awe-inspiring, deafening, colossal; but Battiscombe, who could detect the difference between unfriendly native noises and the other kind, appeared satisfied.

He turned to Standen.

"Where's that damn' girl?" he demanded. "If we could only show her to 'em now, we'd beat that brute Samar all hands down."

The professor raised a warning finger.

The high-priest was speaking again.

The guide leaned across.

"I told you so," said Battiscombe again. "He's asking for Dara. If she doesn't show up inside a couple of minutes—the game's up."

He began shouldering his way towards the shrine with the friendly native at his heels.

"Follow me," he shouted back. "If the worst comes to the worst, we'll make sure of the high ground. We may find some sort of sanctuary up there."

"The horns of the altar!" murmured Standen, as he caught him up.

A few paces from the high-priest himself, Battiscombe bowed politely.

"O wise one!" he began in Malay, assuming him to be a man of superior education. "Dara—the goddess of the Butterfly—is here."

The priest regarded him suspiciously.

"You have said that Abu-Samar is a liar," he reminded the Englishman, "also the son of liars. Abu-Samar, on the other hand, insists that it is you who lie and that it is you who have stolen the sacred pendant which should adorn the neck of our goddess. Restore to us Dara—and the pendant, and all will be well. Otherwise—"

Abu-Samar, still in the European garb he affected, drew himself erect.

"Battiscombe," he called insolently, "you are a brave man and an optimist, but Abu-Samar holds your fate in the hollow of his hand. Yes, I stole your wife from Jelandang. You can shout it to these people again and again, but they will not believe you. They have waited for a white goddess all these years and, now that I have brought her to them, do you imagine they will let you take her away? In a moment I shall move one finger and you and your little party will be blotted out. I am lending your wife to these people. They shall keep her until I am ready to spirit her away, as I took Dara the brown girl." He pointed at Battiscombe's band contemptuously. "It will take more than that to arrest Abu-Samar. Seven little soldiers in round hats! It is an insult—the second time you have insulted me, Battiscombe!"

The magistrate held his head on one side.

"I'm afraid I shall have to inflict a third insult on you, Abu-Samar, for to-night I take you back with me—to be hanged like the dirty cut-throat you are!"

Samar drew in a deep breath and his eyes flashed.

"Dara!" he shouted to the crowd. "Where is she? They, who say they have brought her back, cannot find her. It is a lie, a trick . . . *Kill!*"

And then, as Battiscombe's automatic leaped from his pocket, as grim little men gripped their rifles and a shrieking mass hesitated before sweeping down on them—a dark figure slipped from behind a rock and, drawing a long knife from her hair, buried it to the hilt in Samar's back.

Abu-Samar dropped forward on to his knees and Dara waved the dripping blade aloft.

"Greetings, my people!" she cried, "Behold! here am I! Dara! I have come back to you. My white friends have brought me here—and he who stole me from you is dead!"

They grovelled before her now, moaning, chanting, beating their heads upon the ground, and Battiscombe, darting forward, snatched Vera up in his arms.

"We have won, *Tuan*," said Kuraman at the professor's side. "The *Tuan-Hakim* has won—and the *mem* is safe again. He is a wonderful man!"

Standen smiled.

"Kuraman," replied the professor, "you are all wonderful men—all of you; do you understand?"

And he lit a cigarette.

CHAPTER XXXV

THE FRUITS OF VICTORY

AS THE DAWN WAS COMING UP, Trevor, red-eyed and weary, saw them straggling back among the rocks.

Two men carried a hammock on a *pikul*, the professor and Battiscombe walked leisurely, laughing over something one of them had just said, and everybody was smoking.

"Hullo!" he greeted them; "what luck?"

Battiscombe threw his arms in the air.

"The very best. We've brought her back, unharmed."

The planter vaulted over the breastwork and ran to meet them.

"Splendid! How did you manage it?"

The professor laughed.

"We'll tell you all about it as soon as we've found somewhere comfortable to sit and something warm to drink. We've had a most successful and memorable outing; but it was touch-and-go at one time, wasn't it, Battiscombe?"

The magistrate grinned.

"Don't I know it! Up to a point we were the two most unpopular people in creation—and give me popularity every time! You've read of minutes that seem like years, Trevor?—well, we had about fifteen of those, with umpteen black giants breathing hate down the backs of our shirts! Lord! professor, didn't they stink!"

"They did," agreed Standen, "horribly!"

"And Abu-Samar?"

Battiscombe took Trevor's arm.

"He's dead; Dara killed him."

"Dara?"

"Yes, stabbed him in the back at a very critical moment. We'd talked ourselves hoarse and it wanted something very decisive to convince 'em of our *bona-fides*. Dara supplied it!"

The last trace of anxiety left the planter's face.

"Well, that's about the end of our job, isn't it! We can burn his jolly old breeding-house at our leisure, and march comfortably back to hear the plaudits of the multitude!"

They all laughed.

"How's Armourer?" asked the professor, as they approached the tent.

"Fine, apparently. The last time I saw Miss Standen she told me he had recognised her and spoken quite sensibly."

The professor rubbed his hands together.

"That's what comes of having a fine constitution!"

"And a fine antidote," added Battiscombe.

"And a fine nurse," said Trevor. "I've pitched the other tent over there. I thought you'd want somewhere to put Mrs. Battiscombe."

Standen stopped outside Armourer's tent.

"I could sleep the round of the clock!" he declared.

Battiscombe placed his hands on his hips.

"I can give you four hours. I'm breaking camp at nine and putting as many miles as I can between us and any possible after-thoughts on the part of our coloured friends."

"I don't blame you," said the other, and went in to look at his patient.

By nine o'clock all that was left of the long hut and its loathsome contents was a heap of smouldering ruins.

It amused Standen to compare the atmosphere of the return march to the outward journey of the expedition.

The men, the bearers, the leaders themselves, laughed and chattered as the long line wound its way westward. The fact that their mission was accomplished and that Abu-Samar was dead had taken a weight from every mind, from the highest to the lowest. He wondered what would have happened if they had failed, if the breeding-house had broadcasted its thousands, if Samar had been free to pursue his campaign of hate!

"What's up, professor?" laughed Trevor. "You look as if you'd something on your mind."

"I had," confessed the older man; "but, thank heaven, it isn't there now!"

On the second day Vera was able to ride.

"Jim," she asked suddenly, addressing the man who walked by her side, "are you really glad to have me back?"

Battiscombe smiled up at her.

"Rather!" he said. "When I heard that he'd taken you, I nearly went off my rocker."

"But I've been such a beast to you. It's no earthly use your shaking your head. I've treated you frightfully badly." She rested a hand on his shoulder. "But I didn't know you, Jim. I didn't know you could do things like that. I was so frightened before you came. I was more frightened still—for your sake—when you walked right through that ghastly crowd. I thought they'd kill you."

"So did I," replied her husband cheerfully.

"But you weren't afraid."

"Wasn't I, though! I was in a deuce of a panic, if you only knew."

"I don't believe it," she declared. "I absolutely refuse to believe any such nonsense. You were an absolute hero—a great, fat, dear old hero—and I don't deserve you a bit. But honestly, dear, I mean to stick to you like anything after this."

"You've jolly well got to," said Battiscombe. "You don't suppose I indulge in jaunts of this sort just for the fun of the thing. In future I'm ruling my household with an iron hand. By the way, I'm sending in my resignation as soon as we get back."

Vera gasped.

"You're not throwing up your career because of me?"

"Not altogether. You see, Vera, the old man pegged out on the day I left Rembakut. I got the news when Armourer's man caught me up."

"Jim!"

"Yes," he continued slowly, "I haven't told a soul about it yet; I was saving it up for you. It'll mean a lot to us. You'll be able to have some decent frocks now and the only occupation I shall want is something to help me keep my fat down! I'm sorry I wasn't home when it happened, though."

It was a week before Armourer talked sensibly again. He opened his eyes wearily and realised that somebody was bending over him. It was evening and the air was pleasantly cool.

He reached out with his hand and touched a white arm.

"Is that you, Joyce?" he asked, in so natural a tone that it startled her.

She had somehow pictured their first intimate conversation as something entirely different from this.

"Yes, Michael," she said, with just a catch in her voice, "I've brought Mickie to see you."

He drew her hand towards him and pressed his lips to it.

THE END

RAMBLE HOUSE's

HARRY STEPHEN KEELER WEBWORK MYSTERIES

(RH) indicates the title is available ONLY in the RAMBLE HOUSE edition

The Ace of Spades Murder
The Affair of the Bottled Deuce (RH)
The Amazing Web
The Barking Clock
Behind That Mask
The Book with the Orange Leaves
The Bottle with the Green Wax Seal
The Box from Japan
The Case of the Canny Killer
The Case of the Crazy Corpse (RH)
The Case of the Flying Hands (RH)
The Case of the Ivory Arrow
The Case of the Jeweled Ragpicker
The Case of the Lavender Gripsack
The Case of the Mysterious Moll
The Case of the 16 Beans
The Case of the Transparent Nude (RH)
The Case of the Transposed Legs
The Case of the Two-Headed Idiot (RH)
The Case of the Two Strange Ladies
The Circus Stealers (RH)
Cleopatra's Tears
A Copy of Beowulf (RH)
The Crimson Cube (RH)
The Face of the Man From Saturn
Find the Clock
The Five Silver Buddhas
The 4th King
The Gallows Waits, My Lord! (RH)
The Green Jade Hand
Finger! Finger!
Hangman's Nights (RH)
I, Chameleon (RH)
I Killed Lincoln at 10:13! (RH)
The Iron Ring
The Man Who Changed His Skin (RH)
The Man with the Crimson Box
The Man with the Magic Eardrums
The Man with the Wooden Spectacles
The Marceau Case
The Matilda Hunter Murder

The Monocled Monster
The Murder of London Lew
The Murdered Mathematician
The Mysterious Card (RH)
The Mysterious Ivory Ball of Wong Shing Li (RH)
The Mystery of the Fiddling Cracksman
The Peacock Fan
The Photo of Lady X (RH)
The Portrait of Jirjohn Cobb
Report on Vanessa Hewstone (RH)
Riddle of the Travelling Skull
Riddle of the Wooden Parrakeet (RH)
The Scarlet Mummy (RH)
The Search for X-Y-Z
The Sharkskin Book
Sing Sing Nights
The Six From Nowhere (RH)
The Skull of the Waltzing Clown
The Spectacles of Mr. Cagliostro
Stand By—London Calling!
The Steeltown Strangler
The Stolen Gravestone (RH)
Strange Journey (RH)
The Strange Will
The Straw Hat Murders (RH)
The Street of 1000 Eyes (RH)
Thieves' Nights
Three Novellos (RH)
The Tiger Snake
The Trap (RH)
Vagabond Nights (Defrauded Yeggman)
Vagabond Nights 2 (10 Hours)
The Vanishing Gold Truck
The Voice of the Seven Sparrows
The Washington Square Enigma
When Thief Meets Thief
The White Circle (RH)
The Wonderful Scheme of Mr. Christopher Thorne
X. Jones—of Scotland Yard
Y. Cheung, Business Detective

Keeler Related Works

A To Izzard: A Harry Stephen Keeler Companion by Fender Tucker — Articles and stories about Harry, by Harry, and in his style. Included is a compleat bibliography.

Wild About Harry: Reviews of Keeler Novels — Edited by Richard Polt & Fender Tucker — 22 reviews of works by Harry Stephen Keeler from *Keeler News*. A perfect introduction to the author.

The Keeler Keyhole Collection: Annotated newsletter rants from Harry Stephen Keeler, edited by Francis M. Nevins. Over 400 pages of incredibly personal Keeleriana.

Fakealoo — Pastiches of the style of Harry Stephen Keeler by selected demented members of the HSK Society. Updated every year with the new winner.

Strands of the Web: Short Stories of Harry Stephen Keeler — 29 stories, just about all that Keeler wrote, are edited and introduced by Fred Cleaver.

RAMBLE HOUSE's LOON SANCTUARY

A Clear Path to Cross — Sharon Knowles short mystery stories by Ed Lynskey.

A Corpse Walks in Brooklyn and Other Stories — Volume 5 in the Day Keene in the Detective Pulps series.

A Jimmy Starr Omnibus — Three 40s novels by Jimmy Starr.

A Niche in Time and Other Stories — Classic SF by William F. Temple

A Roland Daniel Double: The Signal and The Return of Wu Fang — Classic thrillers from the 30s.

A Shot Rang Out — Three decades of reviews and articles by today's Anthony Boucher, Jon Breen. An essential book for any mystery lover's library.

A Smell of Smoke — A 1951 English countryside thriller by Miles Burton.

A Snark Selection — Lewis Carroll's *The Hunting of the Snark* with two Snarkian chapters by Harry Stephen Keeler — Illustrated by Gavin L. O'Keefe.

A Young Man's Heart — A forgotten early classic by Cornell Woolrich.

Alexander Laing Novels — *The Motives of Nicholas Holtz* and *Dr. Scarlett*, stories of medical mayhem and intrigue from the 30s.

An Angel in the Street — Modern hardboiled noir by Peter Genovese.

Automaton — Brilliant treatise on robotics: 1928-style! By H. Stafford Hatfield.

Away From the Here and Now — Clare Winger Harris stories, collected by Richard A. Lupoff

Beast or Man? — A 1930 novel of racism and horror by Sean M'Guire. Introduced by John Pelan.

Black Beadle — A 1939 thriller by E.C.R. Lorac.

Black Hogan Strikes Again — Australia's Peter Renwick pens a tale of the 30s outback.

Black River Falls — Suspense from the master, Ed Gorman.

Blondy's Boy Friend — A snappy 1930 story by Philip Wylie, writing as Leatrice Homesley.

Blood in a Snap — The *Finnegan's Wake* of the 21st century, by Jim Weiler.

Blood Moon — The first of the Robert Payne series by Ed Gorman.

Bogart '48 — Hollywood action with Bogie by John Stanley and Kenn Davis

Calling Lou Largo! — Two Lou Largo novels by William Ard.

Cornucopia of Crime — Francis M. Nevins assembled this huge collection of his writings about crime literature and the people who write it. Essential for any serious mystery library.

Corpse Without Flesh — Strange novel of forensics by George Bruce

Crimson Clown Novels — By Johnston McCulley, author of the Zorro novels, *The Crimson Clown* and *The Crimson Clown Again.*

Dago Red — 22 tales of dark suspense by Bill Pronzini.

Dark Sanctuary — Weird Menace story by H. B. Gregory

David Hume Novels — *Corpses Never Argue, Cemetery First Stop, Make Way for the Mourners, Eternity Here I Come.* 1930s British hardboiled fiction with an attitude.

Dead Man Talks Too Much — Hollywood boozer by Weed Dickenson.

Death Leaves No Card — One of the most unusual murdered-in-the-tub mysteries you'll ever read. By Miles Burton.

Death March of the Dancing Dolls and Other Stories — Volume Three in the Day Keene in the Detective Pulps series. Introduced by Bill Crider.

Deep Space and other Stories — A collection of SF gems by Richard A. Lupoff.

Detective Duff Unravels It — Episodic mysteries by Harvey O'Higgins.

Diabolic Candelabra — Classic 30s mystery by E.R. Punshon

Dictator's Way — Another D.S. Bobby Owen mystery from E.R. Punshon

Dime Novels: Ramble House's 10-Cent Books — *Knife in the Dark* by Robert Leslie Bellem, *Hot Lead* and *Song of Death* by Ed Earl Repp, *A Hashish House in New York* by H.H. Kane, and five more.

Doctor Arnoldi — Tiffany Thayer's story of the death of death.

Don Diablo: Book of a Lost Film — Two-volume treatment of a western by Paul Landres, with diagrams. Intro by Francis M. Nevins.

Dope and Swastikas — Two strange novels from 1922 by Edmund Snell

Dope Tales #1 — Two dope-riddled classics; *Dope Runners* by Gerald Grantham and *Death Takes the Joystick* by Phillip Condé.

Dope Tales #2 — Two more narco-classics; *The Invisible Hand* by Rex Dark and *The Smokers of Hashish* by Norman Berrow.

Dope Tales #3 — Two enchanting novels of opium by the master, Sax Rohmer. *Dope* and *The Yellow Claw.*

Double Hot — Two 60s softcore sex novels by Morris Hershman.

Double Sex — Yet two more panting thrillers from Morris Hershman.

Dr. Odin — Douglas Newton's 1933 racial potboiler comes back to life.

Evangelical Cockroach — Jack Woodford writes about writing.

Evidence in Blue — 1938 mystery by E. Charles Vivian.

Fatal Accident — Murder by automobile, a 1936 mystery by Cecil M. Wills.

Fighting Mad — Todd Robbins' 1922 novel about boxing and life

Finger-prints Never Lie — A 1939 classic detective novel by John G. Brandon.

Freaks and Fantasies — Eerie tales by Tod Robbins, collaborator of Tod Browning on the film FREAKS.

Gadsby — A lipogram (a novel without the letter E). Ernest Vincent Wright's last work, published in 1939 right before his death.

Gelett Burgess Novels — *The Master of Mysteries, The White Cat, Two O'Clock Courage, Ladies in Boxes, Find the Woman, The Heart Line, The Picaroons* and *Lady Mechante.* Recently added is A Gelett Burgess Sampler, edited by Alfred Jan. All are introduced by Richard A. Lupoff.

Geronimo — S. M. Barrett's 1905 autobiography of a noble American.

Hake Talbot Novels — *Rim of the Pit, The Hangman's Handyman.* Classic locked room mysteries, with mapback covers by Gavin O'Keefe.

Hands Out of Hell and Other Stories — John H. Knox's eerie hallucinations

Hell is a City — William Ard's masterpiece.

Hollywood Dreams — A novel of Tinsel Town and the Depression by Richard O'Brien.

Hostesses in Hell and Other Stories — Russell Gray's most graphic stories

House of the Restless Dead — Strange and ominous tales by Hugh B. Cave

I Stole $16,000,000 — A true story by cracksman Herbert E. Wilson.

Inclination to Murder — 1966 thriller by New Zealand's Harriet Hunter.

Invaders from the Dark — Classic werewolf tale from Greye La Spina.

J. Poindexter, Colored — Classic satirical black novel by Irvin S. Cobb.

Jack Mann Novels — Strange murder in the English countryside. *Gees' First Case, Nightmare Farm, Grey Shapes, The Ninth Life, The Glass Too Many, Her Ways Are Death, The Kleinert Case* and *Maker of Shadows.*

Jake Hardy — A lusty western tale from Wesley Tallant.

Jim Harmon Double Novels — *Vixen Hollow/Celluloid Scandal, The Man Who Made Maniacs/Silent Siren, Ape Rape/Wanton Witch, Sex Burns Like Fire/Twist Session, Sudden Lust/Passion Strip, Sin Unlimited/Harlot Master, Twilight Girls/Sex Institution.* Written in the early 60s and never reprinted until now.

Joel Townsley Rogers Novels and Short Stories — By the author of *The Red Right Hand: Once In a Red Moon, Lady With the Dice, The Stopped Clock, Never Leave My Bed.* Also two short story collections: *Night of Horror* and *Killing Time.*

John Carstairs, Space Detective — Arboreal Sci-fi by Frank Belknap Long

Joseph Shallit Novels — *The Case of the Billion Dollar Body, Lady Don't Die on My Doorstep, Kiss the Killer, Yell Bloody Murder, Take Your Last Look.* One of America's best 50's authors and a favorite of author Bill Pronzini.

Keller Memento — 45 short stories of the amazing and weird by Dr. David Keller.

Killer's Caress — Cary Moran's 1936 hardboiled thriller.

Lady of the Yellow Death and Other Stories — More stories by Wyatt Blassingame.

League of the Grateful Dead and Other Stories — Volume One in the Day Keene in the Detective Pulps series.

Library of Death — Ghastly tale by Ronald S. L. Harding, introduced by John Pelan

Malcolm Jameson Novels and Short Stories — *Astonishing! Astounding!, Tarnished Bomb, The Alien Envoy and Other Stories* and *The Chariots of San Fernando and Other Stories.* All introduced and edited by John Pelan or Richard A. Lupoff.

Man Out of Hell and Other Stories — Volume II of the John H. Knox weird pulps collection.

Marblehead: A Novel of H.P. Lovecraft — A long-lost masterpiece from Richard A. Lupoff. This is the "director's cut", the long version that has never been published before.

Mark of the Laughing Death and Other Stories — Shockers from the pulps by Francis James, introduced by John Pelan.

Master of Souls — Mark Hansom's 1937 shocker is introduced by weirdologist John Pelan.

Max Afford Novels — *Owl of Darkness, Death's Mannikins, Blood on His Hands, The Dead Are Blind, The Sheep and the Wolves, Sinners in Paradise* and *Two Locked Room Mysteries and a Ripping Yarn* by one of Australia's finest mystery novelists.

Money Brawl — Two books about the writing business by Jack Woodford and H. Bedford-Jones. Introduced by Richard A. Lupoff.

More Secret Adventures of Sherlock Holmes — Gary Lovisi's second collection of tales about the unknown sides of the great detective.

Muddled Mind: Complete Works of Ed Wood, Jr. — David Hayes and Hayden Davis deconstruct the life and works of the mad, but canny, genius.

Murder among the Nudists — A mystery from 1934 by Peter Hunt, featuring a naked Detective-Inspector going undercover in a nudist colony.

Murder in Black and White — 1931 classic tennis whodunit by Evelyn Elder.

Murder in Shawnee — Two novels of the Alleghenies by John Douglas: *Shawnee Alley Fire* and *Haunts*.

Murder in Silk — A 1937 Yellow Peril novel of the silk trade by Ralph Trevor.

My Deadly Angel — 1955 Cold War drama by John Chelton.

My First Time: The One Experience You Never Forget — Michael Birchwood — 64 true first-person narratives of how they lost it.

Mysterious Martin, the Master of Murder — Two versions of a strange 1912 novel by Tod Robbins about a man who writes books that can kill.

Norman Berrow Novels — *The Bishop's Sword, Ghost House, Don't Go Out After Dark, Claws of the Cougar, The Smokers of Hashish, The Secret Dancer, Don't Jump Mr. Boland!, The Footprints of Satan, Fingers for Ransom, The Three Tiers of Fantasy, The Spaniard's Thumb, The Eleventh Plague, Words Have Wings, One Thrilling Night, The Lady's in Danger, It Howls at Night, The Terror in the Fog, Oil Under the Window, Murder in the Melody, The Singing Room.* This is the complete Norman Berrow library of locked-room mysteries, several of which are masterpieces.

Old Faithful and Other Stories — SF classic tales by Raymond Z. Gallun

Old Times' Sake — Short stories by James Reasoner from Mike Shayne Magazine.

One Dreadful Night — A classic mystery by Ronald S. L. Harding.

Pair O' Jacks — A mystery novel and a diatribe about publishing by Jack Woodford.

Perfect .38 — Two early Timothy Dane novels by William Ard. More to come.

Prince Pax — Devilish intrigue by George Sylvester Viereck and Philip Eldridge

Prose Bowl — Futuristic satire of a world where hack writing has replaced football as our national obsession, by Bill Pronzini and Barry N. Malzberg.

Red Light — The history of legal prostitution in Shreveport Louisiana by Eric Brock. Includes wonderful photos of the houses and the ladies.

Researching American-Made Toy Soldiers — A 276-page collection of a lifetime of articles by toy soldier expert Richard O'Brien.

Reunion in Hell — Volume One of the John H. Knox series of weird stories from the pulps. Introduced by horror expert John Pelan.

Ripped from the Headlines! — The Jack the Ripper story as told in the newspaper articles in the *New York* and *London Times.*

Rough Cut & New, Improved Murder — Ed Gorman's first two novels.

R.R. Ryan Novels — Freak Museum and The Subjugated Beast, two horror classics.

Ruby of a Thousand Dreams — The villain Wu Fang returns in this Roland Daniel novel.

Ruled By Radio — 1925 futuristic novel by Robert L. Hadfield & Frank E. Farncombe.

Rupert Penny Novels — *Policeman's Holiday, Policeman's Evidence, Lucky Policeman, Policeman in Armour, Sealed Room Murder, Sweet Poison, The Talkative Policeman, She had to Have Gas* and *Cut and Run* (by Martin Tanner.) Rupert Penny is the pseudonym of Australian Charles Thornett, a master of the locked room, impossible crime plot.

Sacred Locomotive Flies — Richard A. Lupoff's psychedelic SF story.

Sam — Early gay novel by Lonnie Coleman.

Sand's Game — Spectacular hard-boiled noir from Ennis Willie, edited by Lynn Myers and Stephen Mertz, with contributions from Max Allan Collins, Bill Crider, Wayne Dundee, Bill Pronzini, Gary Lovisi and James Reasoner.

Sand's War — More violent fiction from the typewriter of Ennis Willie

Satan's Den Exposed — True crime in Truth or Consequences New Mexico — Award-winning journalism by the *Desert Journal*.

Satans of Saturn — Novellas from the pulps by Otis Adelbert Kline and E. H. Price

Satan's Sin House and Other Stories — Horrific gore by Wayne Rogers

Secrets of a Teenage Superhero — Graphic lit by Jonathan Sweet

Sex Slave — Potboiler of lust in the days of Cleopatra by Dion Leclerq, 1966.

Sideslip — 1968 SF masterpiece by Ted White and Dave Van Arnam.

Slammer Days — Two full-length prison memoirs: *Men into Beasts* (1952) by George Sylvester Viereck and *Home Away From Home* (1962) by Jack Woodford.

Slippery Staircase — 1930s whodunit from E.C.R. Lorac

Sorcerer's Chessmen — John Pelan introduces this 1939 classic by Mark Hansom.

Star Griffin — Michael Kurland's 1987 masterpiece of SF drollery is back.

Stakeout on Millennium Drive — Award-winning Indianapolis Noir by Ian Woollen.

Strands of the Web: Short Stories of Harry Stephen Keeler — Edited and Introduced by Fred Cleaver.

Summer Camp for Corpses and Other Stories — Weird Menace tales from Arthur Leo Zagat; introduced by John Pelan.

Suzy — A collection of comic strips by Richard O'Brien and Bob Vojtko from 1970.

Tales of the Macabre and Ordinary — Modern twisted horror by Chris Mikul, author of the *Bizarrism* series.

Tales of Terror and Torment #1 — John Pelan selects and introduces this sampler of weird menace tales from the pulps.

Tenebrae — Ernest G. Henham's 1898 horror tale brought back.

The Amorous Intrigues & Adventures of Aaron Burr — by Anonymous. Hot historical action about the man who almost became Emperor of Mexico.

The Anthony Boucher Chronicles — edited by Francis M. Nevins. Book reviews by Anthony Boucher written for the *San Francisco Chronicle, 1942 – 1947*. Essential and fascinating reading by the best book reviewer there ever was.

The Barclay Catalogs — Two essential books about toy soldier collecting by Richard O'Brien

The Basil Wells Omnibus — A collection of Wells' stories by Richard A. Lupoff

The Beautiful Dead and Other Stories — Dreadful tales from Donald Dale

The Best of 10-Story Book — edited by Chris Mikul, over 35 stories from the literary magazine Harry Stephen Keeler edited.

The Black Dark Murders — Vintage 50s college murder yarn by Milt Ozaki, writing as Robert O. Saber.

The Book of Time — The classic novel by H.G. Wells is joined by sequels by Wells himself and three stories by Richard A. Lupoff. Illustrated by Gavin L. O'Keefe.

The Case in the Clinic — One of E.C.R. Lorac's finest.

The Strange Case of the Antlered Man — A mystery of superstition by Edwy Searles Brooks.

The Case of the Bearded Bride — #4 in the Day Keene in the Detective Pulps series

The Case of the Little Green Men — Mack Reynolds wrote this love song to sci-fi fans back in 1951 and it's now back in print.

The Case of the Withered Hand — 1936 potboiler by John G. Brandon.

The Charlie Chaplin Murder Mystery — A 2004 tribute by noted film scholar, Wes D. Gehring.

The Chinese Jar Mystery — Murder in the manor by John Stephen Strange, 1934.

The Cloudbuilders and Other Stories — SF tales from Colin Kapp.

The Compleat Calhoon — All of Fender Tucker's works: Includes *Totah Six-Pack, Weed, Women and Song* and *Tales from the Tower*, plus a CD of all of his songs.

The Compleat Ova Hamlet — Parodies of SF authors by Richard A. Lupoff. This is a brand new edition with more stories and more illustrations by Trina Robbins.

The Contested Earth and Other SF Stories — A never-before published space opera and seven short stories by Jim Harmon.

The Crimson Query — A 1929 thriller from Arlton Eadie. A perfect way to get introduced.

The Curse of Cantire — Classic 1939 novel of a family curse by Walter S. Masterman.

The Devil and the C.I.D. — Odd diabolic mystery by E.C.R. Lorac

The Devil Drives — An odd prison and lost treasure novel from 1932 by Virgil Markham.

The Devil of Pei-Ling — Herbert Asbury's 1929 tale of the occult.

The Devil's Mistress — A 1915 Scottish gothic tale by J. W. Brodie-Innes, a member of Aleister Crowley's Golden Dawn.

The Devil's Nightclub and Other Stories — John Pelan introduces some gruesome tales by Nat Schachner.

The Disentanglers — Episodic intrigue at the turn of last century by Andrew Lang

The Dog Poker Code — A spoof of *The Da Vinci Code* by D.B. Smithee.

The Dumpling — Political murder from 1907 by Coulson Kernahan.

The End of It All and Other Stories — Ed Gorman selected his favorite short stories for this huge collection.

The Fangs of Suet Pudding — A 1944 novel of the German invasion by Adams Farr

The Finger of Destiny and Other Stories — Edmund Snell's superb collection of weird stories of Borneo.

The Ghost of Gaston Revere — From 1935, a novel of life and beyond by Mark Hansom, introduced by John Pelan.

The Girl in the Dark — A thriller from Roland Daniel

The Gold Star Line — Seaboard adventure from L.T. Reade and Robert Eustace.

The Golden Dagger — 1951 Scotland Yard yarn by E. R. Punshon.

The Great Orme Terror — Horror stories by Garnett Radcliffe from the pulps

The Hairbreadth Escapes of Major Mendax — Francis Blake Crofton's 1889 boys' book.

The House That Time Forgot and Other Stories — Insane pulpitude by Robert F. Young

The House of the Vampire — 1907 poetic thriller by George S. Viereck.

The Illustrious Corpse — Murder hijinx from Tiffany Thayer

The Incredible Adventures of Rowland Hern — Intriguing 1928 impossible crimes by Nicholas Olde.

The Julius Caesar Murder Case — A classic 1935 re-telling of the assassination by Wallace Irwin that's much more fun than the Shakespeare version.

The Koky Comics — A collection of all of the 1978-1981 Sunday and daily comic strips by Richard O'Brien and Mort Gerberg, in two volumes.

The Lady of the Terraces — 1925 missing race adventure by E. Charles Vivian.

The Lord of Terror — 1925 mystery with master-criminal, Fantômas.

The Melamare Mystery — A classic 1929 Arsene Lupin mystery by Maurice Leblanc

The Man Who Was Secrett — Epic SF stories from John Brunner

The Man Without a Planet — Science fiction tales by Richard Wilson

The N. R. De Mexico Novels — Robert Bragg, the real N.R. de Mexico, presents *Marijuana Girl, Madman on a Drum, Private Chauffeur* in one volume.

The Night Remembers — A 1991 Jack Walsh mystery from Ed Gorman.

The One After Snelling — Kickass modern noir from Richard O'Brien.

The Organ Reader — A huge compilation of just about everything published in the 1971-1972 radical bay-area newspaper, *THE ORGAN*. A coffee table book that points out the shallowness of the coffee table mindset.

The Poker Club — Three in one! Ed Gorman's ground-breaking novel, the short story it was based upon, and the screenplay of the film made from it.

The Private Journal & Diary of John H. Surratt — The memoirs of the man who conspired to assassinate President Lincoln.

The Ramble House Mapbacks — Recently revised book by Gavin L. O'Keefe with color pictures of all the Ramble House books with mapbacks.

The Secret Adventures of Sherlock Holmes — Three Sherlockian pastiches by the Brooklyn author/publisher, Gary Lovisi.

The Shadow on the House — Mark Hansom's 1934 masterpiece of horror is introduced by John Pelan.

The Sign of the Scorpion — A 1935 Edmund Snell tale of oriental evil.

The Singular Problem of the Stygian House-Boat — Two classic tales by John Kendrick Bangs about the denizens of Hades.

The Smiling Corpse — Philip Wylie and Bernard Bergman's odd 1935 novel.

The Spider: Satan's Murder Machines — A thesis about Iron Man

The Stench of Death: An Odoriferous Omnibus by Jack Moskovitz — Two complete novels and two novellas from 60's sleaze author, Jack Moskovitz.

The Story Writer and Other Stories — Classic SF from Richard Wilson

The Strange Case of the Antlered Man — 1935 dementia from Edwy Searles Brooks

The Strange Thirteen — Richard B. Gamon's odd stories about Raj India.

The Technique of the Mystery Story — Carolyn Wells' tips about writing.

The Threat of Nostalgia — A collection of his most obscure stories by Jon Breen

The Time Armada — Fox B. Holden's 1953 SF gem.

The Tongueless Horror and Other Stories — Volume One of the series of short stories from the weird pulps by Wyatt Blassingame.

The Town from Planet Five — From Richard Wilson, two SF classics, *And Then the Town Took Off* and *The Girls from Planet 5*

The Tracer of Lost Persons — From 1906, an episodic novel that became a hit radio series in the 30s. Introduced by Richard A. Lupoff.

The Trail of the Cloven Hoof — Diabolical horror from 1935 by Arlton Eadie. Introduced by John Pelan.

The Triune Man — Mindscrambling science fiction from Richard A. Lupoff.

The Unholy Goddess and Other Stories — Wyatt Blassingame's first DTP compilation

The Universal Holmes — Richard A. Lupoff's 2007 collection of five Holmesian pastiches and a recipe for giant rat stew.

The Werewolf vs the Vampire Woman — Hard to believe ultraviolence by either Arthur M. Scarm or Arthur M. Scram.

The Whistling Ancestors — A 1936 classic of weirdness by Richard E. Goddard and introduced by John Pelan.

The White Owl — A vintage thriller from Edmund Snell

The White Peril in the Far East — Sidney Lewis Gulick's 1905 indictment of the West and assurance that Japan would never attack the U.S.

The Wizard of Berner's Abbey — A 1935 horror gem written by Mark Hansom and introduced by John Pelan.

The Wonderful Wizard of Oz — by L. Frank Baum and illustrated by Gavin L. O'Keefe

Through the Looking Glass — Lewis Carroll wrote it; Gavin L. O'Keefe illustrated it.

Time Line — Ramble House artist Gavin O'Keefe selects his most evocative art inspired by the twisted literature he reads and designs.

Tiresias — Psychotic modern horror novel by Jonathan M. Sweet.

Tortures and Towers — Two novellas of terror by Dexter Dayle.

Totah Six-Pack — Fender Tucker's six tales about Farmington in one sleek volume.

Tree of Life, Book of Death — Grania Davis' book of her life.

Triple Quest — An arty mystery from the 30s by E.R. Punshon.

Trail of the Spirit Warrior — Roger Haley's saga of life in the Indian Territories.

Two Kinds of Bad — Two 50s novels by William Ard about Danny Fontaine

Two Suns of Morcali and Other Stories — Evelyn E. Smith's SF tour-de-force

Ultra-Boiled — 23 gut-wrenching tales by our Man in Brooklyn, Gary Lovisi.

Up Front From Behind — A 2011 satire of Wall Street by James B. Kobak.

Victims & Villains — Intriguing Sherlockiana from Derham Groves.

Wade Wright Novels — *Echo of Fear, Death At Nostalgia Street, It Leads to Murder* and *Shadows' Edge*, a double book featuring *Shadows Don't Bleed* and *The Sharp Edge*.

Walter S. Masterman Novels — *The Green Toad, The Flying Beast, The Yellow Mistletoe, The Wrong Verdict, The Perjured Alibi, The Border Line, The Bloodhounds Bay, The Curse of Cantire* and *The Baddington Horror*. Masterman wrote horror and mystery, some introduced by John Pelan.

We Are the Dead and Other Stories — Volume Two in the Day Keene in the Detective Pulps series, introduced by Ed Gorman. When done, there may be 11 in the series.

Welsh Rarebit Tales — Charming stories from 1902 by Harle Oren Cummins

West Texas War and Other Western Stories — by Gary Lovisi.

What If? Volume 1, 2 and 3 — Richard A. Lupoff introduces three decades worth of SF short stories that should have won a Hugo, but didn't.

When the Batman Thirsts and Other Stories — Weird tales from Frederick C. Davis.

Whip Dodge: Man Hunter — Wesley Tallant's saga of a bounty hunter of the old West.

Win, Place and Die! — The first new mystery by Milt Ozaki in decades. The ultimate novel of 70s Reno.

Writer 1 and 2 — A magnus opus from Richard A. Lupoff summing up his life as writer.

You'll Die Laughing — Bruce Elliott's 1945 novel of murder at a practical joker's English countryside manor.

RAMBLE HOUSE

Fender Tucker, Prop. Gavin L. O'Keefe, Graphics
www.ramblehouse.com fender@ramblehouse.com
228-826-1783 10329 Sheephead Drive, Vancleave MS 39565

www.ingramcontent.com/pod-product-compliance
Lightning Source LLC
Chambersburg PA
CBHW030409020726
47493CB00003B/998